BOOKS BY RICHARD BISSELL

A STRETCH ON THE RIVER

7½ CENTS

HIGH WATER

SAY, DARLING

In the *Rivers of America* series

THE MONONGAHELA

Say, Darling

Say, Darling

A NEW NOVEL BY

Richard Bissell

An Atlantic Monthly
Press Book · Little,
Brown and Company
Boston · Toronto

W

ATLANTIC–LITTLE, BROWN BOOKS
ARE PUBLISHED BY
LITTLE, BROWN AND COMPANY
IN ASSOCIATION WITH
THE ATLANTIC MONTHLY PRESS

*Published simultaneously in Canada
by Little, Brown & Company (Canada) Limited*

•

PRINTED IN THE UNITED STATES OF AMERICA

To Bobby Griffith

"Have you been taking more interest in baseball since your marriage?" she was asked. "Well . . ." Marilyn hesitated. "Yeah."
—An interview with Miss Monroe

As anyone on Broadway can tell you, none of the fictional characters in this novel resembles anybody living or dead on the main stem. They are all too lovable. At any rate, the only place they have ever lived is in the author's imagination.

Say, Darling

Chapter 1

> *Man, when you got to ask what is it, you'll never get to know.*
>
> — LOUIS ARMSTRONG

I DON'T THINK I ever was cut out for it in the first place. Frankly, New York makes me nervous.

It was just as pleasant as you would expect in the Pennsylvania Station, and I began to sweat inexpensively but artistically in my genuine tropical worsted (Marshall Field $55.00). A redcap agreed to take on my bags and I walked up the length of the train and into the station.

I went into a booth and called Frankie. I had to spell out the name of the town pretty carefully and to point out to the operator that it was in *Indiana*, not *Indianapolis*. The operator got the routing and dialed direct and I could hear the phone ringing way out there by the fields of new-mown hay.

"Hello," she said.

"Hello, honey," I said. "What's the latest? How's the price on hogs?"

"Jack!" she said. "What's the matter?"

"Nothing's the matter," I said. "I'm just lonesome is all. I thought I would let you know I got here all right."

"Thanks. I sure was worried," she said. "There's so many young fellows getting kidnaped these days on the trip to New York."

"Well anyway," I said, "how the hell are you?"

"Just the same as I was yesterday morning this time — sleepy," she said.

"What did you do last night?" I said.

"Listen, did you see them yet?"

"No. I just got here. I'm still at the station."

"When are you going to see them? How's New York?"

"Today sometime. New York doesn't show up so good from inside this railroad station, but maybe it will look better when I get outside."

"Are you scared?" she said.

"Now what the hell should I be scared about?" I said quite loud.

"Well I guess you are then," she said.

"Don't be so goddamn ridiculous," I said. "I've been in New York before."

"Not on a deal like this," she said. "You look out for those boys."

"Frankie, do you miss me?"

"Uh-huh. Say, Jack, where do you think they'll take you to lunch, Sardi's?"

"Yeah I suppose. Or 21 or someplace."

"Isn't it wonderful!" she said.

"I don't know yet, honey," I said. "I might be right back home again tomorrow night, sitting around the saloon listening to the boys."

"Oh, by the way — Cousin Archie called," she said.

"All right, let's have it," I said.

"He says you won't like it in New York. He says you can't get a square meal there, but he says to tell you there's a wonderful place to eat in Newark. He says Newark is a lot more interesting than New York anyway."

"Yeah, that's what everybody says," I said. "Leave it to Archie. Say, honey, do you miss me?"

"Give me some time," she said. "Say listen, what kind of a shirt have you got on? You better wear a white shirt when you meet them. I s'pose you've got on one of those crazy shirts. You better wear a white one. What are you wearing?"

"Well, the one I got on is kind of a candy stripe with an overplaid, and I have on a cravat with a hand-painted hula girl on it that lights up when I press a concealed switch. That okay?"

"Well," she said, "my advice is wear a white shirt."

I had left my bag standing over against a pillar and at this point a colored boy came along and picked it up and started off at a brisk pace in the direction of Harlem.

"Hey, rube!" I said. "So long, baby, there's a fellow going off with the well-known valise. Bye-bye!"

"Wait a minute — Jack, listen . . ." she said.

"So long, hotstuff," I said and hung up and busted out of the booth and took off after the case. I caught up with him and tapped him on the shoulder.

"Where you going with the trunk, buddy?" I said. He didn't say nothing.

"See I keep my razor in there and I might want to shave tomorrow A.M.," I said.

He dropped the case and got off in a hurry. I picked it up and walked for a cab.

"Oh say, folks, it's a big friendly town," I said. "Underneath this seemingly cold metropolitan exterior there beats a warm and friendly heart. Because folks are just folks, folks, whether it's mighty Manhattan or that old home town."

A lad from sunny Puerto Rico ran past, pursued by two cops with drawn service revolvers.

"They say this Macy's is some store," I said, and got into a cab.

I told the driver to haul me up to the Algonquin, where they had reserved a room for me.

"Well is it hot enough for you?" the driver said as we waited for a light.

"I'll say," I said.

"It was worse yesterday," he said.

"No kiddin'?" I said.

"Yeah, jeez it was awful," he said.

"It don't sound good," I said.

"I hope it don't get no worse," he said.

"I seen in the paper," I said, "where it was 101° down in Phoenix yesterday."

"Yeah, but that was more of a *dry* heat. That dry heat ain't nothing like this."

"It's the humidity does it," I said.

"You can say that again," he said.

I took it all down and later on I mailed it to the *New Yorker* but I never heard from them.

By this time we were up around 50th Street.

"Say, buddy," I said, "the Algonquin is on 44th, isn't it?"

"That's right," he says. "But you see with the traffic like it is at this hour why we make it faster this way."

"Well do me a favor," I said, "and take a right down 50th here and a right down Sixth and a left at 44th. First thing you know we'll be in Armonk and there ain't no good hotel there."

"Okay, okay," he said, and we completed the voyage in comparative silence except for the rear transmission, which had some loose rocks in it.

The Nedick's attendants had shaved, some of them, but not the fellows staring into the windows of the joke and novelty shops on Sixth Avenue trying to make up their minds whether to invest in some back numbers of nudist magazines or in *Diana, A Strange Autobiography*. Half the streets were torn up as usual and they were putting up a new building on the southeast corner of 44th and Sixth and the jackhammers were going full blast. Dust filtered through onto the Fabrikoid upholstery of Cab #23406 as we whipped past, clipped the rear end of a truck bearing the legend M. BLUMENTHAL SONS INDUSTRIAL SEWING MACHINES and landed with a resounding klunk in front of the Algonquin. I gave Irving Golub, driver, a quarter for his very own self just to prove I wasn't mad.

"You picked a real boob trap here," he said.

A man with a cane and a Homburg hat helped a dame loaded with *embonpoint* into Irving's cab. Two lovely girls with arms around each other's waists emerged from the hotel and paused.

"Cab, miss?" said the doorman.

"I really should call Josh," said the petite blonde to the music of her tinkling bracelets.

"Darling!" said the petite brunette. "Don't be silly. Talk to Liebling *first*."

One of those personality-loaded bellhops grabbed the case and I followed him into the Fun House.

Chapter 2

*The secret of my success is clean living and a
fast outfield.*

— **LEFTY GOMEZ**

So I went to my little room, and the handy bellhop with the receding hairline pulled up the Venetian blinds
for me so I could get a better view of the brick wall facing the
window.

"Say, if they charged according to the view a man could
get this room fairly cheap, couldn't he?" I said.

"You must be an actor," the bellhop said.

"Musician," I said. "I play two cornets at one and the same
time."

"They keep you pretty busy?" he said.

"You can say that some more," I said, and gave him thirty-
five cents — which was way too much, considering he needed
a shoeshine. "You know any good places to eat in Newark?" I
said.

"No, I never bin there," he said.

"Well," I said, "my cousin Archie says there isn't anyplace
to eat in New York City and the best place around here is to
go over to Newark."

"Where does this cousin of yours reside at?" he said, turning on the water tap to see whether the authorities had shut

off the water yet. "Myself I come from Snowflake, Arizona. Very small place."

"Why he lives out in the Golden West, way out in the glorious state of Indiana," I said.

"Why don't he go home for lunch when he's in New York?" he said. "It would be a good deal quicker than going to Newark.

"However," he added, opening the closet door just in case I wouldn't be able to find it, "one thing, they do have a pretty good burlesque show over in Newark."

"Archie doesn't care much for the theater," I said. "I went to *South Pacific* with him and he slept halfway through it."

"Whereabouts was that?" he said.

"Columbus," I said.

"Well them road companies are no good," he said. "If you want anything leave me know." And he departed.

I hung up my various suits and articles of finery and the phone rang and it was the desk and they said they had a telegram for me and I told the girl to send it up.

Pretty soon the boy showed up so I gave him a quarter.

"Where do you come from?" I said.

"Munising, Michigan," he said, and retired to the lobby.

I laid the telegram on the bed and went to drink in the view. By craning my neck I could see down onto the tops of some buildings with little chimbleys sticking out. An odor of chop suey and exhaust fumes wafted itself gently upwards toward the far-off sky, pausing briefly in my room en route.

NA752   CGN   PD-26

JACK JORDAN

ALGONQUIN HOTEL

GOOD LUCK HONEY YOU CAN DO IT TALK RIGHT UP

TO THEM LOVE

FRANKIE

I lay down on the bed and lit a cigarette and the telegram fluttered to the floor.

"Yeah, sure I can do it," I said. "I can ride a unicycle too if I try hard enough."

Two fire engines went up the street. I thought for a minute they were coming right up the hall. Somebody dropped a pile of plates somewhere. I closed my eyes and wished I could take a nap. My watch said 10 A.M. I decided to call them up; I thought about it for a while. I thought about Frankie, too, and about Indiana — Indiana where I knew everybody and everybody knew me, where everything was easy and it didn't matter too much, nobody was straining themselves, nobody ever expected to be able to get out anyway, so they just went on from day to day in noisy desperation, carrying the empties to the grocery store on Mondays.

"Take it from me, you'll never be happy down East," they said to me before I left. "This is the only place for you. Why, this place *is* you."

"You mean I'm just a natural small-town jerk?" I said.

"Aw not that. Heck no. You been around plenty. It's just . . ."

Twenty-six years is too long *anyplace*.

I went in the bathroom and dropped a couple of aspirins on top of my Pennsylvania Railroad headache, and went back and flopped down on the bed again and thought about what they would be like.

I had all these guys pegged out in my mind. I could see them as clear as the picture of "The Berkshires in Winter" over the writing desk.

Sam Snow, Producer: About 50, short, round, red-faced, wearing a signet ring and smoking a cigar with the band still on it. Custom suit in dark blue. Likes cheesecake at Lindy's.

Ted Crosby, Producer: About 35, gray flannel suit, pink

shirt, black knit tie, horn-rimmed scopes. Knows the "little" French restaurants.

Richard Hackett, Director: The great man of the theater. Double-breasted vest, eyeglasses with ribbon. Gold pencil and alligator-skin notebook. Possibly spats, cane and Homburg.

Oh yes, I knew perfectly well what they would look like, for I haven't spent half my life sliding lower and lower in my seat at the movies for nothing; I know what people are supposed to look like and the minute I had first heard Sam Snow's voice from New York over the telephone the true image appeared in my mind, even way out there on the edge of the Indian territory.

"Do you think you can do it?" Sam Snow said. "We'd like to talk to you."

"I don't know anything about that sort of thing," I said. "I'm just a small-town boy."

"Well, we'd like to talk to you about it," he said, avoiding reference to the yokel act.

"I guess that wouldn't do any harm," I said.

"When can you come in?" he said.

"Come in where?" I said.

"I mean, to New York," he said.

"Hell, can't we talk about it over the phone?" I said. I could see him chewing on that cigar, and I figured Ted Crosby was tapping him on the shoulder and giving him instructions on what to say. "I don't have to come clear to New York to tell you I don't know the first thing about a job like that."

"That's just it — if we talk it over together we feel that perhaps we can develop some ideas."

"What kind of ideas?" I said. "I don't very often have any ideas, to tell the truth."

"Wait a minute," he said. "Hold it a minute," and then I could hear him talking to somebody else, good old Ted Crosby no doubt — anyway the other guy said (and it came over the phone hollowly, from an empty room), "Tell him to get off his can and get to New York, for godsake, we got to get moving."

"Hello," says Sam Snow into the phone again. "Listen, we feel . . ."

"Will you pay my expenses?" I said.

"Of *course!*" he said. "My god, of *course* we pay your expenses. *Sure* we pay your expenses."

"Okay then," I said. "But listen, I can't come right away, I can't get away right now."

"Oh-oh, that's bad," he said.

"Tell him we gotta get moving," Ted Crosby said in the background.

"Shut up, for godsake will you, Ted?" Sam said. "Listen, Jordan, we gotta get moving. If you can't get down here now, when can you get here?"

"Not until day after tomorrow," I said. "I'm grinding the valves on my cousin Archie's Locomobile and we're right in the middle of the job."

"Yeah. Okay, okay," he said. "What did you say you were doing? Well never mind, I thought you said something about a Locomobile."

"Locomobile?" I could hear Ted Crosby saying in a peevish voice. "Oh-oh. One of those nuts. Better call it off. Tell him to stay there until he hears from us."

"Shut up, Ted, will you *please?*" Sam said. "Now listen, Jordan, when you get here you go to the Algonquin Hotel, 44th Street. We'll make a reservation for Monday. Got that?"

"Yeah. Okay," I said.

So from a conversation like that, being very keen and clever in such matters, I was able like the F.B.I. to construct a perfect image of both Mr. Sam Snow and Mr. Ted

Crosby, co-producers of, up to that date, nothing. And here I was in this nice room about to go up to see them.

The picture of the Berkshires was certainly an incompetent job; the Pfister Hotel in Milwaukee would not hang a picture like that even in a sample room. The birch trees were too skinny.

The phone rang and it was another gram so I told them to send it up. I gave the boy another quarter and in answer to my quiz he allowed as how he was a native of Kalispell, Montana.

This one was from Archie.

NA673 CGN PD   26   9:17 AM
JACK JORDAN
ALGONQUIN HOTEL

CANT FIND HEAD GASKETS LOCOMOBILE SEE WHAT YOU CAN DO NEW YORK MODEL TWENTY-THREE SERIES AB PHOOEY

ARCHIE

So that sheet of yellow paper drifted to the floor also and I reached over languidly and picked a book off the bedside table and it seemed to be a book by the manager of the hotel *about* the hotel, as follows:

> My old pal Gene Markey came one night and brought his wife, who happens to be Hedy Lamarr, and it so happened that Garbo came the same night. . . . And of course Tallulah, Helen Hayes, Ruth Gordon, Dennis King, Gertrude Lawrence, Walter Huston . . .

How the hell did I manage to get a room here, I wondered, and I looked under the bed to see if Noel Coward or somebody was there.

The back end of this book is full of letters to the author

(some bird named Frank Case) telling him what a peach of a guy he is and how dandy his hotel is. This book was published by Frederick Stokes & Co. in 1940 if anybody wants to look it up. Like for example Judith Anderson says:

"I like you and the Algonquin.
"I dislike anybody who dislikes you or the Algonquin."

I went and had another glass of water and felt better.
But wait, look out!

"I like baked potatoes.
"I dislike fish served with the heads and tails on."

MARY PICKFORD

Well, perhaps that's all I better read this morning, with this headache and all.

Chapter 3

AFTER recovering from Mary Pickford's trouble with fish I pulled myself partly together and called the office.

"They taking good care of you down there? Is your room all right?" Sam said.

"Sure. Fine. Everything's fine," I said.

"Well they've got some pretty rugged rooms down there so if you don't like it make a noise and they'll change it."

"The room's okay," I said. "It's got a bed and everything. When do you want to see me?"

He told me to come right on up so I did.

New York is the best place, it's the only place, and what I like about it is the dandy sophisticated conversations you hear all over town, such as this one in the elevator on the way down:

"I tried to make him see it my way, Ed."

"I don't know whether we can do that kind of a selling job, Frank."

"The way I see it, Ed, is like this . . ."

"An operation like this takes know-how, Frank."

"The whole selling picture has changed, Ed."

"There's new factors involved, Frank."

"You can say that again, Ed."

The lobby was jammed with celebrities, slumping in those easy chairs and divans. I wormed my way through, keeping a sharp lookout for Judith Anderson, but she must have been off duty. No telling what her reaction would have been if she'd found out I didn't think too highly of the view from my room.

I walked up Sixth Avenue humming various New Yorkish songs: "42nd Street," "45 Minutes from Broadway," and "How You Gonna Keep 'Em Down on the Farm?" It's a great street, Sixth Avenue, and you can buy a raincoat at a cut price or a secondhand E flat alto saxophone or most anything, but it's lost a lot of color since they hauled down the El. Wait until they scrap the El on Wabash Avenue in Chicago — what a dopey street *that's* going to be.

But the sun was shining and the sky over Horn & Hardart and the Empire Loan Co. was as blue as Lake Superior; and the bums shuffling along with puke on their vests wore a happy carefree air as they worked the street or ate hot dogs, dribbling mustard on their chins. And what dames! Beat-up old tramps dating back to the Yukon, little Puerto Ricans, regal colored girls, Chinese girls, show girls, dance hall kids, mean-looking bobby soxers, luscious blondes without benefit of foundation garments — all kinds, take your pick, boys. And meanwhile the traffic rumbled, brakes screeched, taxis ricocheted off each other, and the New York perfume, exhaust fumes from a million internal combustion engines, filled the air.

The office was in Rockefeller Center. I walked past Manship's fountain and Maxie Rosenbloom was standing there looking down at the eaters.

He turned to continue on his way as I came along and we bumped into each other.

"Hi, Maxie," I said.

"Hi, buddy," he said.

I went into the building and there was a newsstand there so I bought a postcard and sent it to Frankie and I wrote on it:

Just said hello to Maxie Rosenbloom. Thought I would let you know before you read it in the papers.

On the way up in the elevator I got in on some more gay cosmopolitan chatter, feminine type:

"Well I'll say one thing, I'll sure be glad to get back to Florida."

"Oh, is that your home?"

"Oh yes."

"Whereabouts in Florida?"

"Whereabouts *is* Florida?"

"No, *in* Florida."

"Oh. West Coast, Sarasota."

(Pause)

"I've got an uncle in Tampa."

"That's about forty miles from us."

Well I got off at the right floor and I found the office and figured well I might as well go on in, it's not the dentist's office after all and remember to talk right up to them like Frankie says after all *they* want *you,* not vice versa, here is the fruits of all your midnight labors to be a writer and a big shot, kid, the worst they can do is throw you out the window into the fountain.

Nowadays I am used to it and I can walk through a sea of fifty or more actresses and never even show that I am about to faint, but not then. There was a reception desk and a girl at it and out in front of the desk on both sides were rows of chairs and a couch and all the chairs seemed to be occupied with beautiful dames all dressed up like December 25. Just like in the movies. They all stared at me. I got over to the

reception desk somehow, wondering if I had a rip in the seat of my pants like Charles Chase.

"I'm Sam Snow," I said. "I mean I'm supposed to *see* Mr. Sam Snow. My name is Jack."

"Is Mr. Snow expecting you, Mr. Jack?" she said.

"Yes he is," I said. "Actually my name is Jordan. Jack is my *first* name."

She looked at me with the resigned expression of one who has to handle nuts all day.

"Oh, Mr. *Jordan*. Yes, Mr. Snow is expecting you. Just a minute," and she went through the telephone bit about "Oh, Mr. Snow, Mr. Jordan is here."

So I looked at the ceiling and the girls looked at me, and I thought: Good god the least I could have done was to get this suit pressed at least.

In a minute a kid showed up, some college boy in gray flannels and a tweed jacket and the blue Oxford button-down collar shirt. Yes and the crew haircut and everything, and I thought: Well this boy sure has a nice summer job, better than making hay out in South Dakota or carrying ice like Red Grange and he will have plenty to tell the fellows when he gets back to Tiger Inn next week.

"Come on in, Jordan," he said, and shoved open the little gate, and he shook hands with me. Very nice friendly young man.

"Nice to see you," he said. "Come on in."

Just so we get out of range of all those dames, I thought, and followed him into a little office with a couple of chewed-up desks in it, and he sat me down in a chair and he sat down at a desk. All over the walls were pictures, show cards and stuff from different Hackett shows, *Crazy People* and *Oh Baby,* and dating clear back to *Hi Jinks of 1919.* And there were signed photos from Merman and Lahr and Cornell and

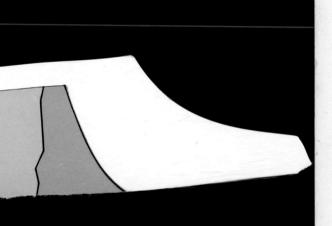

Ethel Barrymore, and rows of books, and scripts piled all over the place.

"Now, how was your trip?" he said.

"Okay," I said. "I got here all right."

"You . . . I suppose you've been to New York before?"

"Yes," I said. "I used to work for the Polarized Light and Power Co., Novelty Division. That was before I went to Guatemala to look for the Lost City of Gold."

"That's funny," he said. "We thought — well — that you — I mean the way you write sounds like you've been in Indiana for — quite a while."

"That's what my friends out there say," I said. "Well, I *have* been there quite a long time — twenty-six years, off and on."

"We certainly are enthusiastic about this property," he said. "We think it has great possibilities."

"Uh-huh," I said. "Say, is Mr. Snow around anyplace? I was supposed to see him I think."

"I'm *sorry*," he said. "*Crazy* of me. Damn silly of me. *I'm* Sam Snow. I just assumed . . ."

There you go. Cheated again; and me so smart about figuring people via the telephone system from their voices. Out the window with fat, ruddy, cigar-munching Sam Snow, fifty-ish — and enter Sam Snow the Boy Producer, with his infectious smile, collegiate garb, and winning ways.

"Oh," I said, looking with utter amazement at his slightly crooked maroon foulard bow tie.

"Well now you don't need to be so shocked as all that," he said.

"You don't look like Sam Snow."

Sam Snow has a theory that it's impossible to size up a man accurately in the summertime, especially on a hot day. "In these seersucker and rayon blend summer suits

everybody looks the same — messy," he says. "Had a fellow in the office one day, wanted to be a producer. Said
he had a lot of ideas and plenty of money available.
Available, he said. He was all wilted and untidy, he looked
like a bum. So I got rid of him. Later on Irv Harris introduced me to the producer of *High and Hot* in New Haven
on opening night. Same guy. Owned three banks and half
the oil in Oklahoma. *High and Hot* ran two years. Road
company all ready to go out *again.* Damn Orlon-nylon
blends."

I didn't know about his theory then, but he was studying
me pretty carefully, and to make it more difficult I had on a
summer suit, the latest thing, Gestron, by-product of the
Shredded Wheat process.

So that's what he was doing now, studying me and my
limp suit and wondering where I got the pretty scar on my
cheek. Heidelberg? Shiloh? Sailor's brawl in Marseilles?

"You know how it is," I said. "You build up these complicated preconceived ideas of people." And I rolled myself a
cigarette. Out the window I could see the Empire State
Building, twenty blocks down the avenue, reminding me of
where I was. In the months to come I was to stare out that
window at the Empire State while squirming through every
chapter of the emotional encyclopedia from triumphant ec-
stasy to the suicide impulse. It was always there, getting
bigger all the time, and more glorious. Mighty Chomo-
lungma, with Mallory and Irvine lost forever somewhere near
the windswept summit . . .

"What do you do that for?" he said, watching me roll the
cigarette.

"Just atmosphere," I said.

"What was your preconceived idea of me?" he said.

"I read too many books, see too many movies," I said. "I

figured you as more of a character actor. Cigar, fat, always interviewing girls and asking them to pull up their skirts so you can see their legs before you give them the job."

He thought this was a good one and he laughed and took off his horn-rimmed scopes and twirled them.

There was a flurry in the outer office. Somebody had come in and it was "Hello dear. No dear. Hello Mara dear. Hello Vivian. Not now darling. No dear."

"Here comes Ted," Sam said, and after striking out on my personality analysis of Sam I was prepared to welcome a midget or an octogenarian in a white beret; the flannels and pink shirt went out the window.

Ted blew in under full steam.

"Ted, this is . . ." Sam began.

"Jordan!" Ted said. "How the hell are you? Glad to see you. Say, is something burning in here?"

I indicated my cigarette.

"What is it, corn silk?" he said. "Listen, hold it a minute," and he grabbed a telephone. "Listen, dear," he said. "Get me Hobe Morrison at *Variety*. Tell them it's J. J. Shubert or somebody, tell them it's Otis Skinner. Get him."

Now this is more like the old Hecht and MacArthur stuff, I thought; why this boy even had a kind of a Lee Tracy hat pushed back on his head and looked as though he'd slept in his clothes, which evidently started life in the Crawford chain.

"Hobe!" he said. "Now listen, pal. Hobe, this is Ted Crosby. That piece you ran this week. I don't know where you got the information but listen, we haven't even *talked* to the guy yet. No, no, absolutely nothing definite, we haven't even *seen* him yet," and he threw me a wink.

"*Variety* had a story about you," Sam leaned forward and whispered.

"The hell they did," I said.

"So, Hobe, lay off, how about it, pal? Give us a break, will you, until we know where we are? Thanks, old boy."

He hung up and turned to me and the phone rang again.

"Oh, goose crap," he said, picking it up. "Hello."

Squawk squawk squawk through earpiece.

"Now wait a minute. Of *course* we read your script. Matter of fact Sam and I are just sitting here talking about it right now . . . Sure . . . Well frankly we'd rather talk to you personally. Basically . . ."

So he went on for a while and finally hung up.

"All these guys think we have to do is sit around here reading their lousy scripts," he said.

The phone rang again.

"I'll get it," Sam said.

"Aha," Ted said.

"Hello," Sam said. "Darling! How are you? Did you get home all right?"

He darlinged it up for about three minutes while Ted held his nose, made faces, and croaked: "Hang up on darling, call it off, will you?" — and Sam kept motioning for him to shut up.

"Wonderful! That's perfect. The St. Regis. Sort of fivish. Swell!" and he hung up.

"Sort of fivish!" Ted snorted. "Get a big load of that, Jordan."

"Oh be quiet," Sam said. "That was Marlowe if you must know."

"Marlowe!" Ted said. "I hope she's put on some weight." He turned to me. "He likes *actresses*. He's stage-struck."

"Never mind that," Sam said. "Let's talk."

"Okay," Ted said and picked up the phone. "No phone calls for a while," he said.

"This book of yours. We think it's terrific. It's very funny stuff. Great characters."

"Offbeat stuff," Sam said. "It has a certain wonderful quality about it . . ."

"I like it pretty well myself," I said. "But — a musical comedy — are you guys serious?"

"Serious? Hell yes. We laid down cash for the option, didn't we?" Ted said.

"And Mr. Hackett has agreed to direct it," Sam said.

"He has? My god," I said. "You mean you're really going to make a show out of that crazy book of mine?"

"Listen, let's go and eat," Ted said. "You hungry, Jordan?"

"Yeah, I guess so," I said and I thought what Frankie told me about remembering to pinch a swizzle stick from 21 or places like that, for little Karen Anne the neighbor girl. She has a collection. Nice hobby for a six-year-old.

"Come on then, we can talk it all over at lunch. Come on, Sam," Ted said.

"Where would you like to eat, Jordan?" Sam said.

"Oh, anyplace is okay with me," I said.

"Swell — let's go," Ted said.

Chapter 4

> "Writers," Ruth exclaimed with a shudder. "I've
> told you not to use that word around here. The
> children might be listening."
>   — AL *and* SHERWOOD SCHWARTZ

I BELIEVE I'll have the Avocado, Anchovy, Pecan and Tunafish Sandwich and a Marshmallow Almond Sundae," Sam said.

"Uh-huh," Ted said. "That sounds pretty good. Let's see . . . What're you gonna have, Jordan?"

"I dig the he-man stuff," I said. "I'm having the Fresh Bartlett Pear Salad Stuffed with Assorted Fresh Fruits and Cream Cheese Nut Balls, and an Iced Luxuro Chocolate with Whipped Cream, with an Ice Cream Cupcake and Hot Butterscotch Sauce for dessert."

"Wow, you're some picker, boy," Ted said. "I'm gonna have the same."

"Hey, wait a minute," I said. "I was just kidding. Some of that real flavorsome Indiana humor."

"Yeah?" Ted said. "How?"

"I mean Cream Cheese Nut Balls, for example," I said.

"Cream Cheese Nut Balls," he said. "That's part of the salad, isn't it?"

"Yeah, silly, isn't it? And Ice Cream Cupcake," I said.

"Uh huh," he said. "Say, it is funny, at that," and he issued a hollow laugh.

"Do they have Schrafft's in Chicago? I can't remember," Sam said.

"Nope," I said. "But they say the ladyfingers at Marshall Field's Tea Room are terrific."

"I get it," Ted said. "You don't like this place, huh?"

"Aw, hell, I was just kidding. I like it fine," I said. "But I don't want no Stuffed Bartlett Pear."

"You talk ungrammatically just to be colorful, don't you?" Sam said, fiddling with the silverware; this boy is the greatest silver twiddler in Gotham.

"Listen, let's order. Come on," Ted said as the waitress got out her little old pad and pencil. "What the hell *do* you want then?"

"Here's an item at the top that interests me quite a bit," I said.

"Where?" he said.

"Right up at the top. See? Where it says 'May We Suggest Gibson Cocktail 65¢.' "

"Aha," Ted said. "You want a drink, huh?"

"I'll have a Gibson with you, Jordan," Sam said.

"What!" Ted said. "You? Drinking cocktails at noon? What's the matter with you anyway?"

"A Gibson will go real good," I said, "with your almond sundae."

About this time an emaciated-looking Size 38 person in a Size 42 camel's-hair coat came stalking boldly down through this long lovely room filled with feminine brouhaha, dodging the waitresses; spotted us, squeezed through and sat down in the number four chair at our table. In wedging himself into place his chair bumped the back of an adjacent chair and a lady with a pheasant feather sixteen inches long in her hat turned indignantly, attempted to glare at our new visitor, failed and glared at me as a substitute receiver. I treated her to a supercilious sneer, and she gave up.

"This is Jordan," Ted said to the oversize topcoat.

"Hey, that's great," he said. "I read your book. Say, is that auto-bio-graphical? You don't have to answer that. Seriously though . . ."

"Did you eat yet?" Sam said.

"I got a date with Maury Converse at Toots Shor's in twenty minutes. Go ahead and order."

We ordered.

"This is Schatzie Harris, our press agent," Ted said.

We shook hands, knocking over a glass of water in the process. Sam began to mop it up patiently. Then we talked for a while about the "property," that's what they called the book, and about how some show on tryout in New Haven was "in trouble," and had canned the choreographer and brought in a new one, and about somebody I never heard of that was getting a divorce from his boy friend. The waitress brought the Gibsons and the food.

"Well, let's have it. What have you got on your so-called mind?" Ted said.

"All right, all right," Schatzie said. "Now listen," he said. "I've got a deal, a pretty slick proposition, on the fire — I want to give it to you while it's hot. It's a big one and I know you'll go along on it — it's one of those quickies — you know what I mean: it just happened, it came to me like a flash and I think you'll see that it's one of those unexpected *breaks*, you know what I mean? It's an idea that could really build, get us nationwide coverage in a big way — all top-drawer stuff and when I say that I'm not just kidding, boys, I handled some big stories, big promotions, in my time you know I was with

Oscar for six years and we cooked up some terrific releases, nothing but the best; I don't have to tell you that, because you know Oscar, you know he doesn't fool around — when it comes to publicity he wants one little thing: Results! And I guess you know what kind of a job I did for him on *Wonderful You;* that two-page color spread in the *Post* made history — didn't cost us a dime and made history in show business. But this little slant I thought up is a new twist — something new, boys, you'll flip when you . . ."

"But, Schatzie, listen, shut up that gab for a minute," Ted said, fiddling with his chicken à la king on spoon bread. "We didn't . . ."

"We didn't even tell you to go ahead yet," Sam said. "Good god, man, it's too early to get on that pitch yet."

"We told you *if* we get this show going," Ted said, picking a piece of pimiento out and laying it aside.

"Would you like your dessert now?" the colleen in the cute apron said.

"Yes, dear, bring us the dessert. And more coffee," Sam said.

"Now, fellows, listen," Schatzie said. "It's never too soon to start laying a foundation. You know what Oscar used to say? I think it expresses very well the whole essence of the publicity field, and I don't think there's a man on Broadway today more competent to sum the whole thing up. When you look at the hits to his credit you have to admit the man knows his business, right? You've got to admit . . ."

"All right," Sam said. "What did he say?"

"Oscar always said, 'Schatzie, you've got to lay a foundation.' He used to drum it into me night and day, he used to . . ."

"Schatzie, listen, let's give Oscar a vacation," Ted said.

Schatzie consulted his wrist watch. "I gotta go," he said,

leaping up. "Nice to meet you, Jordan. This is just the beginning, boy, just the beginning," and he trailed off down
the line.

"Say, are you sure we hired the right press agent?" Sam
said.

"Relax, I worked with him on lots of shows for Hackett.
He's all right," Ted said. "In fact, he's terrific."

Around us on all sides, one half of the entire tuna fish catch
of the year was being consumed. Mink, let-out muskrat, and
squirrel capes and stoles hung languidly from the backs of
chairs, slipped to the floor and were retrieved. Cute hats en-
livened the scene; 5,000,000 cigarettes were lighted, had their
brief fling, and went down the long, long trail from beyond
whose bourne no cigarette returns. Hogsheads full of iced tea
were wheeled in and disappeared as though by legerdemain.
In this whirlwind of sheer joy voices were raised in gay ex-
pectancy as thrilling escapades for the afternoon ahead were
planned: matinees at the Music Hall, auction sales of Swansea
platters and Tabriz rugs, Gloria Swanson at the Museum of
Modern Art, marked-down alligator handbags at Ohrbach's.

"Maurice was terribly amusing last night" — from a nearby
table. "You know how terribly amusing he can be. Well, for
some reason after we left Adèle's we ended up at the Blue
Angel. And you know how small the tables are there? Maurice said, 'If these tables were any smaller they'd be . . .'
Let me see, what was it — Oh something amusing anyway and
it's really his manner, that droll way he has . . ."

"I'll bet Maurice is a bird from Birdville," I said.

"What's that?" Ted said.

"Oh nothing," I said. "Tell me about Hackett. What kind
of a guy is he? Is he going to scare me to death?"

"Oh certainly not, don't be ridiculous," Sam said.

"He's the finest man I've ever known," Ted said solemnly. "He has absolute integrity. He's the most honest man I've ever met."

Well, I thought, I didn't expect he would be a crook.

"Do I understand," I said, "that he's agreed not only to direct this epoch-making musical smash but to collaborate with me in writing it?"

"Do you realize what that means?" Ted said, forgetting to eat he was so overcome with awe.

"No I don't," I said. "Except that I can't imagine collaborating with anybody, with my peanut brain. What *does* it mean?"

"It means that Richard Hackett, author of *Bright Lights,* author of *Home Again,* author of *Lovely Lady,* author of *Love Me Yesterday,* director of twenty-eight Broadway hits, has read this property and consented to collaborate on a stage adaptation, with *you.* It means that . . ."

"Good god did he write *Lovely Lady?*" I said. "That's the greatest show that ever was. I saw that when I was twelve years old."

"I'll say he wrote it," Sam said.

"It wasn't easy to get him," Ted said. "He hasn't collaborated with anybody since *Lazy Day.* He thought this over for weeks. Finally he said, 'Call Jordan. I'll work with him.'"

"Boy did we flip!" Sam said.

"I'll bet," I said. "But listen," I said. "I don't know a damn thing about writing a show and I believe I'll go home on the four o'clock train. This is 'way too much for Jack. I don't want to overreach myself just because I wrote a book. I don't know the rules, boys, I don't . . ."

"Leave that to Mr. Hackett," Sam said. "*He* knows the rules. He *makes* the rules."

"He's the greatest man that ever . . ."

"This man is so terrific he . . ."

"Wait a minute," I said. "He sounds like Jehovah. But what's he going to think of a bum like me?"

"He's worked with bums before," Ted said.

Chapter 5

Now now Waldo, people will think you never had no toys at home.

— J. R. WILLIAMS

ALL of us aborigines from out in the tall grass we love New York, and the natives they rave about it too. It sure is beautiful here and all you have to do is walk through Times Square to get the full charm of the place. For one thing the sidewalks on the Great White Way have more gum, mashed popcorn and asst'd crap on them than any place in the world. They hold the World's Record. Now if you just keep looking up at all the electric signs at night it is an inspiring view similar to the midway of a good traveling carnival, but if you do this you will soon get a crick in your neck and also run the risk of bumping into people; watch this, because there is a number of nasty diseases going around these days as a result of collisions. Often overlooked in the travel folders is the fact that Times Square is a linguistic student's paradise as not more than .005 per cent of the rubes in the crush are talking English; they are talking mostly Spanish, Italian, Yiddish, French, German, Finno-Ugrian and such things, and even the ones talking American are jabbering away in some incomprehensible dialect, so the whole effect is that you are not in the U.S.A. at all but in some international bull pen of lost foreigners all bent on buying a tin replica of the Empire State Building and a piña colada.

So hurry up, folks, there is no waiting for all seats and you can witness James ("Jimmy") Stewart in his latest opera for a mere $2.00. That's why there is no waiting.

What the city authorities ought to do actually is to quit spending money promoting juvenile delinquency and see if we can't get less unpopped kernels in the giant 25-cent bag of Times Square caramel popcorn.

I walked through the square with Sam. It was after midnight but the crowd was still trudging relentlessly up and down, the old folks from Kankakee, and the British sailors with their girl friends.

Sam was about ½ inked up. We had been to Sardi's, squeezed in the Little Bar, at the end of which Cole Porter had sat unsmiling and unexcited, and Sam had had three gin and tonics which was the same as a dozen to most people. He was up in a balloon.

"Isn't it the greatest!" he said. "What a glorious, beautiful city, what a town. It's so exciting. Don't you agree it's the greatest?"

"Yeah, it's the greatest," I said.

"I'm glad you agree with me," he said. "Because I think it's the greatest."

The blind men tapped their canes, the legless man dragged himself along the sidewalk, and over our heads that lovable moppet, Little Lulu, advertised Kleenex in electric lights.

"Let's go to the Stork," Sam said.

"I don't look so good," I said.

"You look great. Come on. Let's walk. I love walking around the city at night. You feel like walking?"

"Sure, let's walk," I said. "I've been sitting around all day.

I'm used to moving around more. Why, in that old iron foundry, I bet I walked ten miles a day."

"I can't get over it," he said as we walked past the Astor. "You really *worked* in that foundry."

"I'll say I worked," I said, and I thought back to that nice cozy little plant, and I thought of Jake and Mabel and Old Man Bliss and the rest of them. So now I was lurching up through Times Square with a crazy producer on my way to the Stork Club.

"How come you quit?" he said.

"I got anointed by a Book Club," I said. "Guess they were hard up."

So we talked about that and we came to an agreement that New York was the Greatest and that we were both pretty marvelous guys. And Sam said what a great thing it was we had Hackett, that we'd have a success and make a lot of money and have our names in the *Times,* but I discounted all that. But one thing I liked was: Sam was a good guy to hang around with and he was loaded over the Plimsoll line with that infectious boyish charm and high spirits. It didn't take much to set him off, he was half-cockeyed most of the time anyway with his own attractions, he appreciated himself 100 per cent.

They looked us over at the Stork Club and took our fingerprints, checked the labels in our suits, asked us where we were born and if we had ever had mumps, erysipelas, or fainting spells, and finally decided to let us into the outer bar.

"It was my Countess Mara tie that put it over," Sam said.

"Don't be simple, Sam," I said. "My bootmaker only turns out two pairs of footgear per annum. Tans his own hides."

We switched to Scotch.

"The whole trouble in a nutshell is, maybe you didn't

know it, Ed, but see Ruth is a Cath'lic, and I'm a Prodes-dent," said a big fellow to my left at the bar.

"Now, Julian, let's not go into that," said his friend.

"I want another drink," the big guy says. "Charlie, give me another bourbon and water."

"Now, Mr. Rand," the bartender said. "I think you better skip this one, Mr. Rand."

"Charlie's always taking *care* of me," the big guy said. "Aren't you, Charlie? He's as bad as Ruth. Aren't you, Charlie?"

"That's right, Mr. Rand," Charlie said.

"Oh my god," Sam said.

"What's up, old bean?" I said.

"It's the end. I can't stand this," he said.

"What's the matter?" I said.

"She will talk and talk and talk," he said, ducking his head into his drink and looking surreptitiously over his shoulder.

"Come, come, now, Noel old chap," I said. "What's biting the ear?"

"I just don't feel like *any* complicated conversation," he said.

"Steady on, old fruit," I said. "Shall we dash for the open air?"

But it was too late.

"Sam darling, what are *you* doing here? I thought you told me this sort of place made you cringe with horror."

"I'm cringing," Sam said.

"Well stop it and come along with us," said Irene Lovelle.

I had never seen her on the stage, but she looked just the same as she does in pictures. Maybe a little better.

"No, no, dear," Sam said. "We're talking."

"That's what you were doing the last time I saw you," she said. "Talking. Haven't you stopped yet?"

"There's something lovely about you," Sam said. "Sort of an ethereal quality."

"You know George Sterling, don't you? George, this is Sam Snow," she said.

"Oh," Sam said — "Hi" — shaking hands with a smallish fellow whose hair had lost the race. "This is Jack Jordan."

There are some ignorant fools in the world who think Monroe is too fat and who think Irene Lovelle is too tall. Well, she is about Ava Gardner's size. Is that bad? Plus the famous blond hair and a falling-off-the-shoulders black dress that kept one on the alert.

So we shook hands all around and Mr. Sterling and I stood foolishly while Sam and Miss Lovelle badgered each other for a while.

"Don't be tedious," she said. "Come along with us to the Bon Mot. We want to hear about the show, don't we, George?"

"Been reading about you in *Variety*," Mr. Sterling said.

"There's nothing settled yet," I said.

So we went to the Bon Mot, which is French for a gin mill sixteen feet wide with a hundred and fifty customers in it.

"Say," I said, after we got jammed into a table. "If these tables were any smaller they'd be . . ."

"Well, *what?*" Sam said.

"I forget the rest of it," I said. "But it's a real keen joke. I overheard it while lunching at 21 this noon with a couple of big producers."

"That's not so very funny," Sam said.

"My stuff goes over better in my native locale," I said. "Say — they don't have much of an electric light bill here, do they?"

"The management are spiritualists," Sam said. "Well, I guess that's not very funny either."

"I've been reading about you in *Variety*," Miss Lovelle said.

"I've been reading about you, too," I said. "In the *Journal American*, *Life*, *Peek*, the *Architectural Record* . . ."

"That piece in *Variety* was utterly premature. They've all gone crazy over there," Sam said.

"And I *dashed* out to get a copy of your book. I *hurtled* around the corner to the Chaucer Head," she said.

"Chaucer Head?" I said.

"Bookstore," she said. "But of course they didn't have it."

"Of course," I said.

"That's Irene Lovelle," somebody said out of the gloom.

"No it isn't, she's in Italy making a picture," a voice replied.

"Why didn't you try a Doubleday store?" I said. "Quite often they keep a copy of the best sellers in stock."

"We were thoroughly annoyed by that piece in *Variety*," Sam said. "Absolutely unnecessary and *meddlesome*. And I called Hobe and told him so, too."

"It won't do any harm," contributed Mr. Sterling. "Don't let it throw you."

"It's *not* throwing me," Sam said, groping in the dark for his drink. "I *simply* . . ."

"Aren't you clever," Miss Lovelle said. "I *went* to Doubleday and they had simply hundreds of copies. I *devoured* your book. I simply adored every word of it."

"Dilute it a little bit, dear," Sam said. "Jack is just in from Indiana and he's under a big strain already."

"Oh, do be quiet, Sammy," she said.

"She calls me Sammy," Sam said to Sterling. "Isn't that cute? What's she call you? 'Georgie'?"

"As a matter of fact . . ." Sterling said. "I beg your pardon, I believe you've got my drink."

"Sorry," Sam said.

"Your characters!" Irene said.

"Isn't that Irene Lovelle?" somebody whispered so you could hear it down at the Battery.

"Couldn't be, she's in London," came the whisper of authority.

"Your *humor!*" she broke down with laughter. "Oh, it's delicious! I can see it all on the stage right now."

"You can?" I said. "I can't. Tell me what you see, will you please?"

"How's your project coming?" Sam said to Sterling. "I think it's a fabulous idea."

"Usual thing. Trouble with lyrics. Trouble with choreographer," Sterling said. "But we think we have something."

"I think it's a terrific concept," Sam said.

"We think it's exciting," Sterling said. "But you never know until you come in. Say, excuse me a minute, there's Freddie over there. I want to speak to him."

He got up and squeezed his way through the mob.

Sam leaned across the table.

"Listen, Irene, how's the show coming?" he said. "How bad *is* it?"

"Incredible," she said. "A real Thanksgiving dinner. In fact . . ." She looked around. "Now don't say anything, but I'm trying to get out."

"No!" Sam said. "But you're sewed up, aren't you?"

"I can get out," she said ominously.

"I *told* you the whole idea was simply *grotesque* for Broadway, didn't I? And you got so sore at me!"

"Darling!" she murmured passionately. "I *love* that tie. Where did you get it?"

"Don't change the subject," Sam said. "I got it at a Cardinal tie shop for a dollar. What about this big serious talk you wanted with me?"

"Why don't we meet tomorrow — just the three of us?" she said.

"Under the Brooklyn Bridge," Sam said.

"You'll come, won't you, Jack?" she said, laying her internationally famous smart-set hand on my sleeve.

"Miss Lovelle," I said, "if you want me to push a peanut up the Post Road to Bridgeport with my nose, I'll do it."

"Nobody uses the Post Road any more," Sam said.

"I know," I said. "And Riverside Drive isn't fashionable. And Scott and Zelda aren't riding around on the roofs of taxicabs any more."

"Oh, did you know Scott?" Irene said, and looked at me tenderly. In this West Virginia coal mine lighting she looked very beautiful.

"How would I know Scott?" I said. "I am only eighteen years of age. Did you know him?"

"A doll," she said. "A regular doll. A sweet, sweet man."

"Oh come on now, Irene," Sam said. "Slow down."

But then our strenuous witticisms were quelled, for the "entertainment" began. It was a rube act, naturally; it was a monologue, of course; by a plain fellow in a plain suit and a plain tie, who said a lot of funny things about the folks back in his home town; like about the plumbing, and the postmaster, and the ticket agent down at the depot. All the glittering girls and boys loved it to pieces and they said he was a fresh talent and that he wrote all his own material. He said about the volunteer firemen's picnic and about his cross-eyed cousin judging the pie-baking contest. George Ade rolled over in his tomb.

Beautiful Miss Lovelle finished her stinger.

"You know what I think?" Sam said in that voice you reserve for talking when the floor show is on. "I don't think he's very funny."

"NBC thinks he's *very* funny," Irene replied. "They're giving him his own half-hour show next month."

"How utterly typical," Sam said.

"I'll call you tomorrow," Irene said.

Mr. Sterling came squeezing back through the cattle and contrived to sit down somehow.

"How's Freddie?" Sam said.

"He must be bored. He's suing the Shuberts again," Sterling said.

"Tell me," I said. "If I become a member of the theatrical profession how much time do I have to spend in the Bon Mot?"

"That is *so* Irene Lovelle," said a girl nearby.

"I'm not sure but I think I'm getting tired now," Sam said.

So the waiter brought us some more drinks as it was only
2:20 A.M.

Chapter 6

We finally got out to the street, not without three full stops where, squeezed against a wall, bumbled into by waiters, I was introduced to shadowy figures whom I would never recognize even if I did ever meet them again. Outside it was cool and clear and late. The traffic had gone beddy-bye and it was a relief; the city was resting up for another big racket and splurge in just a few more hours when all hell would bust loose again and all the cross-streets would be filled solid from curb to curb with trucks which never moved at all.

Sam insisted on climbing the fence in the *middle* of Park Avenue, and singing the entire score of *Wonderful Town*. ("I think Lenny did a *marvelous* job. And Roz is *so* great. Don't you think she's just Great?") Nobody paid any attention. When he wasn't singing he was saying, "Isn't this town the greatest! Look at those lights! Look at the sky! Oh god what if we lived in Albany! Listen to the heartbeat of our wonderful town!"

"That's no heartbeat," I said. "That's a train going underneath us into Grand Central."

But the city *was* beautiful and quiet as we worked our way west toward the Algonquin. Anyway it was quiet. Nothing doing in Cartier's. In Rosemarie de Paris the fancy gift packages, the dolls and toy rabbits waited for the lady customers and the uncles with tiny nieces by the hand. Rockefeller Plaza was empty — all the RCA boys and the agency boys and the TV fast talkers who described their triumphs to each other at 5 P.M. in the men's bar were tucked in their W. & J. Sloane trundle beds out in New Canaan and Westport. I looked up up up at where our office must be, on the 565th floor.

"It simply flattens you, doesn't it?" Sam said. "Nothing like that out in Indiana, hey kid?"

"Nope," I said. "But we've got the old shot tower, that's quite a sight."

"I'll bet," Sam said. "What's it for?"

"Why it just stands there. It don't do a thing."

"Well, you won't see the old shot tower any more. You're going to *love* New York."

"It's not love at first sight," I said.

"Why, what's the matter?"

"Aw hell," I said. "It's all too complicated. Too complicated for me. I'll never make it."

"*Complicated?* What's *com*plicated about it for godsake?" Sam said.

"Everything," I said. "Now you take that problem in the *News* tonight, for example. It says, 'In boarding a bus or any public conveyance should the gentleman assist his companion on first, or should he get on first?' Suppose I and Miss Gloria Vanderbilt was boarding a bus to go have a Giant Idaho Potato at Toffenetti's and I fouled up the embarkation rites. She would tell Sinatra and everybody that I was as square as a coffee table."

"You are quite a cut-up, aren't you?" Sam said.

"All right, smarty," I said. "Here's another one that is keeping the readers of the *News* on the edge of their seats: 'Does a gentleman walk on the outside when with two ladies?' The only way out I personally can see is for the gentleman to tell the queens he has got a dental appointment and bow out."

"But that wouldn't work after 5 P.M.," Sam said. "He had better call a cab."

"Sure, I thought of that. But then," I said, "that raises the question: 'When riding in a cab with two ladies, should a gentleman sit on the left, the middle, the right, on a jump seat, or up in front with Melvin Rench the driver?' See what I mean about this metropolitan life? 'Way too complicated."

We passed Black Starr & Gorham. They had a display of a fancy table setting, the grand feature being some extra-special champagne glasses. For the realistic touch the glasses were filled with genuine flat golden ginger ale or possibly fuel oil.

"That's the way we'll live someday," Sam said, peering into the window.

"You write lyrics, too, I see," I said.

Eventually we tottered to a halt in front of the Algonquin. A cab drew up and a man with a goatee and a cane got out and, having paid the driver, entered the historic portals.

"I'll grab this," Sam said, leaping into the cab.

"Well so long, it's been keen," I said as the cab took off up 44th Street with all jets wide open. By the time it reached the Royalton it had broken through the sound barrier. "Quiet, boys," I said. "You'll wake Mr. Nathan up."

I collected my mail and went up to the home away from home.

So there I was in my nice little room, alone at last away from all the crazy people of the big city. There is nothing so wonderful in this new and jumbled-up, slightly terrifying life of tinkling water glasses, antipasto and French pastry, Italian waiters and plates, glasses, menus, napkins, pots of *espresso* and meal checks incessantly being placed in front of you — not to mention the incessant sound of clever voices yakking on on and on and expecting you to regurgitate something brilliant — nothing so wonderful in this let's-everybody-scream world as to be all alone. One takes off the necktie and no one says "I adore that tie." The tie goes over the back of a chair. One flops in an easy chair, removes one's shoes and rolls a cigarette. No one says "Can you do that with one hand?" The silence is noble, a regular gift from the Almighty; it is worth all the money in the East River Savings Bank. It fills up the room. It's so thick you can reach out and grab a handful.

I sat down and read my letter first. It was from Cousin Archie.

DEAR MR. MAUGHAM:

You are not doing any good on that Locomobile gasket which is the only sensible reason for you to be down there on the world's most repulsive peninsula so why not come home and lend me a hand? The xylophone attachment on your electric piano went out of whack last night and needs your attention. Uncle Fred's hearing aid is on the bum again and all he can hear on it is the chimes concert from WOC Davenport and Little Jack Little the Whispering Piano Player. Everybody wants to know did you meet Richard Hackett yet? Who the hell is he? Forget about this twerp and get over to Egg Harbor City and locate the guy with all the Locomobile parts or else get aboard the steam cars and come home.

Have you ever considered enrolling at the National School of Meat Cutting in Toledo, O., where you get your training under actual Meat Market Conditions? You can pay your tuition in 8 easy installments AFTER you graduate. Think it over, Hemingway.

ARCHIE

"You are always reaching too hard, Archie," I said.

Cousin Archie is a compulsive letter writer and a frustrated vaudeville artist. He can play the musical saw and imitate Eddie Cantor singing "Whoopee" and has a lot of funny jokes. The only thing Archie needs is a job and it's the last thing he wants as he says he is too busy on his projects. One of his projects is trying to see if he can repeat the hole-in-one he made in 1934 at the South Shore Country Club. He works pretty hard at this and you have to give him credit. That's all Archie wants, credit. Someday Archie is going to invent the Perpetual Motion Machine and then we're going to be proud of him.

If I don't go to bed pretty soon, I thought, it will be time to turn on the TV set and see what Dave Garroway, Jack Lescoulie and the chimp are up to because it's TODAY in good old New York and the housewives out in Conneaut, Ohio, are donning their gaily printed housecoats and can't wait to see what Dave has up his sleeve and hear about the Morton folks down Louisville way and their frozen chicken pot pies all chock full of big hunks of white meat.

So now the telephone rings. Oh hell, this is New York — we just call each other up all night — nobody goes to bed in Big Town.

"Hi!" says Sam in gladsome tones. "What are you doing?"

"Oh me and Ina Claire we are just setting around here in our BVD's having a cold bottle of Schaefer's beer," I said. "Where are you at, General MacArthur's suite?"

"No," Sam says. "I am *at* home."

"Well, that's a nice place to be," I said. "What the hell do you want?"

"Oh, I just wondered if you got home all right," he said.

"Why goddamn it, you left me right here," I said. "I

couldn't hardly get lost after entering the magnificent lobby."

"Listen, Jack," he said, "I hope you are thinking *seriously* about the show. I mean *really* seriously. Please get *very* serious."

"Yeah," I said. "Okay."

"Oh *god*," he said. "I *mean* it."

"*Okay!*" I said. "Gee, pal, I'll get serious."

"You can do it," he said. "We need you, boy."

So I picked up that book written by the hotel manager and figured it would put me to sleep better than any pill. Right away I ran into trouble:

Here are a few names known to everyone . . . together with the handier affectionate terms used by their intimates:

Sinclair Lewis	Red
Brailsford Felder	Tom
Samson Raphaelson	Raph
Theresa Helburn	Terry
G. Selmer Fougner	Baron

Right then the phone rang and I figured it was Sam again so I picked it up and said, "This is G. Selmer Fougner speaking, but my intimates call me Baron."

"Is Mr. Jordan there?" the operator said. "Long distance, please."

I admitted that it was really me after all and then Frankie was on.

"Frankie! Hi, baby — say, what time is it out there anyway?"

"It's 3 A.M. I just couldn't wait. Did you meet Mr. Hackett? What happened? Are you going to do it? Did they like you? What's Richard Hackett like?"

"He's kinda like Gary Cooper only better-looking and he doesn't wear levis."

"Did you really talk to him?"

"Why hell yes, honey. That's what I'm down here for, isn't it?"

"Oh, Jack, tell me all about it."

"Listen, did you reverse the charges?"

"No, I didn't."

"Too bad. They would have had to pay for it."

"Never mind that. Tell me. Where did you eat?"

"At Schrafft's — we ate at Schrafft's. I had chopped chicken livers on healthy toast and we all got gay on iced tea."

"Now quit the funny stuff and save it for the show. Omit the jokes and just tell me exactly what happened."

"All right. I went to the office. It's all filled with dames like in the movies. I met Sam Snow and he is just a kid, he looks like he's just going out to buy a new Yo-yo. Guess he's about twenty-five. Gray flannels and Shetland jacket. Then Crosby came in, he's kind of a straight man. Been working for Hackett for twenty years. Nice guy. Lunch like I said at Schrafft's. Blah blah blah we think your book is terrific, fresh, captivating, different, and literate."

"What's that last?"

"Literate. They are all the time saying 'literate.' That's the new word down here. Opposite of ill-literate, get it? Very powerful word down here."

" 'Literate.' Okay. Go on."

"After lunch we went up to the office and I met Richard Hackett. He's about six feet I guess, looks taller. Athletic — graceful walk — he walks better than any man I ever saw. Handsomest son of a bitch in town. Nice dresser — nothing gaudy — gray herringbone, regimental tie."

"How's he talk, Jack? New York?"

"Huh-uh. He talks normal, hits his r's and everything.

Strong quality to his voice. Doesn't shoot off the yap much. And oh boy is he literate."

"Say, is he married?"

"I don't know, baby, but I'll bet he's a Kansas twister with the ladies. Wait till you see him."

"Am I likely to? Oh, Jack, for heaven's sake get on with it. What happened?"

"Well they don't play anything in three-quarter time down here. We talked for a while about the 'property' — more blah blah blah. Then they yanked me out of there and they pulled, hauled and shoved me over to the theater and plunked me into the front row of *Can-Can* for the matinee. Pretty crummy show but very high underpants content."

"Don't tell me you didn't like it — I've seen all the publicity shots. I bet you were in heaven."

"Now now, Miss Glutz, relax. All right — so then there were faithful friends Snow and Crosby waiting for me. 'Come on,' says Crosby, 'we'll have a drink at Sardi's.' So they shoved me across the street and we had a drink. Sardi's is no Empire Room by a long shot, but it's fun there — everybody looking at everybody else. Well, you know how I feel about *one* drink, but just as I was about in the mood for a repeater we are gone again and in a cab. Zoom! Up to the office. Hackett says, 'How'd you like it? Think you can write a musical now?' 'No,' I said. 'I can't write gags.' 'Hmmmm,' says Hackett. 'Sure you can write gags,' says Sam. 'Your book is funny as hell.' 'No,' Hackett says, 'you can't write gags.' 'Well, maybe not gags,' says Sam. 'But you've got something better than gags,' says Hackett. 'That's right,' Sam says. 'You've got an individual style,' Hackett says. 'Your people are real people not cardboard cutouts,' Crosby says. 'We want a literate script,' Sam says. 'Humor from within,'

Crosby says. 'All right, boys,' Hackett says, 'hold everything. I knocked out a rough scenario this afternoon. Suppose I give Mr. Jordan an outline of the first scene and some nice clean sheets of paper and a lovely pencil and leave him in sublime isolation for an hour or two and see what happens.' "

"Oh, Jack, weren't you terrified? I mean — you don't work like that. What did you say?"

"Well, I was about to explain that I was pooped out, that I wasn't in the mood, that it was too hot, that I had a headache, that my feet hurt, that I only write on alternate Thursdays and all that but by god I looked at Hackett and I was just plain afraid to say No."

"Looks like you are in good hands," Frankie said. "I want to meet Mr. Hackett. Maybe I can pick up some pointers."

"Write it down," I said. "That's very funny. Maybe you should write this show instead of me."

"*Are* you going to write it?" she said.

"Yes," I said. "If you'll let me tell you about it without the comical rejoinders."

"I'm sorry. Go ahead," she said.

"Well I wrote some stuff and it was terrible but Hackett said it was on the right track and he said he would *collaborate* with me, get that, he said he and I would write it together."

Frankie didn't say a thing.

"You hear me?" I said.

"Well I'll be goddamned," she said.

"Yeah, me too," I said.

"This is the end," she said.

"You said it, blackie," I said. "Now listen, before the telephone company has all my royalties. Are you listening? Point A: Call Dude Silver and tell him to rent the house. Point B: Start packing. Point C: I'll be home tomorrow night on the flying machine. Point D: We leave for New York a week from today. Now, any further questions, lovebug?"

"I can't believe a word of it," she said.

"And listen, honey," I said. "You better go to the hardware store and get four switch-blade knives for the kids. It's standard equipment in the public schools down here."

Chapter 7

AT HOME things were the same — just think, in five days they hadn't changed a bit. The salesmen hadn't moved an inch from the leather chairs down at the hotel where they sat with their hats on, looking at Main Street or hunting patiently through the Indianapolis *Star* for a message of hope.

"What happened in New York?" said the friendly Naborhood Druggist. "You honestly moving East?"

"That's right," I said. "Gimme some razor blades."

"Look sharp, be sharp," he said. "Keep your eye on those babies down there in New York."

"I don't know," I said. "Wouldn't be surprised if they'd whip me."

"I got a cousin lives in Schenectady," he said.

I spent the week running through a Laurel and Hardy two-reel skit called *Moving Day* in which I got trunk and self stuck in attic stairs, ran into closed doors, locked thumb in suitcase, and blew up cellar while turning off the gas. The kids, numbering four, got into their Our Gang Comedy makeup and put on a competitive show of their own by planting roller skates at the foot of staircases, and getting the Baby lost under the hood of the car.

"The trouble is," I said to Frankie, "I haven't got enough kids. We should have some more of the dumplings. They are an inspiration to me and when I see them tearing the joint apart it puts me in a very creative mood."

"Well," says Frankie, "in only eighteen years the Baby will be twenty-one."

"I hope he votes the right ticket," I said.

"Do you want to take the *Encyclopaedia*?" Frankie said.

"Hell no," I said.

"Well, you just paid the last installment. It cost nearly four hundred dollars. How are you going to get any good out of it if . . ."

"Honey," I said, "we're not taking it. We're not taking the piano, the motorboat, or the lawn roller, either."

"But what if you want to look something up when you're writing the show?" she said.

"Listen, if I need the *Encyclopaedia Britannica* to write a musical comedy I have got the whole thing figured wrong from the start."

"Well, I'm just trying to be helpful."

"That's fine and you are some dandy little wife, but now I have to go meet Link Howard. Link says he has been asking me to Rotary for fifteen years and I have been putting him off. So in a weak moment I told him okay."

"Have you been taking your vitamin pills lately?" says Sweetyface.

"Link has been a pretty good friend," I said. "Don't forget that."

"I didn't realize that they served Martinis at the Rotary," she replied.

We had about three at the Elks Club first and at the luncheon we sang some songs including "Smiles" and then we ate up our lunch, following which we got in on a mighty good talk on the growth of the cigar industry which had reached the point where 43 million dollars' worth of 5-cent cigars and 45 million dollars' worth of 10-cent cigars were being sold annually, or more than 6 billion cigar butts. The speaker, who was equipped with a handy kit of demonstrator cigars, also corrected various misconceptions and "erroneous attitudes" concerning cigars which are sweeping the country and giving cigar manufacturers plenty of gloomy moments when the struggle for increased panatela volume hardly seems worth while — such as he pointed out the fact that *the color of the wrapper*, for instance, has *little to do with the degree of mildness of the cigar.*

"Link," I said, "he's going pretty far with that statement."

"Jack," Link said, "please don't judge Rotary by that remark. While we don't necessarily endorse Free Thinkers, we believe every man has a right to his own opinion."

"That's a liberal attitude, Link," I said.

"It's the American Way, Jack," Link said.

"Hush," said Fatty Boland, who was next to Link.

I filed away the cigar statistics in my head for possible use later on, just in case some party up on Park Avenue should begin to drag a little bit.

That night my mother called up at 6:30 while we were eating dinner; my mother has telepathic powers in regard to our mealtime, as no matter how we juggle the hour she always calls when we are eating. One time we decided to fool her and we ate the evening meal at 3:15 P.M. The Baby had not even warmed up to throwing his dish on the floor for the first time before Mother was on the phone wanting to know if I could remember the name of those people from Evanston who we met at the Yellowstone Hot Springs in 1924.

Well, this time she called at 6:30.

"Jack, I know you're awfully busy," she said, "but you *should* go to Engelden's Funeral Home and see poor old Mary Faulhabber. You know she was with your grandmother for over fifty years. She . . ."

"Oh, Mother, I can't . . ." I said.

"She simply *adored* you, you know," she said. "The family will expect it, I'm sure."

"Oh god," I said.

"Jack," she said, "please don't curse at me."

"Old Mary didn't adore me," I said. "She detested me and I did her. Ignorant German pig. What about the time during the First World War when she dumped the mashed potatoes on Grandpa's head on account of the Kaiser or something? Damned Prussian. Fat old thing."

"Oh my dear," said my mother with sweet gentle reproach. "Oh my dear."

"Well I'm not going and that's that," I said. "I'm trying to get off to New York and close this crazy house. I . . ."

"Just as you like, my dear," she continued, the voice of patient suffering. "I try so hard, but I guess I've been a failure as a mother."

She developed this theme for a while and hung up. So after supper I washed up and put on a tie.

"Where you going?" Frankie said.

"Down to see the remains of Mary Faulhabber," I said.

"Can I come?" said Tom.

"Can I come?" said Nat a little louder.

"Can I come?" shrieked delicate, tiny, rosebud daughter Katie like a steam whistle.

"Me tum!" roared the Baby, battering at the screen door and knocking the screen out.

I couldn't seem to locate the Faulhabber remainders at the funerary homestead or House of Good Cheer, so when one of the hired ghouls showed up I accosted him.

"Is er, um, Mary Faulhabber here?" I said. "I mean the er — remains?"

"Oh no," the kindly chap replied, "she's at Schroader's. She ain't here."

"Oh," I said. "Thanks."

"But we got Old Man Kleinpell and the Infant Bodenheim," he said. "Youse can see them as long as you're here."

"No, thanks," I said.

"That's up to youse," he said. "Youse might as well."

"No. Thanks just the same," I said. "Perhaps some other time."

"They say Old Man Kleinpell left it all to the Holy Name Society, the Rosary Confraternity, and the Order of Foresters. Homer and Roy never got nothing."

"That's tough on Homer and Roy," I said. "So long."

"Say Daddy, listen Daddy, hey Daddy, Daddy listen, are all the people in that house Dead?" Katie said when I got back in the beat-up station wagon.

"Yes, honey," I said. "They are all dead."

"See, see what I told you," Tom screamed. "Ha ha I told you so. I told you so."

"Katie said they *weren't* dead," Nat said.

"Told you so," Tom said.

"I DID NOT DID NOT DID NO-OT!" steam-whistled Katie.

"The heck you didn't," Nat said.

"They're all dead, aren't they, Papa? Ha ha, just as I said," Tom said.

"All dead!" howled the Baby.

"I DID NOT DID NOT DID NOT DID NOT DID NO-O-O-O-OT!" screamed Katie.

"They're alive," I said. "Everybody in there is alive. Now be quiet."

"Oh, Daddy," Tom said. "You told a lie."

"See, ha ha-ha haaa ha," sang Katie the way she does.

"Katie's crazy," Nat said.

"You take that *back*," Katie screamed.

"The people in that house are *dead*," Tom said.

"Dead-dead-dead," chortled the Baby.

"Where are we going, Papa?" Katie said.

"Crazy," Nat said.

"Oh you paste your blabbermouth shut you dumb old Nat you," Katie said.

"Temper, temper, dimple darling sister dear," Tom said.

"Let's go to the Rexall store and see if they have a sale on ice-cream cones," I said. "And let's be friends, shall we? Let's observe a minute of silence for the World War dead."

"Yaay!" screamed All.

"Me want mines soda, Ba-Pa," said the humorous Baby in his screamingly funny dialect.

So I never did see that stubborn old Luxembourger and I am sorry I didn't for the family's sake, but one embalming garden per day is all I can stand.

However, I did hear Frank Carideo at the Elks the next evening and Frank was okay. He is in Football's Hall of Fame and has adopted the Tall Corn State as his home. Is ardent Hawkeye rooter. Frank kicked four consecutive punts on first down against Northwestern on November 22, 1930, all four of which went out of bounds inside the one-yard marker. Think that over for a while. It was a pretty good treat to be in the presence of one of the great Rockne's pigskin immortalities.

I picked up Frankie after the Elks and we went over to Cousin Archie's. Things started slowly but then everybody who passed the house saw my car standing there so they had to come in and give me some advice about what highway to take through Ohio and on arrival in New York not to eat oysters only in the months with *r* in them. So before long everybody was having a good time, which means getting loaded; in this game the object is to see what way it will hit different members of the group and how terrible they can get — or how dull and repetitive — or how silent and in-jured — and the winner is awarded his choice of a German silver pickle fork or a souvenir ash tray of the Wisconsin Dells.

There is not much use in going through this farewell rodeo inning by inning, but I will say that Boots Remington got a good deal more slobbery than usual, and, boys, when she plunks herself down in your lap and gives you the googoo talk it is just too bad. I wish she would get married again, or else hunt up that ex-husband of hers called Antipasto or whatever it was, and quiet down a little bit; or else take off 25 to 50 lbs. if she is going to continue with the lap-leaping act for the next three decades. The rest of the gang were doggedly drinking; Archie had been in and out of two slumps already and was heading for a third, during which he would sit silently for perhaps a half an hour with an expres-sion of amused condescension on his flushed but handsome and ever-youthful face, terribly, terribly sophisticated and im-mune to the yokel babbling of these Poland Chinas; what could they know of the delicious wit, the cold clean intellect that he was with royal dignity keeping to himself?

Most of the girls wanted to go home to bed, but they couldn't go home because this was a Party and it was Lots of Fun, and they might miss something, too, because it was always when you went home that something happened. If you stayed, nothing happened, but if you went home it did. You never could tell when Sam Black's new wife from Kansas City would get a skinful and start telling everybody what she thought of them before she got sick and had to be carried out to the car. So you had to stick around.

Everybody was telling me what a dope I was to leave the greatest little old town in the world, because there's noplace where people have as much Fun. And the big shots other places wouldn't even give me the time of day, much less invite me and Frankie to their parlors for Martinis made of House of Lords gin. But here, why, I was right in the swim with the sawdust aristocracy, the plumbing, dry-battery, wallboard, disk-harrow and axle-grease aristocracy; they accepted me as one of themselves even if I did write books and read the New York papers. Friendship like that — where else would I find it?

More beverages were passed around and Archie woke up and turned on the electric piano and it played "Bambelina," followed by "Yacki, Hacki, Wicki, Wacki, Woo."

Lovable Gene Zuppke, Vice President of the Rendering Works, told me I was in for a cleaning in New York. He said so what if you did write this book what's that prove why anybody can write a book. He said brother you better wise up. He said personally he hadn't read my book but he understood there wasn't much to it. He said why anybody can write a book what the hell is all the excitement about.

"You are right," I said, "and I could be the Vice President of the Rendering Works if I wanted to but I don't want to."

"All you Jordans are so goddamn bright," he said.

"Come on, Frankie," I said. "Let's go home and get the baby sitter and her boy friend up off the couch."

"I was just kidding, you know that, don't you," Zuppke said.

"Sure," I said, "everybody around here is always just kidding."

"No hard feelings, eh, Jack?"

"Don't push it, cowboy," I said.

My face was an impenetrable mask, not unlike Alan Ladd's.

Our hegira coincided with the worst heat wave in twenty-four years. We had a trailer behind us with everything in it from home except Milo O'Brien's wooden Indian and the cast-iron horse-watering trough on Minnesota and 18th Street. The car boiled the entire distance of 900 miles except for seven minutes in a cloudburst on the outskirts of Masillon.

All the way across the fruited plains of Indiana, and Ohio, and through the verdant hills and dales of Pennsylvania, a junior size civil war broke out several times daily between Tom and Katie, climaxed by screams from Katie of "No you won't! If you do I'll *kill you!*"

Finally as we were careening up the Jersey Turnpike I said, "Say, what's this all about anyway? You shouldn't kill your brother, honey. Mother wouldn't like it. Now what seems to be the trouble?"

"Well, Papa," says Katie, "he says he's going to tell my doll what I'm going to give her for Christmas. And I will too kill him, if he does."

And on this note of impending tragedy we swept aboard the George Washington Bridge. Halfway across, the car gave up and stopped dead. That is a very busy street.

Chapter 8

I prefer the theater to night club work because the customers are sober, there's no heckling, and there's nobody named Rocky giving orders.
— JACK WALDRON

PEOPLE are always telling me they have a swell idea for a story only they can't write very good and I'm supposed to write it up for them and we'll both get famous, especially the idea man. "My grandfather was Buffalo Bill's barber and say, some of the stories he told were rich. I'd like to sit down with you sometime . . ." "Dear Mr. Jordan: I read your story in *Holidays* and it was very interesting. I was a rural mail carrier in Tibet for nineteen years and I had many interesting experiences which people tell me would make an interesting book. Would you be interested . . ."

After you get into the theater business it is just the same thing, everybody has got some swell ideas, all they need is me on the typewriter for an hour or two in order to show up Rodgers and Hammerstein and make Arthur Miller take a back seat. One of these barroom playwrights wanted me to drop everything and knock out a libretto on a real funny Western where the action takes place in a soda fountain instead of the usual saloon. Pretty comical twist with all

the hard-case cowpokes belting sodas instead of that rye —
then we'll put in a takeoff on William S. Hart as the Silent
Soda Jerk, Yul Brynner as a humorous laundryman, and Vera
Zorina as a lady sheriff and, say, how can we go wrong?

Well, these happy-faced folks are barking up the wrong
writer, because I still don't have a very clear picture of how
we ever put this play into one piece. Because, gents, it don't
go together so easy as what you might expect and in my case
if it wasn't for Dewar's White Label and Bayer quality pills
it would never have got there at all. I was uneasy most of the
time — hardly breathed a natural relaxed breath for months.
Take living down in Connecticut by the soothing Merritt
Parkway, for example.

INDIANA
*(Sound effects: Meadowlarks warbling;
corn growing.)*

FIRST KID: What's your Dad do?
SECOND KID: He's a writer.
FIRST KID: What's that?

CONNECTICUT
*(Sound effects: Cars crashing; police
sirens screaming.)*

FIRST KID: What's your Dad do?
SECOND KID: He's a writer.
FIRST KID: So's mine.

The way I used to get to the factory out home was to walk
five blocks to the plant. It took about ten minutes.

The way I got to work in Eastern Dreamland was like this:
First round up Frankie and the Baby and push and shove
them into the car, then drive like mad three miles over heav-
ing, weaving blacktop roads bordered by stone walls and
minor executives' phony ranch-type homes, to a funny little

place called Springdale. At Springdale I bought a *New York Herald Tribune* so as to keep up with John Crosby's and Art Buchwald's latest merry quips, and boarded a two-car juice unit with green plush seats for the trip to Stamford. At Stamford I got off the puddle-jumper and stood around the station for from one to sixty minutes waiting for the New York train. When the New York train arrived everybody made a mad dash for seats, using handy weapons such as umbrellas, attaché cases and sword canes in the fight. Fifty-three minutes and two or three nauseating cigarettes later I was in Grand Central Station gazing at the largest American flag in the world and the constellations twinkling in the ceiling. Plunging into a strange tunnel, I made my way for several miles, emerging under the Hotel Roosevelt where, if in the mood, I would stop to case the windows of the lingerie shops. Then up steps, through a revolving door and out into Madison Avenue and the silver shop that is going out of business weekly and has sterling silver crumbers at ridiculously low figures. Brief pause to inspect crumbers for comparison with shop up on corner of 50th and Madison who are staging a crumber price war. Cross Madison at 50th, cruise west on 50th. Hesitation step at Sig Buchmayr's sports shop, then past Saks Fifth Avenue, windows full of beautiful things for beautiful people with beautiful incomes, cross in front of St. Patrick's, cross Fifth Avenue, pass giant bronze statue, enter building, enter elevator, rise 145 stories, walk down corridor, and I arrive at Brain Factory.

Elapsed time from home to place of business: 98 minutes. Condition of feet and nervous system on arrival at work: Poor. Permanent addition to one's valuable store of information from reading newspapers two hours per day: Doubtful. Friendly companionship on train: Zero. Views of sordid home life through track-side windows between 125th Street and 101st Street: Excellent. Status of Anxiety Neurosis: Thriving.

On arrival on September 18, I greeted the office girls and hung up my coat and strolled out of the office and up the hall to the Men's Room to comb my hair. Sam Snow was in there looking at himself in the mirror.

"I see you've got on a pink shirt," I said. "I think I should get one of those."

"My god I look awful," he said. "Do you think I look awful?"

"You look lovely," I said. "Is Mr. Hackett in yet?"

"I think I look *awful*," he said. "I had the most fantastic experience last night. Absolutely the end. Did you rewrite that scene?"

"I took a whack at it," I said.

"Good," he said. "Mr. Hackett didn't think the girl was strong enough."

"She's very strong now," I said. "I left her on Hackett's desk. What did you do last night?"

"Oh *god*," he said. "I was at Sardi's until all hours with Erich and Nancy, and dozens of other people. And when they all went home I got this *crazy* idea. See, I've been living with this girl — she's in *Can-Can* — but her mother's been here from Toledo or someplace — staying with her. So *I* got the idea I had to see her and went to her place and simply *pounded* on the door. I was terrible. I look awful, don't I?"

"You look okay," I said. "So what happened?"

"Well, after a while the door opened and my suitcase came *flying* out into the hall. A respectable apartment building, mind you. And then my clothes came *flying* out after it, and the door slammed shut. So there I was, on my *hands* and *knees* in the hall, stuffing things into my suitcase. A lovely tableau."

"Lovely," I said.

"So at this point this oafish elevator operator appeared and got *very* incensed. 'Hey, buddy, what the hell do you think you're doing?' *That* kind of talk. 'I'm going on a trip, can't you see?' I said. I thought that was pretty funny, but he didn't. Well, anyway, *somehow* I got home. I feel just perfectly *awful*."

"Come on," I said, "we've got work to do. You've got to produce this big smash hit and get your name in the *Times* and the *Little Rock Globe-Gazette* and all, remember?"

"I wish you wouldn't be so funny," he said.

"That's what you hired me for," I said. "Come on, we better get back to work."

"And that damn girl stole my best necktie, too. Anyway, I can't find it."

"You've got to watch these *Can-Can* girls," I said. "Girls always showing off their underpants all the time — they'll do anything."

Mr. Hackett was waiting for us and Sam and I went in and sat down. He was tilted back behind his desk looking at the ceiling.

Sam went into his act, which was to relate funny incidents of the previous evening — what somebody said to somebody else about Jimmy's new girl friend, a new night club act he had seen with somebody in it "worth keeping an eye on," an old-time actor he had run into at The Lambs and the funny things he had said about Jed Harris, what George Kaufman had said about another producer ("He's Jed Harris rolled into one"), and so on and on. Hackett liked having Sam around, he was funny and he kept things livened up, he was all over New York all the time and every morning he had a report which he delivered with all his violent boyish enthusiasm, exploding his sentences, underlining words, faking indignation, stuttering with excitement, laughing, changing the subject.

"And I saw Vivian, with some perfectly absurd little guy — can't imagine where she found him."

"How'd she look?" Hackett said.

"Just ghastly. Overdressed as usual, outlandish hat of course."

"Has she taken off any weight?" Hackett said. "Last time I saw her she was ruining her figure."

"She's *enormous*," Sam said. "And drinking like mad."

"Too bad," Hackett said. "She had such a fresh, lovely vitality. When I first had her she was perfectly lovely. Is she getting any work?"

"Oh — you know — TV stuff," Sam said.

"Too bad," Hackett said.

"Then I saw Benny. He was with that tall redhead that was in the chorus of *High Button Shoes* — remember?"

"Holden — Lydia Holden," Hackett said. "Well, she'll run Benny ragged. He's an idiot anyway. It always amazes me, the men that women will go out with for the sake of their careers."

Then Ted came in and sat down.

"What happened to you?" he said to Sam.

"Let's get started," Sam said.

The way we worked — struggled would be a better word for it — was like this. We had a complete outline of the action, a scenario. This we had sweated over for a couple of weeks. It seemed like a phony plot full of phony situations to me, but I didn't understand then what you can get away with in Musical Comedy. After we got the scenario, we started with Act One, Scene One, and we talked it over and Hackett said,

"Now here's what we want," and he told me what we wanted, and I took notes which I never could understand later when I referred to them. Then we would have a thinking session where we all sat and you could hear a pin drop, down on 42d Street, for five minutes at a time. Hackett would lie back in his swivel chair and look at the ceiling and think. Sam would bite his nails and think. Ted would smoke cigarettes and think. I would sit and try to think but I couldn't figure out what to think about.

Usually something crazy would start to go around and around in my head such as "The sins of Kalamazoo . . ." or "*Utor, fruor, fungor, potior* and *vescor* take the ablative," and I would wonder how that book by Thomas Wolfe ever came out that I never finished reading. From Wolfe I would wander to Maxwell Perkins, which would lead me to wondering whether I should switch to Scribner's.

Meanwhile my colleagues were thinking. Well, friends, I can't think in tandem. I can't think too good, any time, much less way up in the air in New York City with the Empire State Building in a pale haze out the window and Sam Snow looking so intense and busy with his fingernails; and Hackett, I suppose he was probably rewriting two or three acts in his head. Whenever Hackett wasn't talking, which was a large part of the time, he was cooking up something. When I'm not talking I'm asleep, a vegetable, I do all my most marvelous thinking while flapping the old mandible. When everybody clams up, boy, I'm gone. This defect in my character went unnoticed, however, and I spent a lot of time on the problem of what Katie was going to give her doll for Christmas. It was as good as thinking about the show, which was all a blur in my mind anyway. The only time I ever got onto the ball and had any ideas was about one A.M. out in the state of Connecticut, seated at the dining-room table completely worn out, but with the compulsion to hold up my end of things and write something.

How these fast thinkers put up with me is a wonder. They were so sure of themselves, so alert, so jamful of ideas about character, motivation, sequences.

"I think Toots is coming out too brittle," Sam said. "You've got to tone her down."

"Audiences won't like her if she's too fresh. She's almost bitchy," Ted said.

"She can't be so rude," Hackett said. "That's not attractive."

"But she's not rude," I said, rousing myself. "That's just the way people talk to each other out where I come from. That's humor."

"It won't do," Hackett said. "Even if they do talk like that."

"But you bought her like that," I said. "She's just a direct person."

So we hashed that over and I rolled cigarettes and spilled tobacco crumbs on the carpet and tried to think about a shadowy figure called Toots. But I didn't argue too much; how can you argue with Hackett when he is nodding at you so reasonably and being so polite about it, and with that voice of his? This guy had the kind of terrific speaking voice that you couldn't possibly think anything spurious could ever be said with it. This is not the case with anybody else I ever met in the profession, but then, Hackett was different every way. He was a guy that after you worked with him for a while you would lie on the railroad track if he told you to, and like it.

That is, if you got the idea he liked you, you would. If he didn't, you might want to shoot him, I suppose, and some people felt that way. Getting him to like you was the thing.

He didn't pass it out very freely, so when you got it you figured you had something. He didn't like a lot of actors and he didn't like actresses much and he didn't want women to have opinions, and he didn't care a hell of a lot for writers and composers, either. He had had it from all of them. It wasn't that he hated all these wahoos, he just didn't have any illusions about their glamour, and he didn't care much for people who made a fuss all the time and had temperament and were worried about their press notices and leaped from table to table at Sardi's. "Just be good, Jack," he told me one time. "Just do your work and be good at it and the rest will all come to you. Never mind the press agents. No press agent in New York ever created any talent." What he admired and respected was performance.

So, working with a guy like this I didn't throw myself around like I used to out in the Golden West. I was pretty dull. But I worked, harder than I ever did before. It was on account of Hackett with that voice of his.

Chapter 9

I MADE a few stops that night on the way to Grand Central, first at the Gaslight Cafe on Sixth Avenue for an economically priced Scotch, then at one of those open-front stores: ANY BOOK IN THE STORE 19 CENTS. Got Katie a book about Tommy Turtle. Next wedged myself into a sec-ondhand bookstore down by 42d Street filled with men thumbing through Audel's *Automotive Mechanics* and flag-ellation monthlies. Bought Nat a copy of *Tom Swift and His Photo Telephone* and Tom a grimy germ-laden copy of *Treasure Island*. ("About time he started reading some classics." However, when I got home Frankie immediately postponed Tom's adventures with Long John Silver by heav-ing the book out with the potato peelings and some used pork chops on account of it was so dirty.)

Had a hot dog with sauerkraut at Nedick's on corner of 42d. Retraced steps up Sixth and had another drink.

Neighbor at bar: "That's what I tole him but you think he believe me? Oh no, not him. He don't believe nothin'. He don't even believe hisself. 'Listen,' I says to him, 'you are so wise and all, ask Carl if you don't believe me.' 'Carl,' he says. 'Him. What's he know about it?' '*Know* about it?' I says. 'That's a hot one. Oh sure, Carl he don't know nothin' about it. *Certainly* not. Carl he would be the *last* person to know.' 'How come Carl he knows?' he says. 'I never said he did,' I says. 'I just got through tellin' you he don't know nothin'. Why, he'd be the *last* person . . .'"

Going east on 42d I stopped and looked at the windows in the Marboro Book Shop and the crowd kept bumping into me and blamming me around. I went in and bought a book about *The Castles of Ireland* reduced from $12.50 to $1.98 with all the lovely sepia plates; I need this book badly, like I need two or three more children; well, I always wanted to know more about the Castles of Ireland and now, boy, I've got the basic text and sometime in twenty-five years I might even have three spare minutes to look at it if I live that long. So I looked in Stern's windows at the furniture displays and figured what they would look like if they were mine, with a tricycle on one of the chairs, comic books strewn all around, and a peanut butter sandwich upside down on the damask love seat. "Then what did he say?" said a girl to her friend. "He said I odda get my head examined," said pert, lovely Sylvia Feinberg of the flashing dark eyes, the madcap of the E-Z Loan Co. office, Your Signature Is All We Want. On the other side of Fifth Avenue I stopped at Grandma Pinsky's Strudel Kitchen and bought Frankie an apricot strudel with which to improve her figure. Making change I dropped *The Castles of Ireland*, picked it up and down went Tom Swift. And then in the roaring street again I tottered eastwards in the radiant evening, glorious with the pulse-quickening beat-beat-beat of the strudel center of the nation, as, in the gathered dusk, the uninviting throng carried me onwards toward the station, now looming above the jam of taxicabs.

Passing Childs, juggling packages, I paused to gaze in at the warm lights and the white-coated bartender, who at that very moment was setting out old-fashioneds for three matinee-weary matrons in identical fur capes. I joined them, stacking my packages on the bar, with the Irish Castles at the bottom.

"I thought it was good, didn't you?" said one of the dolls eating a peanut daintily.

"Oh, very good," said another.

"I thought the dress she wore in the last act was very unbecoming," said Number Three.

"Oh, but her *hat*, in Act One."

"Do you think that hair is natural?"

"Certainly not. I saw her in Westport last summer and she was brunette."

"I must say I don't see what all the excitement is about her."

"The critics just dote on her, though."

"Well, anybody that flutters her hands like that all the time — they make me nervous."

"I didn't care much for her voice."

"I thought it was awfully good, though."

"Oh, I thought it was terribly good."

"I thought it was marvelous."

"So did I."

I drank my sarsaparilla in a dreadful depression as the gentlewomen plucked the maraschino cherries from their glasses and ate them carefully.

"We're the only big agency that gives out the figures, Fred," said a neat Macclesfield tie on my left. "J. Walter Thompson doesn't, Batten Barton doesn't, Kudner doesn't . . ."

"I'm not saying that, Jerry," said his friend with a jumbo Martini. "I'm just trying to light a few protective smudge-pots around this idea before it freezes up."

"Well, the whole project needs a valve-and-ring job," said Macclesfield.

At the end of the bar two large, prosperous fellows got up to go; as they passed me one of them said:

"Ted, short-selling is the thing that keeps the market in balance."

"I know, I know," said the other.

The advertising boys from the big agency departed and their stools were instantly occupied by a grizzled customer in a brown topcoat and a younger one with a pleasant, eager, wide-open-spaces face.

"You see that simply means like somebody very crafty and scheming up something all the time," said the older man. "It comes from Machavellio, he was a very sharp Italian prince back in the old times who was always cooking up some wise deals in these court intrigues and all that."

"I figured it was something along those lines," said South Dakota, "only I never heard that expression before."

"After you've been around here awhile you'll pick up a lot of this stuff. Don't let it throw you."

Well, that is a pretty good reason for coming to New York at that. You certainly don't pick up much dope on Machavellio out there around Yankton and Sioux Falls.

One likes to dream of New York at twilight in the snow à la Childe Hassam, of hansom cabs, tea served on Fifth Avenue by maids in lace aprons, oyster suppers at Delmonico's, of children in neat pinafores in the nursery at lamp-lighting time, of a good cigar before an open fire in a marble fireplace with the fall rains beating on the windowpanes. But where do you find these lost treasures of living? Noplace that I know.

"Now you take philosophy," said the sage. "It sounds complicated but there's nothing to it. It comes from the Greek words *philo* and *sopho*, and what it means is simply the study of human nature."

"Is that a fact?"

"Sure, that's all."

So I finally wend my way stationwards and add a *New York Post* and an *Evening American* to my burdens and make for the train, the New Canaan Express, which if the combined incomes of the passengers was laid out sideways in nickels it would reach to Arcturus. Brooks Brothers has an agent on the platform next to the conductor and if he spots any males attempting to board the train without garments from the home firm he tips off the conductor and the faulty ticketholder is routed onto the New Haven Local Express and has to ride with the Browning King group.

The critical point arrives when you get inside and find that there are no seats left except alongside somebody else.

The password is: *"May I share this?"*

Now get that, if you have any ambitions to be a successful commuter and make everybody think you are cutting the mustard on Madison Avenue or down on good old Wall Street. And remember not to put any interesting light variations on this slogan — for example if you say:

"Is this here seat occupied?"

Or:

"Is anybody setting here?"

Or:

"Do you mind if I park it here alongside of you, pardner?"

— Why, right away they will figure you come from the wholesale grocery business or own real estate in Sandusky and the offended party will move to another car or see that you are put off at 125th Street.

Having passed the test I sat down and began my tour of the papers. On the front page of the *American* it seemed that three dames had been assaulted the night before in the subway, four candy-store owners in the Bronx shot dead for sums never higher than 85 cents, two babies had been kidnaped by childless women, a former Pulitzer Prize Winner had been discovered in a flophouse on the Bowery, and a kid fell out of a third-story window but wasn't hurt (picture of kid in hospital with happyface nurse).

On Page 3 Pegler had some startling revelations about a letter Eleanor Roosevelt wrote William McKinley the day before he was shot, linking McKinley with the Kerensky Government and the Electrical Workers Union. Pegler was pretty sore about it, too.

But by this time we had emerged from underground and were joggling along the elevated tracks to 125th Street among the most woebegone scenery ever invented. If you are already beat and smudged and depressed by a day of torture in the City of Golden Dreams you may find suicide the only reasonable solution if you look out the window and study the view between 101st and 125th Streets. This devastated area would put Sunshine Sue into the dumps. The colored boys lean against the crumbling brick buildings to hold them up, inhaling the sour zephyrs coming out of the doorways, while soiled urchins, scattered recklessly, finger assorted trash on the pavements. Here again one sees the economic and cultural advantages of big city life, the triumphant urban glory in all its *schöne wirklichkeit*.

Back to the paper, quick!

QUESTION: My husband and I fell madly in love and had a truly romantic courtship and marriage. But after only a few months as a "bride" I find my husband is so wrapped up in his sister and her family he is practically never at home. Also he is terribly stubborn and gets very mad about money problems. He has become very sloppy whereas he was formerly a neat dresser. He does not want to go out like

he used to and wants to go to bed about 7:00 P.M. And he
wants to make love to me all the time no matter how I may
be feeling. My mother-in-law does not care for me and . . .

I just wonder if this girl has married Mr. Right.

The chap next to me sees I am reading the *American* and
lights a large briar pipe in self-defense.

Let's check with Cholly to see who was at that party I
didn't go to last night.

> Greek shipping tycoons Stavros Niarchos and Basil Gou-
> landris, Sylvia Gable and fiancée Prince Dmitri Djordjadze,
> the Alfred de Liagres, the Italian Dukes of Torlonia and
> Canevaro, Anita Loos and Cecil Beaton, His Royal High-
> ness Prince Christian of Hanover and stately cover girl Nina
> Devoe, Iva Patcevitch, Bootsie Hearst, Oleg Cassini . . .

Also Czar Nicholas the Second of Russia and Mr. and Mrs.
Clarence Sodawasser of Battle Creek, Michigan. Sorry I
missed it. But where the hell was Truman Capote? That boy
is slipping.

Oh-oh, Pietro Mele has resumed his pursuit of Tootie
Forbusche. Wonder what beautiful Brenda Frazier Kelly is
going to think of that? Maybe she should call up the fire
department and lodge a complaint.

Now here in the back of the paper at the advertisements of
the public dances and social clubs and all that, it says I
should go to The Friendship Club where "Folks over 28 make
friends and dance. No Jitterbugs. No Liquor. No tipping."
In other words if you want to get in here and have some fun
and meet friends you have got to start tapering off on the
booze about 27½ and learn how to do the twostep. It says
they have television on the premises, so you can follow a
Charlie Chan movie while you are not drinking or tipping or
jitterbugging. Playing Put and Take is allowed and com-
munication is via the Language of Flowers.

It also says here that at a recent party the Duke and Duchess of Windsor pulled off a hot one by wearing paper crowns of gold paper. If I was the Duke I believe I would not bring up the subject of crowns too freely myself.

There is so much smoke in the car by now that the bridge players can't see their cards very well and begin to overbid. The man next to me with the briar pipe is all wrapped up in a spicy article in the *Kenyon Review* and has to bring it closer and closer to see the print. Several boys who have been to the bar are beginning to act like they were in the last stages of the Odd Fellows' Picnic and their conversation doesn't match their clothes any more. The only thing holding them back is that there are no lampshades available to wear for hats.

So at last I am in my little old station wagon zipping gaily between the stone walls, picturing the tender scene as Dear Old Dad arrives home from the city. The way this works out is that when I get home the kids are all looking at Captain Video.

As Sam Snow would say, "The scene didn't play as expected."

(Father enters from Left, crosses Center, blocking television.)

FATHER: Yay, good old Pop is home.

TOM: Get out of the way.

KATIE: You're in the waaaay!

NAT: Gee whiz, Pop, you're spoiling everything.

BABY: *(Scream!)*

FATHER: Look, presents!

EVERYBODY: GET OUT OF THE WAAAAY —

NAT: Gee, Pop, you're always wreckin' everything.

(Adorable Little Daughter rises from floor where

*she is sitting on a cushion, crosses to Father, kicks
him sharply in shins.*)

A.L.D. (*screaming*): If you don't move I'll *hate you all my
life!*

FATHER: (*crossing R to kitchen*) Goddamn ungrateful
bunch of little moron bastards.

(*Mother appears suddenly from kitchen.*)

MOTHER: (*with loathing*) Well, if that's the kind of mood
you're in, maybe you better go right back to New York.

CURTAIN

Chapter 10

*Perhaps the town of Carbondale, Ill., would prove
less obscure in the public mind if it were generally
known that a scintillating screen star was born
there . . . her real name was Agnes Ayres, the
cognomen which she carried to the silver screen.*
— BLUE BOOK OF THE SCREEN, 1926.

ONE THING I hate is getting my hair cut but it
seems the correct thing is to get cut every week or so instead
of every 42 days like I do, sometimes longer. So I submitted
to a supercilious barber at BAILEY'S BARBERSHOP, ENGLISH
HAIR CUTTING A SPECIALTY. Actually I have very English
hair. They put a vibrator on your head here at Bailey's,
which makes a buzzing noise like a giant bee and shakes the
fillings in your teeth loose, an English specialty which may
explain some aspects of British policy. How can anybody who
has had a brain-rattling vibrator applied to his head every
week since he was old enough to hold on to a cricket bat have
any sensible ideas about what to do with India?

And then the hot towels, just for a haircut, mind you, and
gently soothing and thoroughly embarrassing manipulations
of the forehead, temples, eyes, etc. Having a man caress my
face is not my idea of a big time. Plus the inevitable sugges-
tion for some stinky hair tonic in order to raise the ante 25¢,

and my rejection of the proposal. Discouraged acceptance of this verdict by barber, who indicates facially that he wishes the clientele were screened by the British consul. Meanwhile there is a large jovial boy in the next chair living it up with shave, haircut, manicure, shoeshine, extensive facial palpations and being served cigars and newspapers. He is kidding the manicurist about her boy friend, joshing the shoeshine boy, giving the barber advice on the horses and the stock market — say, how do you get that way anyhow? When I left they had him bent double over a washbowl and were giving him a shampoo and getting him ready to lie down and have I Love You Myrtle tattooed on his stomach. And people wonder why I keep putting off getting my hair cut.

'Cause When It's Hair-Cutting Time in Gotham My
Heart's 'Way Back in Indiana
Price .50

In dreams I see it once again
That two-chair shop on Third and Main
Where a Man's a Man
And the tonic is free
Oh there's no head vibrators
In the West Countree.

Over at the office there is a new receptionist with 14K solid gold hair, moist lips, and a patent bra built on the cantilever principle. Sun streaming in the windows and bathing the scene in nature's finest.

TED: What's the big idea, going Big City on us and getting a haircut?

SAM: You don't have to get a haircut on *our* account. I was sort of hoping you'd come in with a pigtail one of these days.

BETTY (*Sam's secretary*): Doesn't he look lovely!

VIRGINIA (*Hackett's secretary*): Mr. Hackett is waiting for you. I like your haircut.

I went into the torture chamber. Hackett was leaning way back in his swivel chair with his hands behind his head and his eyes closed, thinking. I said Hello and he said Hello and went back to his thinking. I studied the picture of Ethel Merman and the picture of Joan Caulfield and the picture of Hackett standing in front of the Belasco Theater with a bunch of people and then Ted and Sam came in and we talked about whether the script was too "episodic" or not, and we talked about "motivation" and how to get more life into the First Crossover and whether the fat girl's lines would register as funny or put the audience into a coma. Then we decided to throw out two whole scenes that had taken weeks to write and use different characters. Hackett rattled off the scheme for the new scenes and I tried to take notes and keep up with him so I would remember what it was all about when I got off in that lonely little room all by myself.

"This scene is in One," Hackett said. "First Janet comes in. Alone. She's upset, downcast, then she meets Freddie, he plants what he overheard in the cabaret between Susie and Chuck and then . . ."

"You mean about the picnic?" I said.

"Certainly," Hackett said. "If she doesn't know what Susie said to Chuck then she can't sing the reprise; and if Freddie tells her what Chuck's reaction was then she won't understand later on what Chuck's real feelings are when they play the scene on the merry-go-round because she'll be under the impression that Freddie only told her to make her jealous because Susie is going to tell her in the next scene, the one on Carl's front porch, what Freddie had already told her before he overheard her in the cabaret talking to Mrs. Fondemeyer."

"Sure, that's clear," said Sam.

"I thought she was talking to Freddie in the cabaret, how did Mrs. Fondemeyer get into the scene?" I said.

"I put her in yesterday," Hackett said. "Thought I told you. Well anyway, you get all that?"

"Well, um, uh, I guess so," I said.

"All right, now let's proceed. Freddie has planted what he overheard in the cabaret and . . ."

"I don't see why this scene has to be played in One," Ted said. "Why can't . . ."

"Because we have to change scenery," Hackett said. "How do we get from the jealous scene to the porch scene without going into One?"

"Oh," said Ted, "I thought this scene came after the scene in front of the drugstore."

"No, Ted," said Sam. "This is the scene just after the new scene between Chuck and the girls."

"*Before* the scene with Chuck and the girls," said Hackett.

"That's what I mean," Sam said.

"You had some awfully funny stuff in your book, Jack," Ted said. "You know where they are on the streetcar and he has this funny conversation with the conductor? I always thought that was wonderful stuff. I think we should get it in someplace. Don't you think so?"

"Well I'm not sure just how we . . ."

"That stuff in the streetcar was great," Ted said. "Don't you think so, Mr. Hackett?"

"No," Hackett said. "It wouldn't work."

"I've always thought it was awfully good," Ted said.

"I don't think it would work, Ted," Sam said.

"All right, boys, let's get back to where we were, I've got to play squash at twelve o'clock," Hackett said.

"In this scene in One," Ted said. "I don't see why Janet and Freddie can't do a number here. Seems to me we have too much exposition. There's an awful lot of yakking going on."

"How can we have another number?" Hackett said. "We just came out of a big number, in the scene before."

"Well, it wouldn't have to be a big number, but it certainly seems to me it would be much more effective if she expresses herself musically at this point," Ted said. "Didn't you say that last night, Sam, down at The Lambs? Remember? We were at the bar talking to old Ferdie, and Archie Guilder came up, and then they went to eat, and you said to me, 'Ted, I think Janet should express herself musically in that scene.'"

"Now, Ted, that's not *quite* what I said," Sam said. "What I *actually* said . . ."

"I thought you wanted to cut down on the numbers," Hackett said. "I thought we agreed at the Palladium last night that we should get rid of a couple of numbers."

"I *do*," Sam said, getting red. "Ted, I wish to heavens you'd quit *quoting* me all the time. Gosh but it's annoying. What I said was, substantially, that I felt that . . ."

"Aw forget it," Ted said. "What's the difference?"

"But I won't forget it. Damn it I want this clear. I get so *bored* having people ascribe things to me that simply aren't . . ."

"Well we can't have a number in here, that's all," Hackett said.

"I agree 100 per cent," Sam said, glaring at Ted.

"Don't mind me, I just came in to empty the spittoons," Ted said.

"Now, Jack, you've got the idea, haven't you?" Hackett said. "You retreat to Connecticut and write these two scenes and bring them in tomorrow. I'll be here at 10:30. Boys, I've got to go, Alfred's waiting for me."

Hackett picked up his hat and went out. I sat looking at my notes.

"Can any member of the class tell me what these two scenes I'm to dash off by tomorrow morning are supposed to be *about*?" I said.

Hackett stuck his head back in.

"And, Jack," he said, "you might put in some funny stuff about Mrs. Fondemeyer's husband; he's a brute, he beats her up. Something like that. You know what I mean."

Hackett left again.

"Sure," I said. "That's a scream."

"Funny stuff about Mrs. Fondemeyer's husband?" Sam said. "Now what do you suppose he meant by that?"

"Oh you know," I said. "Like 'Gee, Mrs. Fondemeyer, where did you get them black eyes? And three of your front teeth is missing.' That'll have Atkinson howling."

So we went back into the other office and I tried to get some sense out of the notes about Chuck and Mrs. Fondemeyer and a lot of other dreary unfunny characters and situations. The boys got on the two telephones and spent a half an hour trying to raise some more money.

". . . and Richard Hackett is writing the script with the author, and will also direct. We're capitalizing at two hundred and fifty thousand with a twenty-five thousand overcall. . . . Is it going to be good? Would I call you if it wasn't, Morty? Ha ha."

". . . and Richard Hackett is going to direct . . . No, we haven't definitely signed a composer yet."

Definitely signed a composer yet, hell, we didn't even have a whiff of a composer yet. Every hot music writer in the business had been approached; they all got very steamed up until they read the plot outline and then they faded out. They were polite about it but they just couldn't see it. We weren't getting anyplace. Looked like we would have to take piano lessons and write the music ourselves.

"No, Tommy, the music isn't set yet, but Hackett is collaborating on the script and will direct the production. We feel that we have one of the most literate . . ."

"Listen, Charlie, whatever you feel you want to do, Charlie. Sure we need money. The units are five thousand. . . . No, no, you can have any part of a unit. . . . Sure Hackett is going to direct it. He's collaborating on the book, too. Jordan? Oh, he's a very talented boy, Charlie. This boy is going places. This show is going to be one of the biggest things ever hit town. . . . No, I'm not kidding. . . . Well, let me know what you want to do, Charlie. Sure like to have you with us."

". . . and Richard Hackett . . ." Sam mopped his brow and stared at the ceiling.

". . . so let me know, Martha. Hackett is very warm on this project, Martha. You know how he is when he gets behind something."

Ted hung up and leaned back and looked out the window.

"Yes, Martha, you damn old bitch," he said. "Turn loose with some of those lousy millions of yours will you?"

"You'll never get anything out of her," Sam said. "She went to six auditions of *Fancy That,* drank up about four bottles of poor old Weintraub's Scotch, and finally put in two hundred and fifty bucks."

"We could use her two hundred and fifty," Ted said. "We could use old rags, bottles, and cast-off shoes."

"My god, we're certainly not getting much money," Sam said.

"It's too early," Ted said. "Christ we haven't even got a script."

"Or a composer," I said.

"Or a star," Sam said.

"Or a choreographer," Ted said.

"Well, Jack's got a haircut, anyway," Sam said. "That's something."

"Frankly, how do you feel, Ted?" Sam said.

"Terrible," Ted said. "I'm going out and buy a new suit and cheer up. Come on. Come on, Jack. Got to keep up that prosperous front."

"If you get another one of those Sixth Avenue Specials of yours we'll never get anyplace," Sam said. "Last time you came into Sardi's I went and hid in the men's room."

"Save the jokes for the script. Come on," Ted said.

"Roll me one of those crazy cigarettes, Jack," Sam said.

We walked over to one of the Fifth Ave. gents' emporiums with plenty of English walking shorts behind the plate glass and a blimp salesman in an iron suit began to give Ted the thread talk. Sam kept telling Ted to get out of this truck-driver's haberdashery and come with him to Brooks Brothers. Salesman didn't dig.

"How do you wise guys like this?" Ted said, clutching a mud-colored tweed with flecks of red in it.

"Just the thing," Sam said. "It sets off your curly hair."

"You're some picker, boy," I said.

So Ted bought the mud number. Sam starts fooling around in the hat department while Ted is getting fitted and walks out with one of these smart little Princeton-boy caps on.

"Listen, walk about ten feet ahead of us, will you?" Ted said.

"Us younger fellows have to keep up with the latest styles," Sam said.

So we walked up Fifth Avenue, Sam with his stylish cap with the little round button on top. Every fifth store was a linen store selling out Puerto Rican handkerchiefs with giant monograms on them and today was the last day of the big sale. It's always the last day. The ladies from Montclair were in there stocking up.

"I wonder if we should send the script to Betty and Adolph?" Sam said. At least once per hour around this business somebody says "Betty and Adolph," it's kind of a nervous habit.

"I wonder if I bought the right suit?" Ted said.

"Why not send the suit to Betty and Adolph along with the script?" I said. "For an opinion."

Garbo went past, dressed for a Halloween party evidently, with Cecil Beaton. Cece had on a little tweed hat like Doctor Watson and a finger-tip coat.

"What do you hear from John Gilbert these days, Ted?" Sam said.

"I understand he's taking voice lessons," Ted said.

"Betty's on the Coast, anyway," I said.

"How do you know?" Sam said.

"How would I know? I read it in *Variety*," I said.

We stopped to look at the furniture in Sloane's window. There was a big burly fellow holding a package by the string standing beside us also looking. Two guys came up, one on each side of him. One of them pulled a gun out from under his arm and shoved it in the first guy's back. The other took the package. The guy with the gun put it away and went to the curb and opened the door of a taxicab. Then they all got in the cab and drove away. None of them had said a word.

"What's Betty doing on the Coast?" Ted said.

"Boy, look at that beautiful sofa," Sam said. "I ought to get that for my apartment. Isn't that handsome?"

"Yeah, some playground," Ted said. "What's Betty doing on the Coast?"

"Mama, look at the man with the funny hat," says a little girl, pointing at Sam.

"Don't point, Sandra," says Mother.

"Cute kid, that Sandra," Ted said.

Sam stopped and looked at his reflection in the store window.

"The hell with you, Sandra," Sam said. "You bad seed you."

"What's Betty doing on the Coast?" Ted said.

"Harry Paige sent for her," Sam said. "I hear they're in trouble on the new musical."

"What new musical?" Ted said.

"Don't you read *Variety?*" Sam said. "It's *The Luther Burbank Story.* Paige has had five writers on it already. Van Johnson was set to play Burbank but he walked off. They're trying to get Joe Ferrer."

"Can he play Burbank on his knees?" Ted said. "Where the hell does Betty come in?"

"They're in trouble on lyrics," Sam said.

"Well I'll send her Burpee's seed catalogue," Ted said, "and the lyrics will write themselves."

"I wonder what was in that package?" Sam said.

A woman with a chartreuse scarf wrapped around her head shuffled past, pulling a little coaster wagon with a Persian cat sitting in it.

"Let's eat," Ted said.

"I've got a date," Sam said.

"A big giggle session at *21,* eh?" Ted said. "Who's the lucky dame?"

"Girl I met last night," Sam said. "This is without question the most beautiful girl in New York. Wait'll you see her."

"I'll wait," Ted said. "I thought that one you had last week was the most beautiful girl in New York."

"This one is better," Sam said. "Listen, I'll see you guys later, at the office." And he darted off across the street.

"Hey," Ted shouted after him. "Better take that adorable cap off or darling will think you're a jerk."

"Say, your partner is quite an active boy, isn't he," I said. "He's after the dames like he was just back from six months up the Amazon in a canoe."

"Very big operator in the Vichyssoise and Clams Casino set," Ted said. "He figures if he doesn't spend twenty bucks on lunch for some dame the whole day is wasted. Say, where do you want to eat?"

"Oh, most anyplace," I said. "I don't care."

"Well, we've got to eat someplace. I've got to get to the theater," Ted said.

We walked through the canyon across 50th Street. I would never stand in line ten minutes, not even to see Ava Gardner in the raw (P. S. I take that back), but here at the Music Hall they stand in a line four-wide, that starts at the box office and bends out to the sidewalk and around the corner 100 yards toward Fifth Avenue. That line doesn't move. They just keep on standing there. They have sold their homes to the Thruway and have come to the Music Hall to pray to Clark Gable and Susan Hayward, and to worship the twinkling toes of the rollicking Rockettes. Perhaps they will stay, setting up pup tents in the lobby and sending out for pizza and pepper steak, newspapers, and the new White White Kolynos toothpaste. Because you can't be too careful.

Ted and I crossed Sixth Avenue and went into the Automat; out on the sidewalk some guy is always selling costume jewelry for fifty cents out of flat paper cartons. Just like over on Fifth Avenue in the Puerto Rican hkchf.

dept., the ladies were in there with elbows up, after the merchandise; they could get it for the same prices by some good taxpaying establishment like Bloomingdale's, but that don't make any ice with them.

And so at the precise moment when Sam Snow was going into Romeo Salta's with the Most Beautiful, his partner Ted and I entered the Automat, having been temporarily blocked at the revolving door by two stocky chaps in Al Capp headgear discussing commissions.

"Look at all that food for only sixty-five cents," Ted said as we sat down and inspected our trays to see just what we had dealt ourselves. He looked tenderly at the lovable little brown pot of baked beans, still the greatest food buy in the whole quivering city.

"You should just see Irving's new house. All the latest modern," said an overstuffed matron at our table as she explored a crumb bun.

"Eating in the Automatic! Some big Producer!" Ted said.

"Best grub in town," I said.

"My boy Sumner, you should see the picture window in his residence," said the opposition matron. "Just beautiful."

Ted Crosby's story was a real life drama suitable for the films (suggested title: *The Ted Crosby Story*; suggested title for sequel: *The "Ted Crosby Story" Story*), demonstrating that on the Association Football Field of Life there is no substitute for old-fashioned pluck. Born in the back seat of a Jewett touring car parked outside a chautauqua in upstate New York, he was raised on a farm in abject poverty. At the age of twelve he had fled from a sadistic stepfather named Noah Beery, and made his solitary way to the big city, living on gravel for over three weeks. He arrived in New York with a stick over his shoulder with his belongings on the end of it wrapped up in a blue polka dot bandanna. Working as a cash boy, a tattered newsboy, and as a train boy on the Erie Railroad he was eventually befriended by a well-to-do merchant with side whiskers whose bulging wallet the honest youth had found in the aisle and returned to him. Followed years of drudgery in his benefactor's countinghouse sharpening quills, when on a sudden impulse he retired from Wall Street to join a Carnival making the smaller towns in Tennessee where he was successively a mugsnapper, spindleman, broad tosser, raghead, squawker, bug man, glim worker, flawny man — learned to swallow the sword and play the steam fiddle and ended up candy boss. From this it was but a step to an association with Richard Hackett, for whom he had acted as stage manager for some twenty-odd years. At present he was stage manager for Hackett's latest hit, *Mambo! Mambo!*

"Listen," I said. "How can you produce a show? I mean — here we are in the Automat for example."

"With other people's money. We just sell pieces of the show all over. Stockholders. Getting them is the tough part," he said. "But we already spent a few thousand of our own money. The option on your book. Your expenses. Lunches for different guys so they could load us with bum advice. And before we got the wild idea of getting you in, we flew one of these hot-shot writers in from the Coast to see if he could write it."

"Well, couldn't he?" I said.

"Sure, he wrote it all right," Ted said. "He thought it was a big howl. It was about as funny as a week end with John L. Lewis."

"But Sam . . ." I said. "He isn't broke, is he?"

"He wouldn't be if he wasn't lunching the quiff all the time and taking them to the Little Club and all that educated crap. Plus the Brooks Brothers act — you can't tell one of those uniforms from another but he has to have a new one every month or so."

"The Brooks Brothers Look is easily recognized at the country's leading Hunt and Country Clubs," I said.

"That reminds me I haven't been out to my Hunt Club for a dog's age," Ted said.

"And he has to have the convertible with the red leather seats," Ted said. "So he can drive these goo-goo dames out to Westport for tea. Let's go. Walk over to the theater with me. I got a matinee."

We walked out onto 50th Street.

We walked west on 50th and met a fellow in a bathrobe passing out salvation handbills, and a man in a Hoover collar wearing a high derby hat, and two beautiful colored girls, and three boys in berets, and five sailors from the Italian Navy, and a girl with long jade earrings and a summer furpiece who was leading three dachshunds on a leash, the dachshunds getting under everybody's feet and causing mingled emotions in the passers-by.

There was a giant truck blocking everything up. On the side it said PAIGE INTERCOASTAL TRANSPORT.

"That guy Paige is fantastic," Ted said. "I knew him when he had to stay in while the landlady washed his shirt."

"*You* know Harry Paige?"

"Why sure," Ted said. "He used to run a girly show when I was with the Mighty Mammoth Shows, Largest Motorized Carnival in South Dakota."

We got down by Roxy's and it said up there:

ALOHA LOVE
Her searing kisses made him forget
the secret shame of his past
RAB WILLCOX   SONIA CALIENTE
A HARRY PAIGE PRODUCTION

We went around the corner and there was one of those crazy shirt shops, with the three-tone shirts, and the shirts with laces, and the shirts with inserts, appliqué, trick pockets — and the sign said:

ANOTHER PAIGE SHIRT BAR
Direct from Hollywood to YOU

"Say listen," I said. "You really know Paige?"

"Goddamn it, of course I know him," Ted said.

"And you're scratchin' for money? What's the matter with your head, boy?"

"Yeah," Ted said, looking at a pink-and-black shirt with soutache braid on the collar. "Harry. The big bum. Yeah. . . .

"Yeah," he said again. "Harry Paige. Yeah."

"That's great dialogue," I said.

"That's quite an idea," he said. "Harry Paige, huh. Yeah."

"Yeah," I said.

Chapter 11

*Once Upon a Time there was a Specialty Team
doing Seventeen Minutes.*

— GEORGE ADE

THAT NIGHT I sweated until 3 A.M. with Mrs.
Fondemeyer and her funny husband, creating hideously dull
dialogue and listening to the beams in the house as they
creaked with fatigue.

At 5 A.M. the Baby woke up crying and throwing up, but
after all, Thomas Edison only used three hours sleep per
night so why shouldn't I, a healthy specimen from the
fresh-air districts, get along okay on two? I didn't have
to invent the incandescent bulb before night must fall.

"Don't give that chile *no meat,*" said the handy colored
girl when she arrived at 8:45 and heard the news. "That chile
has got a congestion into his *blood* from eatin' so *much meat.*
Take that meat *away* from that chile."

So we took all that meat away.

But at 9:05 Mrs. Pusateri arrived to do the ironing.

"Put an egg in the oven and bake it until this egg turns
green," she said. "Give this egg to the Baby and it will draw
out the fever."

"I believe I need a green baked egg myself," I said. "I just didn't get a hell of a lot of rest last night."

"You've been eating too much of that *meat*," Frankie said, the colored girl having disappeared upstairs to see whether she could drag out the bedmaking until noon.

"It's just something that's going around," said the milkman. "There's a lot of it going around. How about some pineapple cottage cheese? It's a special this week. Comes in these here genuine aluminium drinking glasses in your choice of six colors."

I'm getting along in years now and I'm telling you for a fact the winters aren't like the ones we used to have when I was homesteading out in the Dakotas. Kids had some respect for their parents in those days, by golly, and the milkman came to the house and he brought *milk*, he didn't bring no cottage cheese in six colors, nor orange drink, chocolate drink, three grades of eggs, or strawberry-flavored yoghurt — just *milk*. I guess I'm just an old fogy, but let me tell you I know when I'm not wanted, I can take a hint.

The garbage truck rolled into the drive and from the kitchen window we could see Mr. Novak and his boy carrying the garbage cans out to the truck and dumping them, and scattering papers and empty Kix boxes around the yard.

"Oh! I forgot to pay the garbage man this month," Frankie said. "Give me five dollars, Jack, will you?"

And another thing, we never paid some foreigner five dollars a month to come and take away the garbage, no sirreebob. A good strong Irish girl was glad to get three dollars a week, too.

Frankly, folks, I don't know exactly whether I'm going to make it or not. I might just fold up most anytime. I started out running and taking the big gulps of air and making love to the stars but by now I'm about slowed down to a walk and the goddamn stars will have to find a new lover because my feet hurt and my head hurts worse trying to keep everything going all at one time. It is no good either, because it can't be done regardless.

"You'll miss your train," Frankie said. "You better get on the ball, honey."

"In due season we shall reap, if we faint not," I said.

"I don't know about that," Frankie said. "Don't forget your briefcase."

When I first rented this house in Stamford I wondered how come the big parking area out by the barn, but I pretty soon realized it was to accommodate the trucks and cars of the repair and service men necessary to keep the place going. Now for example on this damp, dreary, typical morning in historic Connecticut there were two panels, a light pickup, and a 1½-ton stake truck, representing the ABC Television Service, McCloskey and Sons Oil Burner Service, the Home Appliance Co., and the United Electric Co. All we needed back there was a lunch wagon on wheels to make the scene look like the advance unit for a carnival. Meanwhile the service men, or "crooks" as they are called, were chatting together amiably and deciding how much to pad their bills before advancing on the house.

"Oh, Mr. Jordan," said one as I edged my way through the crowd to my car. "I was telling the Missus. On the TV set. You're gonna need a new grid-leak on the condenser and your capacitor is taking a deflection off the rectifier." I could feel his heater kissing my belly.

"Listen, Jordan," said another, caressing a blackjack. "That electric dishwasher is all gone. Whatcha gonna do about it? Christ, don't just stand there, say something."

"I hate to tell you this, Mac," said a third, whose knuckles seemed to be covered with a strange brass device, "but it's either a new oil burner for you, or . . . well, you're pretty fond of that little daughter of yours, ain'tcha? Be a pity wouldn't it, if anything happened to the kid?"

"Don't bother me with details, boys," I said. "You boys know what you're doin'. Fix 'em up boys. Go to it, fellows."

"And don't let it happen again," said the TV man as I backed out of the drive.

However, before I could get to the main road Frankie popped out the side door and gave forth with a set of squawks and hand signals. So it was Ted on the phone and I went into the house.

"Listen," he said. "Don't say anything about what we talked about yesterday, you know, about Harry Paige."

"Okay," I said. "What's the idea?"

"I don't want to build it up until I see Harry. He probably won't even know me."

"See you at the office," I said. "I gotta catch the train."

"Got any stuff on Mrs. Fondemeyer?"

"Yeah, I was up all night," I said. "I've got some stuff."

"Attaboy," he said.

"You tell her, 'cause I stutter," I said.

One thing Groucho Marx and I have in common is turning off lights, so now, although late, I rushed around in a frenzy and turned off a few thousand watts which would have cast their cheery glow all day long in my absence had I not doused them. My little hummingbird thinks the Power Co. is a benevolent institution and she has never turned off a light in twelve years of wedded blissfulness. Another thing is, she cannot fit a new roll of toilet paper when the old one is gone; I get quite a bit of credit for doing this at our house, explaining that it is because I went to M.I.T. The fact is, although dames look a good deal like men in a general over-all way, they might as well be trilobites as far as mutual mental processes go. For example take this one: Frankie and I were on a fishing trip way the hell up in the backwoods of Minnesota for ten days one time clean out of touch with the world. Finally we got out of the wilderness and back to a little jerk town on the railroad track and I spotted a store and said, "I am going to see if I can buy a paper." The trilobite says: "What for?"

Well anyway I finally got away and drove to the station. I made a flying leap and caught the train like Dagwood, with my body suspended horizontally in mid-air — went inside and read some more about Pietro Mele's problems in the paper. Now this poor guy had been banned from El Morocco for socking a cop up at Brenda Frazier's pad and was pretty sore at the Cossacks and was taking it up with the U.N., only trouble being that by the time he got dressed and shaved every day the U.N. was already closed. On top of that it looked like this Maguire Sister wasn't going to marry Julius La Rosa after all, on account of Godfrey effecting a reconciliation between Maguire and her estranged husband of the U.S. Army. The only bright note, in fact, was that Debbie Reynolds said she was mighty warm on the subject of Eddie Fisher and Eddie said he thought Debbie was some kid. However, Hedda denied both statements while Lolly endorsed them, so we ended up in a tie.

"Well, let's see your homework, Jack," Hackett said when I came into the thinking room.

I gave it to him and went into Sam and Ted's office and lay down on the couch. I was tired. Ted came in and sat down in his mud suit.

"You're a hell of an inspiring sight," he said.

"Say things to me, Geraldine," I said. "Things about us."

"Did you give Hackett the stuff?" Ted said.

"The stuff is there," I said. "And it's very ripe."

Hackett came in. He had put on his gray topcoat, and his hat was on, but pushed back on his head rakishly. This indicated he was about to go but not until after a little dialogue.

"I think most of this is usable, if not noble, Jack," he said. "Tell you what we'll do. I'll take this home overnight and work it over, and you take a crack at the finale, how's that?"

"That's okay," I said. "How'd you like the Fondemeyer stuff?"

"I'll have to think about it and read it again. I have a feeling maybe you gave it too much."

"Well you go ahead and cut it down then," I said.

"I've got to go," Hackett said. "Alfred's waiting for me." He pushed his hat down where it should be. "By the way, Ted, I auditioned Rex Ives yesterday. It was really an R. and H. audition. Dick asked me to drop in. I certainly like that boy's singing voice. Of course he's such a cheap actor. Has anybody seen him in his new picture? Well, he's been out barnstorming with *Oklahoma* for two years. Can't expect too much. Keep him in mind. You know him, Jack?"

"I saw him in Indianapolis," I said.

"We might do worse," Hackett said.

"He's pretty square, Mr. Hackett," Ted said.

"I know, I know," Hackett said. "Well, I'll toddle off, can't keep Alfred waiting."

"Well, we're almost done with this crummy script," I said after he had gone. "And am I sick of it."

"Yeah, almost time to write the second version," Ted said.

"Second version? Oh hellkite! I wonder what is doing out in the cornfields," I said.

"I still think that funny stuff in the streetcar where you have that crazy conductor oughtta be in someplace. That's awfully rare stuff. And it's different, you know what I mean?

That's real humor. No gags. Just real humor from people. Human values."

"Hackett don't like it, Ted, so that's that. What's the use of fighting it? You heard how he dusted you off the other day."

"Well I still think it's just terrific stuff," Ted said. "Hey, where you going?"

"I'm going down to 42d Street," I said.

"What the hell for? You going to a movie?"

"No, the public library and do a little work on the finale."

"What the hell you wanna go down there for? You can work right there at Sam's desk."

"No, thanks, junior," I said. "Too much traffic up here. Not to mention Miss DeVere with the golden hair out there at the switchboard. I can't write with that hair around, and those moist rosebud lips — because it's Love, man, Love."

"Maybe you better go to the library at that," Ted said.

And then it was the phone and the blond Venus said it was Mr. Snow and it was Mr. Snow.

"Meet me at Torino's at two o'clock," he said. "Listen, I'm worried. It's the script. I think we're muddy in spots."

"Yeah," I said. "And the rice with the cheese in the middle."

"Two o'clock at the bar," he said.

So I winked at all the girls and threw a rose to Miss De-Vere, and stepped off gracefully to the library, twirling my Malacca cane; and Fifth Avenue was a whispered promise, a sliver thrown up from a bar of gold, bronze by gold, with the spurs steelyringing across the secret sands.

Out in Indiana after the movies we used to go across the river to Ollie Schneider's place and sit around waiting to see who would come in. Because Everybody went to Ollie's. No

one knew how it got started; Ollie himself was fat and had
pig eyes. So there we sat looking over ourselves and the other
local celebrities: Chick Baker, slightly punchy, all American
(Oklahoma, '37), now selling insurance; wealthy Alice Free-
bles and her untidy girl friend; Doris Pelt, who owned the
cannery and who could knock off a pint of bourbon in an
hour; Roger Kunkel and his hot girl friend from Rock Island,
an ex-hustler as everybody from Rock Island explained, but
Roger didn't care just so long as it irritated his father; Buster
Corrigan, who once shot a man in Oskaloosa or maybe was
shot by a man — all sorts of famous characters. The drinks
were higher-priced than any other joint on the strip and
that's why we went there.

Well listen they are not giving anything away at this
Torino place, believe me, even smiles, but we went there and
sat around looking at each other just like at Ollie's, and kept
coming back, too. When Ted was charged thirty-five cents
for a second cup of coffee after buying drinks at the bar for
an hour followed by a nine-dollar dinner, he got pretty sore
and said he was through. In a few days he was back though,
saying "Hi, Morty, how's the rack look?" and "Say, Melvin,
I sent a tap dancer to you today," and combing the menu
desperately for something to eat for lunch that would cost
him less than $3.75, as he didn't much like parmegiana,
loathed beef bones no matter with what flourish they were
served up, and had had enough chicken pot pie in his life to
float along on without giving up $2.50 for some more of
same, especially when you could get it from behind one of
those little rectangular glass pop-up windows over on the
square by placing a quarter and a dime in the slot.

And as he fished around hopefully under the Bordelaise
sauce Ted would think back to the old days when he used to
sweep the sidewalk in front of McGinty's — for wasn't he the

most popular soprano singing waiter in the Tenderloin, and how the merry harlots, the pretty dumplings, spoiled him; with comfits and roguish kisses, they love love loved him so sweet. Big Daddy, tell us some more about your European trip. . . . Watch it now. Here comes waiter. The Bordelaise torture. Slowly drown him in vat of sauce. Better still: all headwaiters in New York. Fill swimming pool with Bordelaise. Force them walk plank. Read menus to victims out loud. Baste them with black butter. Bring them wrong desserts. Careful. Headwaiter suspicious. Smile. Close thing, that. All clear.

I went into the bar to wait for Sam and there was a girl and a fellow there on the long side of the bar having some Manhattans and the girl went to the ladies' room and when she came back she stopped and did a long inspection of the dining room. Then she came back and sat down.

"Guess who's out there," she whispered.

"Who?"

"Red Buttons," she said. "I'm not kiddin'."

"Aw he is not."

"Go and have a look for yourself," she said.

So he got down and went and had a look.

"It's him all right," he said.

"A lot of them come here," she said. "I always heard that but I din't really believe it. What was he doing when you looked at him?" she said.

"Just talking to that other guy."

That's where these kids missed it, because when he's feeling good this fellow can turn an ordinary piece of Melba toast into a giant ruby, throw his voice all over the room causing many a humorous effect better imagined than described, and play the 1812 Overture on six water glasses until you'd swear it was Sir Thomas Beecham and the whole bunch. Because when it comes to wit and talent, you can't get a table in the front room in this restaurant without first giving an audition of your stuff, and no excuses allowed such as "I just got in from the Coast and my Indian clubs are still at the depot" or "I've got laryngitis and my voice coach says I really shouldn't sing at all this week."

That's why the prices are so rugged. On account of the free entertainment at each and every table, why, gents, it's better than George C. Tilyou's Steeplechase combined with the genuine French novelty booklet, and another thing, you never know which one of the delicious milk-chocolate Hershey Bars has got the dollar bill hidden in it.

We sat down over in the corner.

"You know who was sitting right here in this same seat yesterday?" Sam said.

"Gertrude Ederle of Channel fame?" I said.

"Monroe," he said. "Oh *god,* but she's fan-*tas*-tic. But never mind that."

"Dreenks jantleman?" said the waiter.

"Two Martinis," Sam said.

"I don't want a Martini," I said. "Make mine a Scotch and soda."

"Thank*you* jantleman," said the waiter.

"Now listen," Sam said. "We're almost finished with the book, right? A few more days. You've done a great job, a *great* job. But I'm worried."

"All right. What?" I said.

"It's Chuck and Janet. I think the second scene on the porch needs building. She needs an added dimension, and a new direction in her emotional involvement, a causative connection . . ."

"Oh christ what have you been eating?" I said. "Listen, bud, get this straight. I wouldn't know an added dimension if one walked in and sat down on my lap."

"That's right. Be crude," Sam said. "But I'm right. And what's more Irene agrees with me."

"Irene?" I said. "Irene . . . ? I thought you hated her. And where did she see any of the script?"

"Well as a matter of fact . . ." Sam said. "And *god* I wish people would quit misquoting me. *Hate* Irene? I'm de-*vot*ed to her. Theatrically, she has a great many brilliant ideas, too, let me tell you that."

"*Gott im Himmel,*" I said, "*mit the vielfarbigen Kunstbeilage.*"

"Weren't you and I at Amherst together?" said a pale fellow from behind a large nose.

"Oh hello," Sam said. "How are you?"

Any minute now Sam was going to start telling me what he "really wanted to do." We always started with talking about the script ("pressures," "internal mechanics," "pace") and before long we were talking about Sam. It seemed that being handsome Boy Producer and luncheon athlete was not enough, and he felt that his creative talents were badly stifled and that he really was a writer when you came right down to it; he had written shows at Amherst and TV scripts at NBC before he got into Hackett's office. On the other hand he had been a pretty good actor if he did say it, and sometimes he felt like going back to acting to achieve a sense of fulfillment. ("I *know* I could be one of the great actors of our time. But is it worth it?") Anyway he felt creative as all get out and he wasn't being creative as a producer, and what he really wanted to do *actually* was direct, he just had the feeling that he could be one of the top directors of our time. Being a great director was something you were born with and he had been born in the Seymour Apartments on 112th Street and Riverside Drive with it. In fact Sam wanted to be everything in the theater all at once except play the French horn in the pit. If anybody paid any attention to the French horn player he would have been one of the great unproved French horn players of our time, too.

"Do you think I was rude enough?" Sam said after Amherst had gone back to his table with a girl who had on a stylish hat resembling an inverted wicker wastepaper basket.

"Well, just barely," I said. "You could have done better."

"I'm not up to par today," he said. "Tell the truth I feel com*pletely* lousy and frustrated."

"The Martinis," the waiter said, putting two Martinis in front of Sam. "And the Scotch."

"There's absolutely nothing creative in my life. But *nothing*," Sam said. "Hey, what's the idea of the two Martinis?"

"Jantleman say, 'Two Martinis,'" the waiter said, shrugging his shoulders up to his ears.

"But we changed the order! We don't . . . Oh god, forget it," Sam said.

"Nice jantleman," I said.

The waiter went away gesturing to himself and wagging his head from side to side as though it was on a spring.

"Stupid ——," Sam said. "Anyway I feel utterly frustrated."

"Well, honey," I said, "the creative stuff is great, it's fine. Only it's a hell of a lot of work."

"Something inside tells me I should write," Sam said. "The creative life is the only self-respecting life, right? Otherwise what is a man, anyway?"

"A producer," I said.

"You think it's funny, don't you?" he said.

"If you wanna create, you silly bastard, go over to the dime store and get some paper and a nice leaky pen and start creating something. You sure as hell not gonna create anything except a head sitting around this glorified Coney Island Lunch."

"You're so right," Sam said soulfully. "Shall I do it? I mean really?"

"No, you have to finish those Martinis and then make some phone calls and get in and out of ten or fifteen taxicabs and smoke a few dozen Parliaments and check Louella's column and go to that experimental play tonight where the audience sits on the stage and the play is played in the balcony, and then there's Irene, you gotta get some more of her brilliant ideas, too. . . . You don't wanna be a writer. It's too tough."

"Well I don't think you're being too funny," Sam said. "What are you a writer for then if it's so tough?"

"It was the only way I could figure out how to make people take notice of me," I said.

"But you like it, don't you?"

"Try it and find out for yourself," I said. "It's a big pain in the . . ."

"Oh sure, sure," Sam said. "Don't make me bust out crying."

The trouble about being creative was that you never knew where you stood. . . .

Now there's a pretty nice lead-off sentence into a good paragraph but I can tell that's about as far as I'm going to get along those lines. When it comes to constructing a good heavy paragraph with some A-1 sauce in it I am left wondering who stole the tire pump. On the other hand I could equally well start the paragraph:

The thing about being creative was that you *always* knew where you stood. . . .

Actually it doesn't matter whether the original premise

makes any sense or not, as long as you can get the brass section to come up loud in what follows.

"The trouble with being creative," I said to Sam, "is that you never know where . . ."

"There's Frank Loesser over there," Sam said.

"Good. Let's send him a poem. Who is he?"

"You certainly overplay the hick act sometimes," Sam said.

"How the hell would I know? Who is he, anyway? I've never been in show business before."

"Never mind," Sam said. "Here comes Josie."

A tall colored girl approached, saw Sam and screamed, "Sammy dear! Lover!" Sam got up and they kissed and hugged and carried on. He introduced me, and she sat down and told us about how she was just back from two weeks at the Palladium in London and Anthony Eden was taking her out all the time to those night spots in Soho and drinking champagne out of her slipper and she was going to do a show with dialogue by W. H. Auden pretty soon if they could raise the money.

"That's brilliant, Josie, just brilliant," Sam said.

"No onions on mine," I said.

"Good-by, boys," Josie said, and rushed off to another table after kissing us both.

Leonard Lyons came in and cased the layout.

"Here comes Peggy Regan," Sam said. "She's a doll. You'll love her."

Peggy sat down with us, brunette, wide-eyed, luscious, bursting a cardigan sweater.

Lyons looked things over and left.

"Were you in *Carousel?*" Peggy said to me.

"I don't think so," I said. "Is that out West?"

"Well I've seen you someplace. Were you in *Me and Juliet?*"

"Look, honey," Sam said, "Jack is writing our show for us. He's a writer. He's not a lousy performer."

"Oh that's nice," Peggy said. "Oh the funniest thing happened at rehearsal this morning . . ."

"Jantleman weesh to order?" said the waiter.

"Very dry sherry," Peggy said.

"Wan sherry."

"And *one* Martini, and *one* Scotch and soda," Sam said loudly and *very* rudely.

"The trouble about being creative was that you never knew where you stood," I said. "And the Cadillac with uniformed chauffeur is outside right this minute because I want to appear on Craigie Street in style."

"You're a writer all right," Peggy said.

"Very talented boy," Sam said.

"But what's he talking about?" Peggy said.

"Just came from a little man-to-man talk with P. L. Nagel," I said, "and it was a great pleasure."

"You sure gather 'em from all sides, don't you?" Peggy said to Sam. "But this one is the mostest."

"I wish we'd gone up in the pine woods," I said.

"You and me in the pine woods — now that would be worth while," Peggy said.

The waiter came and set the sherry in front of Sam, the Martini in front of me, and the Scotch in front of Peggy. We rearranged the glasses as though we were playing Pollyanna, the Glad Game.

"I have a mad desire for a sidecar," Sam said.

"Bring Mr. Harcourt a sidecar," I said.

"Now we'll never get any more work done," Sam said. "If I drink that sidecar."

"What work were you planning?" I said. "Something worth while I hope."

"Dear, what are you doing here if you're in rehearsal?" Sam said to Peggy.

"This is the break," she said.

"Fifty-five dollars a week and you take your break at Torino's?" Sam said. "What if we hadn't been here to buy you that nice sherry?"

"Then I say, 'Just a cup of coffee, Pierre old chap!'" Peggy said. "By the way, have you got a script yet? When are *you* going into rehearsal?"

"Sure we have a script," Sam said. "A marvelous script. Howard Ullman says it's great."

"How much did he put in?" Peggy said.

"He said the script was perfectly marvelous."

"How much?" Peggy said.

"He's letting us know this week," Sam said.

"Uh-huh," Peggy said.

"Oh don't be so smart," Sam said. "Anyway we've got Rudy Lorraine for music and lyrics. Anyway we've almost got him. We think."

"Rudy Lorraine! What! That schmo? Sam, are you boys all out of your minds?" Peggy said. "He's never done a show has he? Why, he's only about thirteen years old isn't he? Oh my God that's the end."

"Mr. Hackett — in fact all of us see in him a brilliant new name."

"Brilliant new name my foot! Did you ever listen to the lyrics in that awful jukebox number of his? I don't believe he could have got past fourth grade."

"I hope you've got some money with you because I've decided not to buy that drink for you," Sam said.

"Rudy Lorraine! Oh, that's the end."

"You don't like him, huh?" I said.

"My dear boy," Peggy said, "he could no more write the

score for a Broadway show — he's just a cheap Tin Pan Alley moron. Someone introduced him to me at a party once and he said, 'How do you do, how about you and me climbing into the sack a little later?' "

"Yeah, well 'Chief of Love' is Number One on the Hit Parade," Sam said. Sam was getting peeved.

"Hackett likes him," I said.

"Peggy is a great picker," Sam said. "She came to Boston and saw *Wonderful Town* and told me confidentially it wouldn't last six weeks at the Winter Garden. She had five hundred in *Can-Can* and after she saw it out of town she sold her interest to Charlie Weinheimer. And she said Pinza was too old for a romantic lead, nobody would go to see an old doddering wreck like Pinza. So finally she put six hundred in *Willing Hearts,* which had a simultaneous Opening and Closing Night."

"So how did I know Dolores was going to pull out in Philadelphia?" Peggy said.

"Rudy Lorraine no good, huh?" I said.

"The worst," Peggy said.

"Well I've gotta go now," I said. "I'm going up to the Museum of Modern Art to see Valentino."

"Wait, wait, I'm coming," Sam said.

"You won't have any fun," I said. "And you'll probably talk all the way through it like my cousin Archie and make a lot of great jokes about the performers."

"Good-by, dear," Sam said to Peggy. "And thanks for the build-up and all the constructive thoughts."

We walked up to Times Square along 44th Street. Where the big trucks bring the rolls of paper into the *Times* I said Hello to the guy in the uniform that stands around there all the time and he said, "How they going?" and I said "Okay."

"Who's that guy?" Sam said.

"He's the man I say Hello to," I said.

We got a cab in front of Whelan's and got out on 53d and Sixth and walked over to the Museum.

Before we went downstairs to the movie we walked around the new exhibit. There was a girl in espadrilles, black wool stockings, a skirt made of burlap, turtleneck sweater, and blue spectacles, standing with dirty fingernails in front of a Mondrian.

"He has so much to say," she said. "But it just doesn't come through."

"Thematically confused," replied her companion, a young man suffering from acne and no haircut.

"Well, that washes up Mondrian," I said.

"Yeah, he's thematically out of the big picture," Sam said. "Let's go to the movie."

Frank Hackenbush of the Sheboygan Sash and Door Co., holding his hat in his two hands carefully as though it might break, passed by and said to his wife:

"I am glad none of the boys down at the Statler can see me now."

"And I am glad I can't see them," replied Mrs. Hackenbush cheerfully.

"Let's go down and see Rudy," Sam said.

Oh, it's a mighty sophisticated audience at those movies at the Museum of Modern Art. The picture that afternoon was Valentino and Alice Terry in *The Four Horsemen of the Apocalypse*.

"Look at the hair-do," said one gay modern artist behind us. "Ha ha."

"I don't think she's much," said Number Two.

"I can't follow this," said Number One. "When did he get into the Army?"

"That isn't him," said Number Two.

"Sure it is," said Number One.

"Maybe it is at that," said Two.

"Sure, I can tell by looking at him," said One.

"But I thought he was supposed to be in Paris."

"Well he must have joined the Army after he went to see her there where she was a nurse."

"Oh. But I thought it was him that went blind."

"No no, that was her husband."

"Look at her hair. You'd think she'd have more sense."

"Well that's the way they used to wear their hair."

"Well it looks silly. You'd think they could give her a better hair-do."

"Your Aunt Emily from Montclair used to wear her hair like that."

"I don't *really* care for these war pictures. Too depressing."

"I wonder if he's going to get killed."

"I don't think he's so much. What did people see in him, anyway?"

"Listen, let's not go to Schrafft's after, let's go to that place on Fifty-seventh."

"Look, there's that hair-do again. What a mess."

"Well that's the way they used to wear their hair, dear."

"Listen," Sam said to me. "I just had a brain wave while listening to the hair debate."

"Yeah, what?" I said.

"I've been thinking about Harry Paige," he said.

"Yeah he does look like Valentino," I said. "Or Alice Terry. What you been thinking about him?"

"I've been thinking about his money," Sam said.

This is getting unanimous, I thought.

Chapter 12

*Back in 1914 a little war was started which rum-
bled on into the greatest struggle the world has ever
known. The same year in Hollywood a man started
a struggle which has rolled on and on until today
he is a star. He is Monte Blue . . .*
— BLUE BOOK OF THE SCREEN, 1926

I<small>T</small> was Valentino's turn to die and he died to a
fine accompaniment on the piano; Marguerite Laurier faded
away and away; tears fell; the play was over and the lights
went up, revealing the sad news that the red plush on the
backs of most of the seats was worn through. Phony accents
filled the aisles and spilled out into the staircase as all the
serious cinema students filed out. Phony opinions floated to
and fro like nickel balloons. Some ascending to the ceiling,
some sinking to the floor among the Capezio afternoon
pumps and ballet slippers. The heavy intellectual groaning of
young men with beards mingled with regurgitations by the
young ladies: such as Kafka, Koerner, Khachaturian, Kant,
and Krylov.

"Nice crowd there at your club," Sam said as we strode
quickly down the Avenue past De Pinna's. "Most of them
friends of yours?"

"What were you saying about Harry Paige?" I said.

"Met him one time. Double-breasted vest. Always talking about 'Vegas' and 'the rushes.' Fantastic what a job he's done as a producer. This man, I'm telling you, has not one iota of taste, personally that is, and yet look at the pictures he's made. Fabulous. Meaningful. Artistic triumphs. Goddamn mystery to me."

We were stopped by a red light and stood teetering on the curbstone while taxicabs, an ancient Rolls-Royce with an ancient chauffeur, and several trucks rushed forward enveloping us in a cloud of blue exhaust fumes.

"Are you there, Sam?" I said.

Voices from behind us:

"I hear Hackett is getting ready to cast. Big musical."

"Let the son of a bitch go ahead and cast. I wouldn't work for him again for all the . . . Say, who's the producer?"

"I don't know. Some new guys. Couple of jerks."

"Well that son of a bitch Hackett can go clear . . ."

We proceeded down the Avenue.

"About Paige," Sam said. "As one jerk to another, now don't tell Ted, but I'm having cocktails with Irene in about half an hour and I am going to get *her* to introduce *me* to Harry Paige."

"And you're going to get him to write you his name on a piece of paper from the Guaranty Trust Co. Good. Why not?"

"Most of these guys in pictures like to be in something on Broadway. It irritates their friends — always desirable anyplace, but especially in Hollywood."

"Sam, there's a tear for every smile in Hollywood," I said. "It's a city of broken dreams."

We got to the office and sat around looking at and complaining about various pieces of paper such as Ted's dentist bill, a letter from Acme Stage Lighting Inc., various notes from actors wanting jobs, and an 8 x 10 glossy photo from an agent, squared off into four sections showing a "very talented" young client in various roles such as (1) smoking pipe in profile, (2) sailor suit and clean-shaven boyish grin, (3) John Garfield sneer ("rocks inside, that's what"), and (4) in checkered shirt with frown indicating serious rural emotions such as in *Ethan Frome* or *Of Mice and Men*. Agent suggests that we place this brilliant young actor at once. Ted places him — in wastebasket, together with several offers to let us in on investing in new shows. One of these new shows strikes its would-be producer, he says, as having "the same quality and feeling as *Winterset*" and he will accept sums as small as $600.

There was even a piece of paper for me and it ordered me to call MUrray Hill something or other, so it said in Miss Receptionist's best Palmer Method.

"Hello," I said. "Somebody there want Jack Jordan?"

"Oh what a surprise. I really didn't think you'd call. This is Aunt Thelma."

"Well my golly! Hello there, honey. How's everything in Kenosha? And what the heck are you doing in town?"

"She's from Kenosha," Ted said.

"Well what I called about, Jack — I know you're busy and I won't take up your time oh we're all so excited about what you're doing you know Uncle Ed was a great one for the theater used to go into Milwaukee pretty nearly every week he just loved it he'd be *so* interested if he'd lived poor Ed was always mighty fond of you Jack you know that he used to tell me you were his favorite nephew of course he didn't show any favoritism between you and Leroy and Orville and poor Earl but he felt it just the same. How's Frances and the kids okay I hope your mother sent one of Frances's letters to

Olive so I heard all about the measles or was that Orville's kids? But what I called about Jack, I'm writing a paper on bells for the P.E.O. and I wonder if you could get me into the carillon at St. John the Divine?"

"St. John the Divine?" I said.

"Hold 'er Newt, she's arearin'," Ted said.

After I got Auntie Thelma subdued by promising to take her to lunch, Sam took me out into the hall.

"I'm going now," he said. "Mum is the word."

"How do you spell that word?" I said.

I went back into the office. Schatzie Harris squeezed past me and we got stuck in the swinging gate together.

"Sorry," he said.

"Say — Floyd Collins he's the boy that really got stuck," I said.

"Is Ted here? Where's Sam Snow?"

He rushed into Ted's office with his overcoat flying in all directions. Hackett emerged from his office, coat also flying, and went out. Two actors arrived and sat down to wait. Goldy powdered her nose. I went into Ted's office.

"A foundation, that's all I want, a foundation. I got to have something to work with. Without a foundation I'm no place. Look at Sam, there's a man with no foundation and look at him he's all over town what's the matter this boy can't sit down? I can't talk to him I can't get anything out of him. 'Let me buy you a drink,' I say. 'Sure,' he says, but can I hold him, can I keep him? Halfway through a Martini his mind is wandering, he's off someplace or he's got to go talk to somebody at the end of the bar why he's worse than Rudy Lorraine and say *listen* now, Ted, level with me please will you honey *What about Rudy Lorraine,* have we got him or not I'm going crazy I bet six or a dozen people last night at Toots Shor's and at Lindy's they're saying 'Hey

Schatzie, I hear Sam and Ted got Rudy for the new show'
and when I go into Moore's after theater I step to the bar
and Vince says to me 'Say Schatzie, you got Lorraine for the
show I hear.' What gives, come on, yield a little, pal, unhook it
for Schatzie, my god I'm only your publicity agent just trying
to lay a foundation, Teddy, that's all. Not trying to fill up a
scrapbook, either, just trying to promote the show that's all,
you know, Jordan, some of the boys they figure they fill a
scrapbook with clippings that's a job well done but believe
me, a scrapbook isn't the answer, it's what good is your
publicity doing the show that counts that's where they are
paying off on the results at the old box office am I right Ted
you know I'm right that's what Oscar always told me and
Oscar ought to know a little about it huh I figure Oscar
should know maybe just a wee little bit about publicity huh
well anyway seriously, and hey here's another thing, come
on now, What's with Irene Lovelle? I hear rumors around
that she's battling with Sterling and Fein something awful
and is trying to get out and that you guys already got her on
paper I even heard the figure, fifteen hundred a week as
soon as she gets clear of Sterling and Fein I don't know how
many people said to me already this week 'I see Sam Snow
and Irene Lovelle hittin' it up. What's the deal, she going
into the new show?' I guess you saw 'Sam Snow and Irene
Lovelle in the clouds at Armando's' in Kilgallen last night
not to mention Winchell on Tuesday what's the Idea? Not
that it's my business or is it? Keep me posted will you? All
right, all right, I'm going, got to meet *This Week* magazine
— boy I'm planting something there that if it works oh boy
will it be sensational and I use that word advisedly this story
will be sensational! And with that stirring thought I'll leave
you, having had none of my questions answered whatsoever
and leaving in utter darkness. How do you like New York by

now, Jordan? Well the trouble and hard work is just starting believe me before this show opens you'll wish you were back out there amongst the alfalfa, kid. So long."

"Come on, Jack, put on the fedora, we're going calling," Ted said when Schatzie was gone.

Out the gate, down the hall, stand by the elevator reading the index of offices on that floor, wait for the red light; oh, man do I get sick of those New York corridors, those elevators to wait for, and then when they come you are in there like you were bound from Platte to Sioux City, courtesy of Armour and Company except that the hogs and the Herefords don't talk about What Charlie McDermott said to Walt Ferlihy after the meeting about the Kreml account.

"Where we going?" I said to Ted as we all spilled out of the elevator and rolled in all directions like peas.

"Going up! Roof garden, ladies' corsets, Chinatown," said the elevator boy, the one that talked like Donald Duck.

"That kid slays me," said a mammoth red-faced executive of obvious distinction, breeding, charm, and culture.

"He'll go places," chuckled his companion, whose horn-rim glasses were black and very, very heavy, and whose shoe soles were of an amazing thickness.

"Where we going, boss? Come on, Mr. Fagin, tell me where we're going," I said.

"To see Harry Paige," Ted said.

"You didn't fool around, did you?"

" 'Lightning,' that's what they used to call me in the Finger Lakes League."

All was hushed, refined, in the lobby of the St. Pierre. For a dollar the bellhops would direct you to the men's room and for another dollar the little man down there in the gray coat reading Louis Sobol's column and picking his teeth would turn on the water faucet for you and hand you a towel. No toothbrushes allowed and shaving frowned on.

In the lobby two or three aged characters in different stages of disintegration were propped here and there. There was a man with spats. There were two boys with longish blond hair, and the cheapest cigar at the cigar counter was twenty cents straight and no make anybody down on the corner ever heard of either. And don't think the boy behind the counter is going to thank you when he gives you your change because without an introduction he is not going to do it so don't get your hopes up even if you buy a couple of those big fat Havanas for a dollar each you're still going to get the dignified not to say sullen silence. That's the way it is up here and if you don't like it maybe you can get work at the Caterpillar Tractor plant out in Peoria as I understand they are hiring this week.

The carpets are very deep here at the St. Pierre, very deep, and the woodwork is cream with gold stripes and there are mirrors around most everywhere, reflecting the gaiety and the colors of the ladies' dresses. Voices are not raised and everybody is polite.

Harry Paige's door was ajar and we pushed the pearl doorbell button and a voice called out "Come on in," quite a good loud male voice, and Ted pushed in with me behind him and we were in a foyer and beyond that was a big room and it was like a stage set for some play about rich people with the Lunts in it. There were flowers in vases, too.

Harry Paige was sitting on a couch with his feet on the coffee table. He had on a tan gabardine suit but the coat was over the back of a chair and he was in his suspenders — beautiful silk brocade ones only not the corny ones with the naked dames or the ones with the playing cards on them.

These were black with a little dark red fleur-de-lis figure in them.

"Hold it, will you, Dory?" he said and put his hand over the phone. "Hello, Ted," he said. "Sit down, I'll be with you in a minute."

I sat down on a big couch and Ted sat in a chair with gilt legs.

"I keep telling you, Dory, that I had absolutely nothing to do with it at all, but nothing. After I saw the rushes I was very upset. Kirk meanwhile had gone to Vegas and I was unable to reach them. I just *happened* to see Louella that night at Jack Warner's and I tried to explain *exactly* what it was all about. . . . Yes. . . . *No,* Dory, I had *absolutely nothing whatever.* . . . Goddamn it, Dory, if you will *not* listen to me or to anyone involved, then how can you *possibly* . . . Oh *screw* that. You've been talking to Van Horne again; that's what this call is all about, am I right? . . . No, it's Van Horne, am I right? . . . The hell you didn't see him. You saw him all right. . . . Yes you did, you saw Van Horne and he told you about the three hundred and fifty thousand so you called me to cry. That's right, isn't it? . . . Sure, I know you did. . . . Well get this, Dory, you tell Van Horne what the Chase Bank told me this morning, you tell Van Horne the Chase Bank said . . ."

I sat there looking around at the furniture and Ted and I carried on one of those great conversations where you haven't a thing in the world to talk about but you don't want to just sit there listening to some other guy's private conversation. Not too loud to bother him but loud enough so he can hear that you're talking.

"Hey this is pretty nice," Ted said.

"Yeah, pretty nice spot."

"Uh-huh. I like those mirrors."

"Flowers too."

"Yeah, they look nice."

"I need a shoeshine."

"I could use one myself."

"That's one thing, you know, I'm always putting it off."

"Me too. My wife says to me yesterday, 'Say,' she says, 'you need a shine. You give me a laugh,' she says, 'you men pay twenty bucks for a pair of shoes and then you let them get to looking all shabby.' "

"I think maybe I'll get one in Grand Central on the way home."

"I can remember when a shine was a nickel."

"Now *listen,* Dory, I'm telling you for the last time that *I personally had nothing* . . . Well why the hell don't you go over to Vegas and find out then? . . . No, no, *NO,* I've got a board meeting of Intercoastal tomorrow. . . . Oh my god . . ."

"Nice rug," Ted said.

"Yeah. Oriental."

"Well, this always was a good hotel."

"It was?"

"Why sure. My gosh this has always been a very fine hotel. Very fine class of people."

"I guess that's right."

"Sure. Always had a *very* fine reputation, the St. Pierre."

"Well, it's certainly okay."

"I'll tell you who always stayed here. Queen Marie always stayed here."

"Is that a fact?"

"Sure. She wouldn't stay any place else. Not in New York that is."

"Queen Marie of Rumania?"

"That's her, sure. Always stayed here."

"Say what ever happened to her anyway? We don't hear so much about her any more."

"Darned if I know. I guess maybe she died or something."

"I suppose she did at that."

"You know. She'd be pretty old now."

"Yeah, she would at that I suppose."

"She was quite a girl."

"Yeah. She sure was. Good old Queen Marie."

"Queen who?" said Harry who had suddenly hung up.

"Oh we were just talking about Queen Marie of Rumania, Harry," Ted said. "She used to stop here, you know, here at the St. Pierre. Harry, I'd like you to meet Jack Jordan."

We shook hands.

"Jack wrote the book for the musical we're doing. You probably read his book, it was a big Book Club selection," Ted said. "Big best seller."

"Glad to know you, Jack," Harry said. "I read the studio synopsis of your book. We couldn't use it. You have any offers from the Coast?"

"I sold it to Ted and his partner," I said.

"Yes I know. Well, don't let it bother you. Maybe next time. I know writers personally that wrote for fifteen or twenty years and no luck. Then, bingo, they make a movie sale."

"I know guys like that," Ted said. "Cyril Brown. He wrote *Noontime*. Won a lot of awards. Big picture."

"Yeah," Harry said. "Big. Every place except at the box office. It was a flop."

"I can still remember that scene where the guy gets shot. Man, what a picture!" I said. "Remember that?"

"It didn't make a dime," Harry said. "Let's have a drink. It's about that time, isn't it? A little Scotch? A little bourbon? What about you, Jordan?"

Harry made us some drinks and we sat down. Harry lighted a Parliament which he stuck right in the middle of his mouth and kept there all the time he was talking, squinting his eyes from time to time on account of the smoke but never taking the cigarette out until he was through with it.

"Well, Ted, I read all about it in *Variety* and you want me to invest in your show I suppose," Harry said. He was a big guy, he looked like he could get in there and wheel one of those Paige Intercoastal trucks right down the line any time. Harry liked yellow shirts and pink shirts and deep violet shirts — I never saw him in a white shirt except when he was in evening clothes.

"Dorothy!" he called out. "Are you still here?"

A redhead came in a door down at the far end of the room.

"Did you want something, Mr. Paige?"

"Get me the file on Hackett, Richard Hackett. You know, that stuff Jerry got together for me?"

Red went out and came back with a folder and handed it to Harry.

"You can go any time, dear," he said. "I don't need you any more tonight."

He opened the folder and took out some papers. Dorothy toddled back to her room.

"Here's the whole story. See, we do things in a businesslike way in Hollywood. The hell with the sentiment, let's see the figures."

"What figures you got there, Harry?" Ted said.

"I asked my boy Jerry Kriebs — you remember Jerry, don't you, Ted — used to chase trouble for Balaban? Well, he's mine now and he's awfully good. Anyway I asked Jerry to get me all the figures on Richard Hackett — sort of a twenty-year batting average, get it? Now what Jerry did was to total up the number of Hackett shows, the amount of capitalization of each, and then he multiplied the number of weeks each show ran by the something-or-other and added the estimated receipts from the road companies and any picture sales or subsidiary rights, and then he divided by the total number of productions, and he comes up here with a figure of 10.956 per cent — say 11 per cent."

"Yeah," Ted said draining his Scotch and clanking the ice around in his glass nervously. "Eleven per cent, huh? Harry, what's that mean? Eleven per cent of what?"

"That's what I call the Success Potential figure, Ted. It's an original with me. I developed it when I was on the Fox lot. Jerry has expanded it and worked out the mechanics. We use it on everything. I wouldn't hire a soul without working out the S.P. Figure first."

"But Harry, how about guys like Don Rixon? The guy himself is always broke, he's always in flops, his record is awful, but he's still a terrific draw at the box office, probably the biggest, and the critics adore him. Man, his Success Potential is about ten degrees below zero but what a star! What an attraction! I wish we could get him."

"In a case like that we have an adjustment formula that we use. Jerry worked the whole thing out. I'm telling you, Ted, it's scientific, it's down to earth. That's the only way to operate in the theater. The hell with the sentiment, let's see the figures."

"Well, I'm going now, Mr. Paige," the redhead said. She had on a pillbox hat tied under her chin and a black coat over her arm, she sure looked too yummy to be a secretary, but she was and that's all she was. I'll tell you one thing I like about those Hollywood boys, they think of things like this. Makes life pleasanter. Little things. "Have you got enough ice and everything? I left your letters to be signed. Or would you like to sign them and I'll mail them? And Mr.

Rhinelander called again. And your theater tickets will be at the box office. Curtain is 8:40. The theater is on 45th West of Broadway. And you have a table for four at 21 for eleven o'clock. I guess that's it."

"Thanks, dear, thanks a lot," Harry said. "By the way, this is Mr. Crosby and Mr. Jordan. You may be seeing them a good deal. Boys, this is Miss Asbury — Dorothy."

"How nice," Dorothy said. "Well, bye-bye. Don't forget the meeting tomorrow, Mr. Paige."

Dorothy went, I wondered where.

"That's a pretty good-looking girl," I said.

"Efficient too," Harry said. "Nice, when it works that way."

"Harry, I need another drink. My goddamn Success Potential is all shot to hell," Ted said.

"Help yourself, boy. It's all right there. How about you, Jordan?"

"What's that 11 per cent mean, Mr. Paige?" I said. "Is that good?"

"Well I'll tell you, Jordan. In order to understand the full significance of the S.P. Figure you've got to take into consideration what I call Constant Variables. Now when I worked the S.P. Figure out on Zanuck, just for fun, you understand — well, it was very interesting — I was amazed, Jordan, simply amazed. Well what I hadn't taken into consideration was the Constant Variable Factor. Now in Hackett's case, an almost identical situation arises. Jerry thinks it's probably based on royalties fluctuation."

Ted had made himself another drink and drained it. He was standing in front of the big white fireplace that had a mirror over it. He was getting pretty red in the face and he had on the mud suit with the flecks of red in it and his tie was crooked like it usually was.

"Listen, Harry," he said. "Harry, listen. I want to ask you something. Okay, Harry? Just one question."

"Why sure, Ted," Harry said, and he got to his feet and headed for the bar. "I believe I'll have another dash myself. What is it?"

"Harry, are you going to put some money in our show?"

Harry was getting some ice out of the big silver ice bucket and he turned, holding a piece of ice in the tongs, and looked at Ted.

"Why sure," he said. "That's what we're talking about, isn't it?"

"Jerry Kriebs-Balaban-Zanuck-Instant Variable — I dunno," Ted said. "What *are* we talking about?"

It turned out to be a pretty big deal and changed a lot of things, because Harry didn't only just put in some money, he became co-producer with Sam and Ted. I guess he did it to raise their Success Potential Figure.

Chapter 13

AFTER our little earthquaking talk with Harry Paige we tiptoed out of the St. Pierre leaving Harry on the phone talking to Paige Intercoastal in Seattle. It was nearly seven o'clock but Ted had to go to the office to sign some letters and wanted me to go along; what with all the highballs and excitement, I was perfectly willing to go any place, including a trip to Hyde Park to visit Fala's grave, so we walked down the Avenue with our feet only touching the sidewalk every other block.

"How do you like that?" Ted kept saying. "How do you like that? Harry Paige . . .

"He could be a big asset, Jack," he said. "Don't underestimate this guy. This guy gets things done. He's got the know-how, boy."

"And money," I said. "And lots of shirts."

"Yeah, how do you like that?"

When we got back to the home grounds it was pretty quiet and only one elevator running. Ted opened the office door with his key and we went into his office and there was a note from Sam on his desk:

TED! *Call me at home! Important!*

So Ted dialed Sam and signed letters with one hand while he talked to Sam, and when he got done he got up and said:

"Come on, Sam's got something hot, he says, got to see me right away. Can't whisper it over the phone. Got to do it the hard way with a lot of taxicabs. Come on."

"I better go home," I said. "I've got twenty-five lines of Caesar to do for tomorrow's class."

"Come on," he said. "Lay off that going home stuff. You can go home next year. Sam will give us a drink."

"You think that's what we need?"

"Sure."

"But you have to make the theater."

"I'll make it. Come on."

"But the little wife is waiting for me by the garden gate in the dotted swiss apron."

"Look, if I tell Sam about Harry Paige he won't believe it. You gotta come and give the story the benefit of your thrilling vocabulary."

So we went up to 69th Street in a cab driven by Harry Micklethun, who stated that he expected rain before midnight for certain sure.

Sam's mother had died a couple years before, and he lived in her apartment. He was always going to "fix up this place and get rid of all this junk" but so far had been too busy calling cabs to do anything except stick up a big abstract painting called "The Subway" which some girl friend of his who was at the Art Students League of Nations had given him to commemorate One Night of Lipstick. Since the rest of the room was done in straight Paramount Pictures 1923 beaded-fringe style, the subway scene, done in a migraine-producing combination of Harrison red and chrome-yellow lemon, was as much at home as an orange whoopee-hat on Hackett's head. The chairs were overstuffed to the bursting point, and the side lights had Tiffany glass in them, right from Knickerbocker Lighting, 781 Eighth Avenue, not to mention round sateen pillows in various colors, and a large pale oil painting of Pierrot and Pierrette over the radio, which stood upon heavily carved legs.

"Listen, I'm going to give you a Spanish shawl for the grand piano," Ted said. "What's the idea anyway, no Spanish shawl?"

"I've heard it all before," Sam said. "So go right ahead. Get it over with. I suppose you guys want a drink."

"How come no mahogany tea wagon?" I said.

"Come on, what do you want to drink anyway?" Sam said. "Scotch, I suppose," and seizing an enormous cut-glass decanter he refilled a wineglass he had been holding in his left hand.

"What the hell are you doing?" Ted said. "What's that you're drinking anyway?"

"Sherry," Sam said. "Anything the matter with that? Any reason why I can't drink a little sherry in my own home?"

"Did I say anything?" Ted said. "I didn't say a word."

"I happen to like it, that's all," Sam said. "One gets tired of all this whisky swilling eventually."

"Yes, doesn't one?" Ted said.

"Irene says . . . well, anyway, there's the stuff, help yourself."

"Skip me. I've got to be at the theater in an hour," Ted said.

Jack helped himself.

"What's Irene say?" Ted said, sprawling on the sofa and picking up a copy of Edith Wharton from the end table.

"Oh, I was just thinking about the script," Sam said.

"Hey, get this," Ted said, reading aloud. " 'When Newland Archer opened the door at the back of the club box, the curtain had just gone up on the garden scene.' Oh baby! Life in the raw department."

"I had cocktails with Irene," Sam said.

" 'The blood rose to his temples and he caught a fold of her cloak,' " Ted read. " 'Ellen, what is it? You must tell me!' "

"What about Irene and the script?" I said.

"Yeah, what's she know about it? Has she read it and if so why?" Ted said, discarding Miss Wharton.

"I gave it to her," Sam said, sipping his sherry. "I happen to value her opinion."

"Uh-uh," Ted said. "Well?"

"Irene thinks it's a very literate script," Sam said.

"She does, hey, that's damn nice of her," Ted said. "It so happens I think it's an illiterate script and I like it that way. Man, the way people talk nowadays about musical comedy it is worse than listening to them slobber over this Faulkner boy."

"Go ahead, be just as crude as possible," Sam said. "Faulkner's only the great writer . . ."

"Yes, he's grand. Only why doesn't he try writing in English sometime?"

"Genius is something you couldn't possibly be expected to under . . ."

"The number to play is O double O," Ted said.

"I've got a rather brilliant idea. Let's drop the subject."

"All right, tell us some more about Irene. My favorite indoor sport is listening to the opinions of actresses on account of they are noted far and wide for their brains. Take Hackett, for example — you notice that whenever he gets into a jam he calls up some actress and asks her advice."

"My god but you're in a repulsive mood," Sam said. "I think I'll go to a movie."

"Oh come on down," Ted said. "Now what's the big news anyway? After you spill, maybe I've got a little item for you."

"In the mood you're in, what's the use? It's just something that could solve all our problems, that's all. Just merely something I set up that could mean the difference between our success and failure, that's all. Let's talk about it tomorrow, what the hell."

"All right, all right, forget all that — I was a bad boy and I just love actresses."

"That's good, because Irene fixed it."

"Fixed what?"

"Well, as a matter of fact it's about Harry Paige."

"Not *the* Harry Paige?"

"You know how he is, always putting money into different things."

"You mean he's like an 'angel,' they call it?"

"Suppose — now there might not be anything in it — but just suppose he got interested in the show. Like if he put some dough in — boy, what a talking point to attract investors — right? Not to mention all his friends and so on — others that he might bring in?"

"Say, you got something there," Ted said. "Why didn't I think of that?"

"I don't know how I got the idea," Sam said, looking as though oleomargarine wouldn't melt in his mouth. "It just came to me out of the blue. But the best of it is — get this — Irene is going to fix it for us to meet him. She worked for him on a picture. You know, she was in *Noontime* — that's where she got her Oscar."

"That picture didn't make a dime," Ted said.

"Oh for god's sake what has *that* got to do with it? So we all *know* that. For heaven's sake can't we *please* stick to the subject?"

"I'm with it," Ted said. "I see indirect lighting, incense,

soft music. . . . Harry Paige is getting groggy. . . . He takes out his fountain pen. . . ."

"So you might just as well quit low-rating this girl all the time."

"She's just trying to be helpful, huh?"

"She certainly is. And I think it's pretty — darn — nice — of her, too."

"I don't suppose she noticed when she read Jack's illiterate script that there was a great big fat lead part just made to order for her?"

"Now, Ted, wait — don't, Ted — please don't say things like that or I shall become *violently* annoyed with you. I just can't *stand* that kind of thinking. Every fiber of me revolts at such sordid innuendo. It's the kind of cheap, nasty talk that makes me feel sort of unclean, sort of . . ."

"Well go wash your hands then," Ted said. "And listen here to me. I used to know Harry Paige pretty well, so today I . . ."

"What! You never told me that!"

"Why should I? I didn't tell you my Sixth Grade teacher's name either. Harry used to be with Mighty Mammoth Shows at the same time I was. Harry had a grind show, with the Men Only deal for another four bits. Funny thing, I saw one of the girls just the other day — she was making change at that Penny Arcade on Broadway and 48th Street, you know, next to the corner there. Frances something, what was her name — Williams — Wilson — something like that. I'll have to ask Harry."

"Better still, let's all grab a cab and go up and ask her, because I can hardly sleep a wink until I know," Sam said, pouring himself some more sherry out of the enormous Bohemian glass decanter.

"So Jack and I went up to see Harry this afternoon at the St. Pierre," Ted said.

"You took *Jack?*" Sam roared. "*I'm* your partner, he's just a lousy . . ."

"Inky-fingered hack writer," I said.

"Thanks, Jack," Sam said. "He's just a lousy hack so you had to take him instead of me. What the HELL kind of a partner are you? Sometimes I think I'm going crazy. It doesn't make sense, it's crazy. What's the idea of taking Jack along, he's only . . ."

"A sorry scribe," I said.

"That's right," Sam said. "Why didn't you take the doorman at Sardi's while you were at it, or Hackett's chauffeur?"

"I wanted to surprise you, dear," Ted said. "And if you'll turn off the blower and cool down the pipes, I'll tell you about kindly old Uncle Ted in Harry Paige-land."

"This stuff tastes terrible — what in hell do I drink it for?" Sam said, looking at his sherry glass with disgust.

"I'll get you a Scotch, Sam," I said.

"Thanks, Jack," he said.

"That's okay, Sam," I said.

"Harry wants to be partners," Ted said.

"Partners?" Sam said.

"Sure. Paige, Crosby and Snow, Producers."

"Make that a double Scotch, Jack."

"Sure thing, Sam."

"He says he'll put in fifty thousand himself and he'll bring in another hundred thousand."

"WOW," Sam said.

"That was more or less my reaction."

"Does this man have any taste?"

"Who won the Cannes Film Festival — first prize?"

"I know, but he's so *Holly*wood." Sam shuddered.

"A hundred and fifty thousand, kid. That means all *we* have to raise is one hundred grand."

"Paige, Crosby and Snow. That sounds ludicrous."

"Harry has some pretty terrific connections, Sam."

"Hackett! What about Hackett? You know how he might feel about somebody like Harry Paige."

"Listen, Harry's not so bad. He's a very literate guy actually."

"I'm afraid of Hackett on this."

"Everybody's afraid of Hackett on everything. That's the whole dang trouble. We've got to let him know we're the producers."

"Yeah, us and Harry Paige."

"Well, I didn't give him an answer. All I said was —"

"What's he really like, is he like that director you introduced me to at The Lambs from MGM that kept talking about 'Metro' all the time and about 'widescreen,' and 'TV program hunger' — God save us from —"

"Harry's okay. Of course he does 'springboard' a bit."

"He whats?"

"He springboards. Like he says, if he gets any ideas storywise when he gets back to the Coast he'll springboard them to us."

"Gawd," Sam said. "Now it begins."

"Listen, I'm going home," I said. "I already missed Buffalo Bob, Captain Video, and Magic Cottage."

"B-O-S-C-O spells BOSCO!" Ted shouted.

"So long, fellow brownies," I said. "See you down at Paige, Crosby and Snow."

Sam groaned.

"You understand, of course," I said, "that we'll all have to wear Paige shirts. Harry will expect it. This month's promotion, for example, is pink raw silk with black collar and cuffs, and black pearl buttons, with a blending harmonizing Paige-ensemble tie."

"But we'll get a discount from Harry," Ted said.

"Maybe we'll even get 'em free," I said.

"A hundred and fifty thousand," Sam murmured. "Paige, Crosby and Snow. Well, where is he? Let's go talk."

Chapter 14

If Adam had been a chorus boy, there'd be no human race.

Hackett said we all needed a three-day vacation so he went to Bermuda while I stayed home in lovely Connecticut over the week end and acted like a writer — that is, I started two short stories and filed them away, wrote down ideas for a couple of great novels and filed them away, walked up and down the road in front of the house kicking stones, looked at the funny pictures in the *New Yorker,* practiced with Katie's Yo-yo for a while, turned the TV on and off constantly and told Frankie I was through, washed up, no ideas, bare cupboard. Monday I stayed home for more of the same, and Tuesday Frankie said she had had enough and I should go into town and look at the tall buildings.

I bought all the papers available at the Greek's in Springdale and boarded the cars. Harry's press agent or good old Jerry Kriebs had not been idle and in Louella's column it said, "Harry Paige has Irene Lovelle in mind for his new Broadway musical. Well, Harry, Irene is a very talented girl, as all of us know who saw her in her Oscar-winning role in *Noontime.*" Hedda said, "Harry Paige and Richard Hackett teaming up to produce a Broadway musical." Winchell said,

"Harry Paige . . ." Hy Gardner said, "Fabulous Harry Paige
. . ." Ed Sullivan said, "Harry Paige and amazing Richard
Hackett . . ."

And so on. I'll say one thing about Harry, he certainly got
everybody jumping up and down all the time over his projects. I went up to the office. As I cheerily greeted Miss De
Vere, the switchboard sweetheart, she made a face at me,
jerked her head toward Ted's office and said, "Watch out,
boy. Bad day at Black Rock."

I went in and tossed my Doug Fairbanks Jr. worsted gabardine trench coat with the belt and shoulder straps onto the
couch and stood by the window looking down, down, down to
the skating rink, a silvery square where a few nuts were
showing off, and I remembered skating in Indiana. That was
a Willa Cather kind of skating, with clamp skates, chilblains,
mufflers, lost mittens, skate keys, rosy cheeks, innocence.
Especially innocence. Well, there's not a dime to be made
with innocence, so that's out.

For we are very, very advanced here at the Rockefeller
Plaza and the Dan Beard projects are taboo.

But definitely. Ask Kriebs.

"I see Harry Paige is producing a musical comedy," I said
to Ted.

"Look, I don't think it's very goddamn funny," he said,
"and Sam's about wild."

"Hey, you're getting sensitive," I said.

"Well maybe I am," he said. "After all the slavery we've
done over this project, what happens? 'Harry Paige's new
Broadway musical!' Hell, he hasn't even read the script. He
had Dorothy get him a synopsis of it. Ever hear of anybody
having a *synopsis* made of a ninety-page musical comedy
script?"

"What's going on, anyway?" Hackett said, standing in the

doorway with his hands on his hips. "The elevator boy, the obnoxious one that imitates the duck, just said, 'I see in the papers you've got Irene Lovelle for the new show.' What's *he* talking about? Morning, Jack."

"Oh hell, it's the Hollywood business already. It was in *Louella's* column," Ted said.

"Who's Louella?" Hackett said.

"Parsons," Ted said. "The columnist. She had it in about Harry Paige. And Sam is fit to be tied because it didn't mention us. The way it was worded it's all Harry's show."

"Well you knew this was going to happen, didn't you?" Hackett said. "Forget it. Nobody reads that Hollywood slop except ribbon clerks anyway. And who cares?"

"I don't care," Ted said. "What do I care? Let 'em print any crazy stuff they want. But I must say Sam's plenty mad."

"Well, what *about* Irene?" Hackett said. "Where'd they get that line? You know, she's got a nice quality. Might be very good, if Hollywood hasn't wrecked her."

"She only made two pictures out there," Ted said. "She wants to get back on Broadway."

"She does, hey? Can she sing?"

"That's what they say."

Sam came in and slammed his briefcase down.

"Well, I just got it from that comical elevator boy," he said. "I knew we should never have teamed up with Harry Paige."

"Come on, boys, I'll take you to the Harvard Club for lunch and we'll discuss all these momentous questions in an atmosphere of utter gloom," Hackett said.

We walked down to 44th Street, Hackett and Ted ahead, Sam and I behind, and I thought Oh boy I guess I am okay after all here I am walking right down Fifth Avenue past Finchley's with two producers and the World's Champion

Director. So I stopped several strangers and said, "Look, that's Richard Hackett, he's the most terrific guy in the world and in the theater he is nonpareil and I not only know him but listen friend, I'm writing a show with him yes that's just exactly what I said of *course* I know him hell I'm going to lunch with him right now at the Harvard Club of the World and I am going to talk to him, going to sit right down there with him. Bill Inge comes from Kansas, by the way, Leland Hayward comes from Nebraska City, Nebraska, Hackett comes from Michigan — why almost all of us merry jesters on Broadway come from R.F.D. Number 1."

The Harvard Club has all the architectural charm of the 12th Street Station in Chicago and is even darker inside; every member is furnished with a licensed guide and a bull's-eye lantern on entering the club. Entertainment consists of a complete line of pinball machines and a booth where you can take your own picture for a quarter.

Hackett conducted us to the bar, where we enjoyed rubbing elbows with several famous statesmen and one failure. Then he took us in to lunch.

"Now you're going to be Paiged to death," Hackett said. "So you might as well get used to it. You went into this for a good reason. Maybe he'll do you some good."

"We got his check this morning," Ted said. "That's something."

"Good," Hackett said. "Now what about Irene . . . ? Can she sing? Any of you boys heard her lately?"

"I saw her on TV," I said. "She sounded okay."

"Big voice?" Hackett said.

"On TV everybody's big," Sam said.

"Well, I think we better audition her if she's at all interested."

"Is she interested, Sam?" Ted said.

"How do I know?" Sam said.

"Didn't she say anything," I said, "when she read the . . ."

"I'll have the veal steak!" Sam shouted.

"Oh-oh," I said.

"You boys are certainly on edge," Hackett said.

"Irene is all tied up contractually with Sterling and Fein," Sam said.

"That's all off," Hackett said. "She broke the contract. The show is on the rocks. They're giving it up for the time being."

"I don't think she's the *type* at all," Sam said.

"I disagree with you," Hackett said, "if there's any sincerity left in her acting. She had a great talent last time I saw her. A natural, believable style."

"She certainly vibrates," I said.

"What's that mean?" Hackett said.

"I mean she's vibrant," I said.

"They're not quite the same thing," Hackett said.

"On *Broadway?*" Sam sneered. "Are you serious?"

"Why not?" Ted said. "She knocked them on their ear in that revival of something up at the Center, didn't she? Not to mention *The Penalty*. What's the matter with you anyway? I thought you and Irene were doing the skit entitled *Just Chums* these days."

"Just because I happen to know her does that mean I'm supposed to — to sign her up — to knock myself out giving her parts — to sabotage this entire project just because . . . ?"

Hackett treated Sam to a curious look. Sam fizzled out and set up a great clatter with the silverware and even drew a few zigzags on the cloth with his table knife.

"Well . . ." Hackett said.

"She's no name on Broadway," Sam said.

"Evie told me a pretty good one," Ted said. "This guy says

to the girl, 'Honey, how would you like to see your name in lights?' and she says, 'Oh lovely. Are you a producer?' and he says, 'No, an electrician.' "

"That's a riot," Sam said. "No wonder Freddie gave Evie the air."

"Maybe we better go over to the Amherst Club," Ted said. "What have you got, the Harvard blues?"

"I'm going to get some cigarettes," Sam said, and getting up quickly he bounced off Hallowell, '31, onto Winston, '13, recovered, and went in search of the cigar counter.

"What goes on here with Sam?" Hackett said. "He seems to be a large packet of nerves. And what's all this about Irene Lovelle?"

"He's been flying around town with her. Gassing it up," Ted said.

"How bad is it?" Hackett said.

"Well, she's got him drinking sherry," Ted said. "And he says he admires her mind."

"Have you met this *femme fatale* yet, Jack?" Hackett said. "She's quite a dame."

"I met her one night when I was first down here. Sam and I ran into her one night. When she first showed up Sam would hardly speak to her. He said she was too impossible, he couldn't face it. She was in some show . . ."

"Sterling and Fein," Ted said.

"But she was trying to get out . . ."

"She's out," Hackett said.

". . . And she was making quite a play for Sam, and she was telling me what a peach of a writer I was and how she had hysterics when she read my book it was so funny — all that."

"Sam was cold to her?" Hackett said.

"Playful rudeness you might call it," I said.

"Well that's got all the elements of a great, soul-searching love affair. Hate turns to love. Our hero devours Miss Lovelle with kisses, he explores her mind; the mind of a great actress: in it he finds a thousand little drawers, each containing a solid gold cliché. He explores her body — he folds his trousers neatly over a chair — they exchange handkerchiefs . . ."

"Then why doesn't he want her in the show?" Ted said. "Wouldn't you think he'd . . ."

"Well it makes it complicated, I suppose," I said. "When your girl friend changes to an employee."

"*Hmm,*" Hackett said.

"I don't think we should worry about that," Ted said. "Boy, if we could get Irene Lovelle we'd be in damn fine shape."

"All right, all right, sign her up," Sam said, sitting down and lighting up a few cigarettes.

"We'll audition her," Hackett said. "When are we having our first auditions?"

"Next week," Ted said. "At the Broadway Theater."

"Nice roomy house," Hackett said. "Couldn't we get the Music Hall? Or the Polo Grounds?"

"They gave us the Broadway," Sam said. "It's dark."

"What about Rudy Lorraine, the greatest composer that ever lived? We got him yet?"

"Almost," Sam said.

"Want me to talk to him?" Hackett said.

"We're going up to his place tomorrow at noon. Come on along."

"Has he calmed down any?" Hackett said.

"You know Rudy," Ted said.

"A bit of a bounder, eh wot?" Hackett said. "Well, he writes damn good tunes sometimes."

"But never a show," Sam said in lugubrious tones.

"This place is not very jazzy," Hackett said. "But I never saw it have this effect on anybody before. Come on, boys, let's get Sam out of here before he starts picking on Charles Francis Adams."

"I think this is a real nice place," Ted said.

"Never again," Hackett said. "Not with you crude oafs from show business."

Rudy Lorraine had what he called a "studio" over on 47th Street so he could go there and work. Some work.

Well maybe he did work there, I don't know. He worked someplace, because he did get those tunes written. But the only times I was ever there without we let him know ahead of time we were coming, there was always some dame getting up off the couch or else one showed up ten minutes after we got there and he'd say: "Not now, honey. I'm busy. I'll call you later. Listen, I'll meet you at Lindy's at 6:30, okay?"

There was a couch and a Schaaf upright piano, which was all the equipment he needed for his two principal activities. Also a couple of chairs, a lot of music sheets lying around, and a record player so he could play his latest platters while visions of royalties danced in his head.

He had his tie loosened and his black hair mussed up, and was smoking a cigar when we got there. He was a dark, good-looking boy with very white teeth, about thirty years old, in a black suit. That was all the stuff then, the black suits.

The boys introduced me and we shook hands while everybody took off coats and hunted for places to put them.

"I read your book when I first heard about this project," he said. "Great stuff, solid, different. It's down, that's what I want, something down. I been working on some special material for Dietrich — up, way up. I wanna get down."

Hackett put his coat and hat on the piano and sat down

in a chair. There was a crunch, and Hackett reached under him and began hauling out pieces of "Chief of Love," now Number One on the Hit Parade.

> From care I'm getting such relief
> Since you became my darling Chief
> Of Love. . . .

But you know the rest. The first week, when it was Number Seven, they did it on the Hit Parade with everybody in Indian costumes and some thrush sang it to the Indian Chief. Pretty cute. The next week it was Number Five and they did it in the County Jail with the song directed at the Police Chief. Then they did it on a sailboat for no good reason, and in a medieval castle with a lot of armor. Where they missed up was not having six teen-agers singing it to the engineer of the Santa Fe Chief, which would have been a neat twist and maybe some nice tie-ins with the railroad like free Santa Fe ashtrays or something.

"Never mind, I've got plenty of them," Rudy said.

"I must confess," Hackett said, "I've been wanting to do that for weeks."

"You don't like it, eh?" Rudy said.

"No, I don't like it," Hackett said. "But don't let that worry you. I'm pretty hard to please. Now play us something you've written lately. Give us an idea. Get us in a romantic mood and then we'll discuss the sordid details."

Rudy sat down at the piano, removed the cigar from his face and began to play for us. He played and he sang. A ballad, then a novelty number, then a waltz even. He was good; he could go out and work the niteries any time — he played his own stuff better than anybody else ever played it. On the ballads he had a straight clear quality with a lot of conviction, and the way he sang that smeller "Chief of Love" you began to believe in it. And on the hot items he could raise his voice and belt along with the best of them. Then he'd switch to a sob number and have you reaching for the kerchief. Tell the truth I never cared much for anything of his I'd ever heard until I heard him do them himself.

Except all the time he was working he kept looking at us just like he was playing to an audience in the Camellia Room, not to four jerks in a dreary pad on 47th Street. The question is, what kind of a facial expression are you supposed to wear when some guy is singing a love song to you three feet away and looking right at you?

I never understand how guys can do that; it's like poets who love to read their poetry out loud to a little group at home. If I ever wrote any poetry I'd be too embarrassed to read it to anybody, even if I did like it myself. Not Rudy. He'd meet you on 45th and Broadway and he'd say, "Hi, kid, listen to this. For that spot where Chuck's got the dame out on the beach in the Second Act," and he'd pull you over to one side of the sidewalk against a mailbox and start singing to you, while you stood there like an idiot, and some dame going by says, "Look, what's that fellow singing to that other fellow for?" and her friend says, "Listen, Mabel, this is New York. See, you got to expect anything."

Hackett sat there like he was a product of the Vermont granite industry, Ted and Sam looked at the ceiling, at their shoelaces, and out the window at the CHOP SUEY sign across the street. The phone rang twice while Rudy was working and each time he picked it up and said, "Not now," and hung up.

"That's enough of a rumble for now," he said after he quit, and the phone rang again. "Hazel, I'm busy. Don't call me any more, will you please! I'll call *you*," he said and he hung up again.

"You think you could do a show?" Hackett said.

"Why not?" Rudy said. "I go to all the shows. I write words. I write music. So that's it, isn't it?"

"Well, we can't use any 'Love Chief's or anything like it," Hackett said. "I'll tell you, we're going to be pretty brutal about lyrics."

"Oh that's all right," Rudy said. "For you, Mr. Hackett, I'll even go to bed early. When do we start?"

"We've got a working script now," Hackett said. "Boys, see that Mr. Lorraine gets a script. Of course Jack and I are going to rewrite it. It's too long. And it's wrong in places. But you can read it. You'll see the song cues. You can start any time."

So then we all had a lot of excitable talk about how great it was going to be and Hackett said Alfred was waiting for him and he had to go and after he left we all had a big yak and Rudy wanted to know about casting and who was going to sing his songs and how many girl and boy singers in the chorus, and how many pieces in the orchestra and who was going to be the musical director and what theater we'd be in and how were the acoustics and who was going to be the arranger and how many weeks on the road tryout and where were we going to rehearse.

Then the phone rang again and Rudy answered it.

"You know something," Sam said. "We're going to have a really exciting score. I just feel it."

"Gladys? Gladys who?" Rudy said.

"I think you're right, Sam," Ted said.

"Oh sure I remember," Rudy said. "When, right now? Hell, I'm busy . . . Uh-huh . . . you bet I remember, honey . . . wait a minute."

"I sure like that last number he played. Has that been released yet?" I said.

"I don't think so," Sam said.

"If it was, I haven't heard it," Ted said.

"Listen, you guys," Rudy said. "How long you gonna be here? Oh hell, never mind," and he said into the phone, "Come on over, baby," and he hung up.

"Listen, you guys," he said. "This is the most beautiful —— in the business. Look, you guys go over to the Chink joint and have a drink. I wanna talk to you some more. I'll be there in twenty minutes."

"Yeah, we gotta go anyway," Ted said.

"No, listen, wait for me over at the Chink joint."

"We better get back to the office," Sam said.

"It's just that this dame . . . See, she's singing with Les Williams's band and they're between trains or something and I gotta see her . . . you know — business."

"We'll meet you at the Chink's," Ted said.

So we went over and had some Martinis and Sam wanted some sweet and sour pork. In twenty minutes Rudy showed up.

"Boy, that was a quick one," Ted said.

"Now listen," Rudy said, "when am I gonna get that script?"

I can see it all now from my armchair as though it were only yesterday — the puddles of sweet sauce and hot sauce, the inscrutable Oriental maiden standing by the booth, Sam Snow, pale, worried, casting a glance of appraisal at Rudy Lorraine, and outside: the restless, faceless figures hurrying past the plate glass in the late fall rain. *Coins, Bought and Sold . . . Any Book in This Rack 15 Cents . . . Hot Pastrami 35 cents . . . Rooms $1.50 . . . Banjo Lessons . . . "Shine 'em up, mister?" . . . Please Sit Back and Enjoy Your Ride.*

Chapter 15

AND when I am too tired to sit around Torino's any longer running down Kazan, and listening to Charlie Hershfield give after-dinner speeches, and sitting on the floor at cocktail parties talking about the Theater de Lys's latest mistake, and looking at the Park while lunching at the Plaza for $28.00, and gazing with pained regret in Cartier's window — and when I am tired of sitting in cold dark theaters in the fifth row staring at the 1000-watt work light while nervous girl singers give us their version of "It's Almost Like Being in Love" — then perhaps I shall say, "I am sorry, friends, but I am in my Second Childhood," and I shall go home and curl up in that big easy chair and read *Paddy Muskrat* and *Kernel Kobb* and *Little Miss Sweet Clover* and *Jeremy Fisher* and *What Happened at Miss Minchin's*. Joseph Wood Krutch and Phyllis Bentley and Sidney Hertzberg and Donald Adams and the Sitwells and V. S. Pritchett and David Daiches and the Alsops and David Lawrence and Sokolsky, they can all go poop, for I shall be playing with my electric train in the attic on rainy days, and I shall rig a market basket and a clothesline on a pulley from my bedroom window and give my guinea pig elevator rides.

"He's gone crazy," they will say at Torino's as they pop the pink pills into their mouths before eating.

"Too bad about Jack Jordan," they will tell their psychiatrists. "He was just as normal as you or — er — I, and then all of a sudden . . . A pity, too. Great talent. Of course he hadn't any *flair*. And his coarseness was rather trying. But still . . . By the way, I understand Josh is upset again."

But in the meantime, before the crash, we have a number entitled:

AUDITIONS FOR FEMALE LEAD

There we were, Hackett and Ted and Sam and Rudy and I, sitting in the fifth and sixth rows of the dark, damp, cold Broadway Theater, looking at the 1000-watt work light. Coats draped over shoulders in the approved manner.

And De Marco was there with us too. He is now a big figure in the group.

Back home we would call him the band leader, but here he's the musical director and he not only conducts the orchestra but he and the arranger pick the singers, with the help of the composer and a lot of cheap advice from all the rest of us including the pianist and the doorman. And for weeks he rehearses them over and over and over until you think maybe he has a screw loose. According to the musical director and the composer the singers never *do* sing it right, even if the show has been playing on Broadway for five years.

De Marco is a pudgy guy with tortoise-shell glasses and is always talking about "the *fermata*." Any reader having information about the whereabouts of the *fermata* please get in touch with the writer c/o the BIJOU THEATER, MUNCIE, INDIANA. All letters answered and photos will be returned.

One of the office girls was up on the stage with a clip board and she came out and asked us if we were ready and we said we were ready and she said "Judith Marlowe" and Miss Marlowe came out in a darling blouse with puff sleeves and pinched-in waist and flaring skirt.

"Skinny legs," Rudy said.

She leaned over and handed her music down to the pianist. He put his copy of *Variety* on the top of the piano, set her music up in front of him and sat down.

"Move back a little please, Miss Marlowe," Hackett said. "We want to see you."

So she moved back where the light struck her better, and went into a very busy number, some special material that she probably had been doing in night clubs.

"That's no good," Hackett said. "Don't you want her to sing something else?" he said, turning around to Rudy.

"Hold it!" Rudy said very loud. "That's enough!"

Miss Marlowe couldn't hear and went right on singing.

"Hold it! Stop!" Sam said, also very loud, and the piano player heard him and quit and Miss Marlowe finally quit too, in the middle of a phrase.

"We want to hear your *voice*," Hackett said.

"Can you sing in your chest voice?" De Marco said.

"Oh yes, very loud," Miss Marlowe said. "I was in *Pink Tights*."

"What the hell has that got to do with it?" Ted said *sotto voce*.

"Well, sing something else," De Marco said. "Sing anything."

"Well — how about *South Pacific*? Something from that?"

"Well, let's see. How about good old 'Blue Skies'? Can you sing that?"

"I think so."

"All right, fine."

"Nice figure except for those legs," Sam said.

"Listen, dear," De Marco said. "Do it in E minor, will you? Johnny, give it to her in E minor."

So Miss Marlowe sang "Blue Skies" in E minor with the chest tones and skinny legs.

"Listen, dear, have you got tones in between chest tones and head tones?" De Marco said when she had finished and was standing there looking out into the black, blinded by the work light.

"Well, I . . . What do you mean? I guess so."

"Does your voice break there?"

"Oh *no*."

"Well, can you make it break?"

"Oh! Yes!"

"Well, we'll give you a call if we want you. And if you come back, bring back all you've got. It's a little weak, dear. Thank you."

"She's pretty cute," Ted said.

"Cheap type," Hackett said.

"I didn't care much for her," Sam said.

"The voice is very good," Rudy said.

Then nine girls in succession came out and sang for us and every time they were done De Marco's voice spoke up loud in the empty theater: "Thank you." And that's all they got for their trouble, the special hair-do, the last-minute advice from the voice coach, the sleepless night, the hunting for the stage door, the standing for two hours in the wings waiting. For "Thank you" means "Good-by." And they would say "Thank you" back and stoop over the footlights and Johnny would hand up their music to them and they would walk off the empty stage all alone and brave. And some of them brought their own pianists, who would appear from below in the pit and make their way to the piano, knocking over music stands; and that was sadder because here the girl had to pay the guy five dollars. For nothing.

All the time the girls were up there dying, it was going like this out front:

HACKETT: She was in *Where's Sally?* Had an affair with the drummer.

DE MARCO: Yeah, I know her. Not much voice there.

SAM: Every time one comes out that I go for you can't hear her voice past the pit.

HACKETT: What's that song, original material?

DE MARCO: That's from *Hazel Flagg.* I made an arrangement of it. In G flat!

HACKETT: I didn't see *Hazel Flagg.*

TED: You didn't miss a thing. I lost five hundred dollars though.

SAM: Hey, look at her. How you like her?

JACK: Cornfed. Too wholesome.

TED: I bet she does this number out on the Post Road on Friday nights.

RUDY: She's an ad for diaphragmatic breathing. Too bad nothing happens.

TED: Another party singer. I bet her friends all told her, "Go ahead, Myrtle, you can sing better than them Broadway stars. Go ahead, take a chance. What have you got to lose?"

HACKETT: Is Irene Lovelle coming?

TED: At four o'clock.

RUDY: Oh boy, there was a flat D flat.

SAM: *Beautiful Sea* is down to thirty-one thousand. They won't last. Poor Shirley.

HACKETT: I like this one. Nice style. How's the voice, De Marco?

DE MARCO: Mr. Hackett, don't take this girl. She's handy to have around a show, but . . .

HACKETT: But what?

DE MARCO: Just *but* . . . She's a troublemaker.

TED: She's been in every show in town.

HACKETT: Well, let's not waste her time calling her back then, if you don't want her.

DE MARCO: I definitely don't want her.

HACKETT: Well, you tell her then.

DE MARCO: THANK YOU!

SAM: I know this girl. Met her at Janet's. Crazy kid. Comes from Utah. She's a Mormon.

TED: Aw come on.

HACKETT: Funny, she doesn't speak anything at all the way she sings. Very crude speaking voice.

RUDY: She's a waste of time.

JACK: I'd like to waste some time with her.

HACKETT: Jordan rides again. Jack always likes those dark, mean-looking girls.

TED: Did you hear about the contract Drake got on *Kismet?* Wow.

RUDY: I saw that show the other night. Boy, what dames.

HACKETT: What was it all about? I still don't know. I couldn't follow it.

RUDY: Who cares, with all those lovely navels winking at you all evening?

SAM: My god, can't we get some heat in this theater?

HACKETT: What's this girl doing here? How did she get in?

TED: MCA called me up about her. Said she had great talent.

HACKETT: They've got a big nerve.

SAM: I'll speak to David about it.

DE MARCO: Too bad. She really has a glorious voice.

HACKETT: Tell her she's the wrong type. Why waste everybody's time? *I'll* tell her.

(Hackett gets up and walks down to the pit and talks to girl. She retrieves music and exits. Nice business we're in.)

HACKETT: *(sitting down again)* Those things are terribly sad.

SAM: Look, there's a wonderful type. Wonder if she'd take an understudy part?

RUDY: Forget it, she can't sing.

TED: Lovely tits.

RUDY: She can't sing with them.

HACKETT: Awfully cute girl. Nice Western type, don't you think, Jack?

JACK: Perfect. Wonderful hard accent too.

SAM: She's a darling.

DE MARCO: I'm sorry, fellows. This voice is impossible.

TED: She's a honey. Couldn't you work on her a little?

DE MARCO: Love to. But it wouldn't help her voice any.

SAM: There we go again. None of the good-lookers can sing.

HACKETT: How bad is she?

DE MARCO: She's not good.

HACKETT: Tell her to come back.

RUDY: She'll never fill a theater.

JACK: Well, we can look at her some more anyway.

HACKETT: Jack's got the idea.

RUDY: I could murder all the voice teachers in New York. They perpetrate such frauds.

TED: This girl was in *Wonderful Town*. Has four kids. You'd never think it, would you?

HACKETT: I would.

JACK: Man, this is a strange way to make a living, sitting around here all afternoon watching a bunch of girls sing. Just think, everybody else is working.

TED: We're working.

HACKETT: We'll put a time clock out by the stage door for you to punch, Jack.

JACK: That would make me feel better.

SAM: My God, isn't anybody else cold? I think it's just *impossible* in here.

DE MARCO: If she had tried for the E I would have told her to come back.

HACKETT: Nice voice but too loud. She's no good for a principal and she'd wreck any chorus.

DE MARCO: (*to stage*) Wait a minute. Wait a minute. You're too low. Try it in E flat.

SAM: There's a nice voice.

HACKETT: But no projection.

RUDY: No chest tone.

JACK: But what a chest.

TED: Not bad. She was in *Allegro*.

RUDY: Can't we hurry this up? I'm recording at Decca in half an hour.

HACKETT: More "Love Chief"'s?

RUDY: No, this is a new one.

HACKETT: Got the deejays all lined up?

RUDY: Well, that's the way we do it. I can't help it.

HACKETT: How do you like *our* business?

RUDY: This is a nice business, Mr. Hackett.

TED: Here comes another fine pair.

RUDY: Adolescent size. I dig that.

SAM: That's Dotty Wilson. What a doll. (*To stage*) Hello Dotty, dear.

(*Girl on stage shades eyes but can't see anything out front. She says, "Is that you, Mr. Hackett? Well, hello."*)

TED: That's what you get for being familiar.

HACKETT: Dotty's putting on weight.

RUDY: She was in *Me and Juliet* wasn't she? Been on the Coast, I think.

SAM: You sure are hep to the shows for a pop writer.

RUDY: I'm in the business.

This went on until 3:45 when Sally from the office came out and said: "Well, that's all for a few minutes. Miss Lovelle isn't here yet."

Sam nudged me and said, "Come on across the street with me and have some coffee."

The stage doorman was sitting in his little hole reading the *Mirror*. Outside it was cold and raining again. We went down the dirty areaway past the rusty trashcans and across the street to the Spanish joint. It was warm and smelly and empty except for one guy and a fat girl at the bar. We got the coffee. The tablecloth had gravy, A-1 sauce, mustard, ketchup, soy sauce, soup, and frijoles on it.

"She'll be great. She'll kill 'em," Sam said gloomily.

"You don't sound like you want her much," I said, blowing on my boiling coffee.

"Oh hell," Sam said.

"We need a big name, kid," I said. "Nobody ever heard of any of the rest of us, except Hackett. And the critics will be out for Rudy with blow guns, with poison darts."

"She's no name."

"Why do you keep saying that? Why of course she is. Even out where I come from everybody's *heard* of her."

"Aw they have not."

"I'm tellin' you."

"Come on. She's probably there by now. Pay the check, will you?"

She had on black slacks and a two-dollar blue chambray shirt; and the longest mink coat I ever saw.

She had blond hair, she had chest tones, she had that E, she could belt, she could project, she could move, she didn't have skinny legs, she wasn't nervous — she was Irene Lovelle and she was good and she knew all about it.

"Oh-h, man," Rudy said, "listen to her holler."

Nobody else said anything. There wasn't too much to say; it was all too obvious that this was the girl, if we could get her to say my lines and sing Rudy's music. Already I could feel all those typewritten sheets begin to come alive. All those lousy lines. Right away I had that feeling that she would make them good lines.

I looked at handsome Richard Hackett. He was looking at Irene Lovelle. She could fill a theater all right, and she was filling it. What a Christmas present.

After she was through singing Hackett got up and went down the aisle and up onto the stage. She retrieved her fur coat and Hackett shook hands with her and they stood there talking.

"She's marvelous," Rudy said. "She's the end."

"I wonder how much she wants?" Ted said. "Think we can get her for a thousand?"

"Don't be silly," Sam said. "You know what she gets in Hollywood?"

"Well this ain't Hollywood, Junior," Ted said. "If she wants that cinema loot then why is she in New York? What'd she come here to this old dark cold theater and knock herself out for?"

"Sam," I said, "she's terrific. She's just the girl, that's all."

"I gotta get this girl to Mitch. With the right number she could rock the industry," Rudy said.

"Never mind the goddamn records," Ted said. "As for Rasputin, keep him outa here."

"Don't be so goddamn stuffy," Rudy said. "You get this baby shouting out of every jukebox in the country and all the deejays behind her, you think that would hurt your dear old B.O.?"

"Rudy, just stick to the show, huh?" Ted said, and he went down to tell Johnny he could go.

"Come here," Sam said to me, and we walked up the aisle to the empty lobby.

The manager came out of the office.

"Now listen, Frank," Sam said. "We have simply *got* to have more heat if we're going to hold our auditions here. It's just not fair to the girls. Mr. Hackett is pretty sore about it."

"All right, all right, just don't give me any of that Hackett stuff," Frank said. "I been Hacketted to death in my time and if he gets chilblains I couldn't care less."

"That's a hell of a fine attitude," Sam said. "Hackett is merely one of the greatest . . ."

"All right, all right, so I talk too much. Next time you get more heat, okay?"

"What's the matter with you and Hackett?" Sam said.

"Just one of those heartrending real life backstage dramas, Mr. Snow. Once upon a time there was a cute kid in the chorus named Dorothy. We will skip the rest of it."

He went back in the office.

"Who's Dorothy?" I said.

"How do I know?" Sam said. "I suppose she fell for The Boss or something."

"Does The Boss like the girls?" I said.

"Are you kidding?" Sam said.

We lit some cigarettes and stood out there in the lobby with the urns with the sand in them, and I could see Ted and

Rudy sitting down there in the fifth row arguing about Mitch, and up on the stage Irene Lovelle talking to Hackett; she was looking up at him and smiling.

"Well," Sam said, "how about it? Everyone's gone crazy over her. Tell me the honest truth. You wrote the part of Susie. Susie is *your* girl. Do you think she can play Susie? No crap now."

"Sam," I said, "this girl doesn't have to play Susie, she *is* Susie."

Sam blew out some smoke and walked up and down dramatically like a producer walking up and down in an empty lobby.

"Her quality is perfect," I said. "She's a strong, direct, the hell-with-you type without being tough."

"Yeah," Sam said.

"Her speaking voice is so right — boy, it floored me. I bet she comes from Peoria."

"South Bend," Sam said.

When we got down again to row E, Irene was gone from the stage and Hackett was back, sitting in the aisle seat with one long tweedy leg thrown over the arm, and Rudy and Ted were standing in the aisle.

"You think she's right, Jack?" Hackett said. "Nice rough speaking voice, didn't you think?"

"I think she's right," I said. "Like we wrote it for her."

"Sam, what did you think?" Hackett said.

Everybody looked at Sam. Sam sat down behind Hackett in row F. Sam put his hands behind his head and looked up at the chandelier, up there in the gloomy mist.

"I think she's right," he said.

After the audition Ted took me over to The Lambs for a drink and we stood at the bar; that's the best bar in New York barring none (get that one) and had some Martinis and listened to the soft click of the pool balls. And let's see, Percy Kilbride was sitting there at the table by the cheese and little round Melba toasts, and Victor Moore, and Happy Felton, and Alan Mowbray, and three or four aging matinee idols, and a lot of young guys all looking like James Dean and John Kerr, or is it James Kerr and John Dean, and the rest of them trying to look like Ben Gazzara, and lots and lots of gray character actors, and plenty Martinis and the little round toasts with the cheddar cheese on top.

And next to me at the bar is a stocky fellow in a loud jacket and he is saying, "And then Rodgers said, 'My God, did I write that?' and I said, 'No, Mr. Rodgers, but you wrote this.'" (Sings):

> I'm gonna poison Ivy
> Before Ivy poisons me.

"See, he wrote that for *me*, he and Larry Hart, 'way back, when they were students. Yes, I was in *Shanghai Baby* too. Oh baby was that awful!"

So he busted out singing:

> Sukiyaki mama
> You're the queen of Yokahama . . .

Meanwhile Fritz Loewe was in the other room playing the piano and Jimmy was rushing the food in. I'm telling you I felt funny considering a few months before I had been in the iron foundry business out in the glorious hot and cold belt under the Hoosier skies. And all the time Ted was introducing me to everybody around there and saying "Jack wrote the book for our new show" and instead of getting bored they all gave me a big hand and looked at me like they thought I was going to do or say something perfectly terrific almost any minute now.

After a few more Martinis I called up Frankie and told her
I was going to stay in town for the night. She took it all
right. Said she was so played out she was going to bed anyway; the Baby had overturned the ink bottle onto the rug and
a few other fast rounds of domestic joy had been fought out
and she was going to lie down and wait for the morning gong.

So we called up Sam and he came down after a while.

"How come you're not giving the girls a break tonight?"
Ted said. "The wine steward from 21 called up a while ago
and was wondering where you was at."

"Well I'll tell you," Sam said. "You know what Hackett
was doing up there on the stage talking to Irene?"

"You tell us," Ted said. "I been thinking too much lately."

"He was asking her for a date," Sam said. "For tonight."

Ted went into hysterics and the only thing that would
bring him out of it was another Martini. So we started out to
paint the town red but the party ended a cerulean blue with
some girls whose activities will remain incognito as this here
is a family magazine.

Chapter 16

So many girls, so little time.
— FREDDIE HEBERT

WHEN it's all said and done New York is really a pretty good place if you don't bleed easy. And one nice thing you find out is, that the dames actually do not all look like they do in those fashion magazines in the dentist's office. I mean it is not a city ordinance that they have got to have eleven-inch waists, barn-door mouths, and stand around on the sidewalks with their feet at right angles to one another. For one thing, an awful lot of girls in New York have to fall back on the subway for transport, and in the subway most of the time there is just not enough room for the right-angle foot position. Not only that, but a good many girls have found out that it is not necessary to look angular and wear a hat resembling an inverted salad bowl in order to interest some young man severely enough to cause him to take steps. Some of the girls in New York are actually fat, and they are getting married every day. When are the dentists going to get wise and go back to the *National Geographic* and *Wallace's Farmer* anyway? They didn't have *Mademoiselle* in old Doc Conzett's office and we got by just fine. Right this minute I have got a rough place on one of my attractive teeth that has been annoying me for days but I keep putting it off on account of *Harper's Bazaar* and *Mademoiselle*.

Take Irene Lovelle for example, with that ground-dragging mink coat: she did not look anything at all like the manufacturers would have liked her to — she just had the Lovelle Look, and too damn bad the boys with tape measures draped around their necks couldn't copy it, but no. Irene had her own style somehow and there she was, following the *maître de* toward us and between the tables and palms for Luncheon at the Plaza, with the first exciting snow flurry swirling outside the tall plate glass. *Segue* to Lem Ayers over in the corner by the window, Fredric March buttering a bun, and Cary Grant behind me where I could not see him without being rude (I simply detest rudeness), with a girl in a hat with brim so fashionable that it sagged to her elbows.

"Hello, you boys," Irene said. "Hold everything, be right back," and she went over and said Hello to Cary.

"Looks good, doesn't she?" I said.

"Oh, well," Sam said. "Look at her showing off. How childish. Look at her grinning at Grant, for god's sake — how disgusting."

"She's not so dumb," I said. "It's all good for business."

"Oh, but it's all so cheap," Sam said, nervously ruining a hard roll. "When I take her to the theater, she stays in the powder room until the last possible moment, and at the precise *instant* that everyone is seated and in the half *second* before the lights go down, she sweeps down the aisle. I don't know *how* she times it so perfectly. Then before sitting down she spots somebody and waves at them gaily — oh, it's a big production, lots of teeth showing. I could just die."

"Look, after you and Irene are married," I said, "then you can change all that. You better marry this dame, Sam, she needs you. Besides, think of all the nice book ends you will get for wedding presents."

" 'Love is the triumph of imagination over intelligence,' " Sam said. "How do you like people who make bright remarks like that?"

"What's she doing?" I said.

"Still grinning like an idiot," Sam said. "Well, here she comes."

"Cary is off for Europe," she said, sitting down.

"Gee, I hope he has a swell trip," Sam said. "And I hope he's got enough travelers' checks, because I always say it's better to have too many than to run out."

"Sam hates Hollywood," Irene said to me. "Terribly, terribly jealous."

"Yes, I need help," Sam said.

"Jack, I just loved the new scene," Irene said. "I think it's out of this world."

"She makes these expressions up," Sam said.

"Drink your drink and be quiet," Irene said. "But, Jack, I mean it. I think the scene will play big. And it builds beautifully."

"I don't know whether it holds, though," I said.

"Of course it holds," she said. "It has drive."

"I felt a falling off," I said.

"You're so wrong," she said.

"Come on now, tell me the truth," I said. "Didn't you feel it was a little too much?"

"No, I certainly did not. I thought it was just right."

"How do you like the script in general? I mean since the new scenes went in?"

"I think it's a *very* literate script," she said.

"You mean it can read and write?" I said.

"Crazy," she said coquettishly.

"Irene, listen, who the hell *is* that with Grant?" Sam said. "All I can see is an amazing chest. It looks like the Himalayas."

"My god, don't you know what that is?" Irene said. "For heaven's sake, where do you keep yourself?"

"Mother doesn't let me go out on week-day nights," Sam said. "And on Saturday nights I go to a social club on Central Park West. Gee, it's a swell bunch. On Thanksgiving we had a candlelight buffet."

"That's Ingborg Ecklund," Irene said, leaning over the recently arrived fruit salad and pronouncing distinctly so we would get the full import and fall back, jaws sagging, in glorious amazement.

"You mean the Scandinavian most likely to make a complete shambles of the entire United States?" Sam said.

"Wait until *Confidential* gets after her," I said. "Oh man!"

"Oh, really?" Irene said, spearing a grape with poorly concealed enthusiasm.

"Certainly," I said. "She's a notorious offender *in re* personal daintiness."

"Is the Plaza approved by Duncan Hines?" Sam said. "I think this lettuce is awfully poor."

"It's supposed to be wilted, you fool," Irene said. "But I thought she was in Rome doing that picture for Rosselini."

"The picture she was making was with De Sica, dear, not Rosselini, and it was in Firenze, not Rome."

"Not Roma, you mean," Irene said.

"Aren't you cute," Sam said.

"Well, I'm *sure* I read in the paper she was on location in Rome," Irene said. "Or maybe that was Hank Fonda."

"Or William S. Hart," Sam said.

"She's beautiful," I said, "and a real dame too."

"How can you tell?" Irene said.

"Why, damn it, because it's a hobby of mine. I study up on it. I got a degree in it from Western Reserve."

"What's it called, this subject?" Irene said.

" 'Girls,' " I said. "I'm working on my Ph.D."

"The first snowfall of the year," Irene said. "Look at the Park."

The waiter came and poured more water, the bus boy stabbed pieces of butter and plopped them on our plates among the crumbs. The Captain looked apprehensively at our noisy table; laughing and high jinks not encouraged here.

Sam and Ted had persuaded the famous Telesco to do scenery and costumes and this was all great so Sam revealed this gem and he and Irene began to gurgle about that for a while.

"I'll bet you had to give him a swell percentage," Irene said.

"We figured it was worth it," Sam said. "We want all the *best* talent we can get. We feel it's . . ."

"You've got *me*," Irene said.

And there was plenty of ice water on the table tinkling cheerfully while the snow flurries swirled above the taxicabs and swept through the iron fence and onto the frozen soiled earth of that dreadful park. And out home in Indiana, down at Tunker or Royal Center or Rome City or Union Mills or Ege, or even at Glendenning Corners or Petroleum, the vet is fighting with some old cow who has et too much silage and has the bloat; and the vet in his overshoes is out in the barn-yard with the frozen clods and the loose corncobs, and he's got her head tied to the top rail of the fence and he's shoving an eighteen-inch tube down the old girl's throat and pumping a half a bucket of red medicine into her; "Hold still, you brute," he says, his breath steaming, and the farmer is there in his overalls shoving the brute's rear end against the fence. The cow's eyes are rolled clear back — all you can see is white. "Hold still you son of a bitch," says the vet from Indiana State who looked so pretty on graduation day — now look at him, he's working, and I'm glad none of the luncheoneers at the Plaza are witnesses, for the crudity of the scene, added to a glorious view of the farmer's greasy neckband, would no doubt cause them to cancel their dessert orders. "I had three cows to bloat on me already this year," says the farmer, "but I never heard of no cow bloatin' in wintertime." "Hold still, you morphidite," says the veterinary M.D.

There is a very high incidence of bloat among the population of New York, as a matter of fact, and almost nothing is being done about it. Sure, they have the reducing pills attractively packaged at Whelan's and Walgreen's, but tell me, what direct steps are being taken besides the drugstores putting on a One Cent Sale of arch supports once in a while?

"And we go into rehearsal in only a week?" Irene said.

"That's the way Hackett wants it," Sam said. "Exciting, isn't it?"

You take Wolfe, for example, he wrote his stuff on top of the icebox on account he was wanting to be near to the refrigerator just in case, whereas Proust confined himself to a room entirely lined with souvenir corks from different Paris cabarets. So there is no accounting, as Cousin Archie says, for how it tastes.

Especially lunch at the Plaza with Sam Snow and Irene Lovelle lobbing the ball back and forth over the waiters' heads, while all the dames in the place divide their attentions between the watercress and trying to figure out who are the two squares with Irene Lovelle.

"Irene, let me tell you, Mr. Hackett is the most Honest Man I've Ever Known," Sam said. These boys should hang a placard around their necks, I thought, with *Hackett Is the Most Honest Man I've Ever Known* printed on it by an artistic sho-card painter with the letters sprinkled with sparkle dust.

"He has absolute integrity," Sam said.

"Now don't get on *that* again," Irene said. "For godsake, he's just a man, and a damn difficult one at that."

"Look out now, honey," I said. "Naughty naughty. Mustn't talk to Mr. Snow like that or Mr. Snow won't pay for your nice lunch."

"Of all the out*rage*ous remarks I've ever heard," Sam said, "that . . . that . . . that's without any question the . . . the . . . the most utterly . . ." he had his fake stammer going and he held up his hands in a dramatic gesture somewhat marred by the fact that he was holding a buttered hard roll in one of them.

"Listen, have you ever spent a week end out at his place in Westport?" Irene said. "Put that bun down, you look silly."

"Yes, my dear," Sam said. "It so happens I have spent *many* delightful week ends at Mr. Hackett's and in my mind he is the perfect host."

"Tell *me*," I said. "Was it an honest week end?"

"It was the goddamnedest experience I ever went through," Irene said. "Now don't get me wrong, I like this man immensely. He's terrific and he's got . . . well . . ."

"Lots of integrity," I said.

"Say, by the way," Irene said to me, "how do *you* get along with him?"

"Just fine. He knows I'm a bum but he never lets on. I think he likes me and I'm a sucker for anybody that likes me. In fact, I think he's the greatest guy I ever met."

"Well, that gets you off the hook," Irene said.

"Tell me about Westport," I said.

"Who else was there?" Sam said.

"Well, it was a cold raw day and I thought we were going to sit around a nice log fire and talk about the theater. There were three or four other people there . . ."

"Such as who?" Sam said. "And how did you get out there?"

"We drove out. My god, what a drive! When he asked me, I thought probably a man of his age —"

"Look out now," I said.

"Well, I mean after all . . . I expected a nice black limousine and a chauffeur; instead he showed up in that crazy sports car with the top down — damn it, if you think it isn't cold on the Merritt Parkway these days you're all wrong."

"And the beret and so forth," I said.

"Sure, he had on the beret, and a camel's-hair coat with the big pearl buttons. You could have knocked me over with a . . . Anyway, we got there somehow, me and my sporty boy friend, but say, have you ever driven with this man? Crazy! But I mean cra-zee! Like High School out in South Bend. This man is driving ninety and a hundred miles an hour whenever he can get in the clear."

"Oh, go on, go on, who was *there?*" Sam said. "Everybody has sports cars nowadays, where've you been anyway?"

"So the last few miles I'm so cold I can't talk. I'm literally shaking. He goes jabbering on — oh, *he* was having a fine time. *Well* — I was thinking 'Oh, that lovely big fireplace with the nice log fire.' — 'Oh, and a hot buttered rum or a shot of lovely brandy!' Now do you know what we did after we got there? Do you know what this wonderful man had us do after inviting us all the way out there, and after torturing me for an hour in that terrible car?"

"Charades?" I said.

"Oh *god,* you've *been* there!" Irene said. "Oh, but that was *later.* *First* he passed out dungarees and old sweaters to everybody and we had to —"

"Clear brush out of the woods," Sam said.

"No, thank heavens!"

"Rake leaves?" I said.

"Nothing so ordinary. That's too easy."

"Oh, *I* know!" Sam said. "Touch football! Well hell, that's fun isn't it? I don't think that's so bad. They all do those things out in the country. I think it's rather nice. We'd all be a lot better off if we did *more* things like that. That's where the English are so much smarter than —"

"We did NOT play touch football!" Irene said, raising her voice.

"Oh," Sam said. "What did you do, dear? Please tell us."

"We went *sailing,*" Irene said.

"I say, this *is* a bit much, you know," I said.

"Oh no, that's ridiculous," Sam said. "He loves that boat I know, but . . . Not in November."

"Oh yes we did," Irene said. "And what a crew! There was a muscular ballerina, and a girl from Warner Bros. with a bad cold, and that gloomy German boy that writes music that nobody likes, and of course our nice Richard Hackett, loving every single moment of it, explaining things in that careful, precise way he has, telling us what to do, getting off some of those dry jokes of his — I must say, the man is amazing."

"I wouldn't have gone," Sam said. "I would simply have said, 'Look here, I really can't . . .'"

"You'd have gone, lover," Irene said.

"I would have said, 'See here, Dick, sailing is out. Got that straight, boy?'" I said.

Cary and the Swede got up to go. Irene twiddled her fingers at Cary. They went out. Outside the snow was falling thicker and the wind was driving it faster.

"Actually it ended up all right. For *me* anyway. I had the best sweater."

"She had the best sweater," Sam said.

"The others were miserable. Of course they didn't *dare* let on. Hackett was having the time of his life. He told me where to find it and I went down in the cabin and got a bottle of Scotch. That warmed us up a bit. By the time we got back to our mooring he was singing about 'Blow the Man Down, Boys' — he was really a lot of fun. The others wouldn't drink out of the bottle so they were not too jovial."

"Hackett slugging out of the bottle — I'd like to see that one," I said.

"When this man gets out of town, Look Out Boys!" Irene said. "Anyway he was just getting warmed up. After that we *hiked* home, a mile and a half — then dressed for dinner; then drinks, dinner, champagne, more drinks — then we get our orders, which is charades for two hours. By this time four or five more people had showed up. Well anyway, I folded at 3:30 A.M. and I think the party was still on. So at 8 A.M. Hackett is knocking on the door — he wants me to go *riding* with him. On horses."

"So you went," I said.

"You know I did," Irene said.

"Well, what's it all prove?" Sam said. "Nothing so unusual about it. That's the way people live out there."

"At his age? Sailing in November? And all that? It just surprised me, that's all. Around New York he seems so conservative."

"Well, he is conservative," Sam said.

"And he had that ballet dancer in his room all night, *too*," Irene said.

"Dessert, sir?" said the waiter.

"I'll have the profiteroles," Sam said gloomily.

"And at his age, too," I said.

We strolled out past the pleasant, comfortable, expensive brouhaha of the Palm Court and found ourselves back again among the raw realities of doormen, cabs, and snow.

Sam and Irene and I stood there a little bit lost, feeling the leaden effect and general letdown following too much lunch, many cocktails, and a check representing two weeks' wages for the boy I used to be with my milk route.

"Well, I have to go back to the office, I suppose," Sam said.

"How dull," Irene said. "Jack, what are you and I going to do?"

"Well gosh," I said, "I suppose I really ought to go back to the office too."

"What for? You'll just sit around there wasting time. You won't do a damn thing," Irene said.

"Of course," Sam said. "We don't do anything down there. We just sit on the floor playing mumblety-peg. Hell, we don't ever do any work. You know how Richard Hackett is, always falling asleep all the time."

"All right, so you work like mad," Irene said. "But Jack hasn't got anything to do."

"Well, that's up to Jack," Sam said. "So long, you two, have fun at the zoo," and he walked off purposefully after a brief New-Yorkish hugging and kissing party with Irene while they both murmured "Darling" and "Marvelous lunch" and "Fun."

"Come on, Hoosier, let's walk," Irene said.

"When it used to snow out in Indiana," I said, "I used to look out the window at the foundry and wish I was in New York. In New York so I could walk up Fifth Avenue to the Metropolitan."

That was all I had to tell Irene; she didn't have to go to Bonwit Teller or Helena Rubinstein like all the dames in New York are always telling you when you want to go to a movie or something. She was ready and always ready.

So we walked up there in the snow and looked at the pictures and the Egyptian stuff and it was quiet in there in the museum and the guards stood around and a schoolteacher was taking a bunch of Steig kids on an educational tour, parking them in front of the Van Dykes but zooming past the nudes.

With anybody else I would have figured she was doing it for me, an act; but Irene, she liked everything. She was fun to be with anyplace.

When we got out it was 4:30 and we got in a cab and went over to her place on Park Avenue. So long, Indiana.

DEAR MARY HAWORTH:

I have a problem and my problem is I am a married man with four children and my marriage has always been a real storybook affair as I am a good husband and father and usually bringing some little trinkets home to the kiddies and never fail to help the little woman with the dishes or other useful household tasks when I find I can be of help. My wife and I were high school sweethearts out in a Middle Western state and she was a "child bride" more or less, having got married when she was only eighteen years of age to me. Our lives together have always been a real storybook romance and our friends always remarked they envied us our "happy lot."

Recently I came to work in New York and I located in one of the suburbs north of town. In other words I am a "commuter." In my line of work I meet many beautiful girls but it has never made any difference until this one girl came along, she is an actress and you would know the name if I told it to you.

The other afternoon I asked her to visit the Metropolitan

Museum with me as I have always taken considerable interest in the arts and always cut out the color pages in *Life* magazine and have them in a big scrapbook. Well that was all right but afterwards she invited me over to her apartment where we had some cocktails and one thing led to another.

My problem is really twofold. In the first place I lost one of my cuff links up at her house, which my mother gave to me when I graduated from college and they are 14 k. gold and I would like to ask her if she has seen anything of the link but I don't know how to go about it. The other thing is, would it be proper to ask her for another date, as I would like to take her to the Frick Museum?

My trouble is I am always falling in love. And when I'm not, I'm trying to.

"I love you, darling," I said, with an ardent vibrato.

"Do you? So do I," she said. "I think I'm terrific."

Chapter 17

THE SCRIPT was done. Mrs. Fondemeyer and all the funny entrances and exits and song cues, all the romance and the kisses and the tears, the partings and musical reconciliations, the costume suggestions and the stage directions, they were all between blue paper covers held together with brass paper fasteners. The scripts were in a pile on the corner of Hackett's desk, numbered Script Number 1, Script Number 2, Script Number 3, and on up to 25. And I in my childish innocence thought that that was that. I thought from now on I'll just coast along, oh what a jolly lark it all will be! It was not that at all. In the next weeks and months whole scenes were chopped out and ended up on garbage scows bound seaward; reams of hilarious dialogue proved to be Academy of Tedium Award Winners and were tossed out onto 50th Street. Characters were withdrawn without ever having lived before the lights, and sent to oblivion in the file marked REJECT STUFF ETC. Mrs. Fondemeyer's husband, originally a low comic buffoon, emerged in the final version as refined as Bert Lytell in his dress suit; while our heroine's young sister, conceived as a tender ingenue, ended up a coarse and horrid little tramp.

Confused and irritated by these constant changes, the famous Telesco, our scenery and costume designer, went wild —

sent ultimatums — sulked — woke agents up at 3 A.M. to re-
vile the management, and meetings would be called for 3
P.M. in Hackett's office. Awed by Hackett's grandeur, suntan,
tailoring and complete composure, the wild 3 A.M. squawks
would fizzle out as Hackett twirled his horn-rim glasses and
stared at him like a Great Dane watching a cricket.

"We are all working together to make this a good show,"
he would say. "I am the director. You've just got to trust
me. Otherwise we'll get noplace."

Meeting dismissed. Exit Telesco, appeased until next incident.

"I told Hackett *exactly* how I felt," he would say later after
the second *very* dry Martini.

"*You* told *Hackett?*"

"I certainly did. I said, 'Dick, we've got to have an under —' "

"You called him 'Dick'?"

"Certainly. What do you call him?"

"I call him You Son of a Bitch."

"Now, Arthur, that was ten years ago, dear."

"He's still an s.o.b. to me."

"Well, I told him *exactly* how I felt about the *entire* setup.
'I simply can't en*dure* any more of this *torture*,' I said."

"I didn't get that, I didn't hear it. Tell us that again,
Charlie. And a VERY dry Martini please. Well, the picture
was a flop but what did he care he got paid it didn't hurt *his*
reputation any. Don't look now but *right* behind you . . ."
"Five years ago she was a BEAUTIFUL woman. How can that
happen so fast? Tell me. Sing it to me with a five-string banjo
accompaniment." . . . "And I always say if the director himself loses control then how can you blame the cast? I'm telling you he made a perfect ass of himself." . . . "And I

suppose you heard the one about the midget and the casting
director. Make mine VERY dry please, Johnny. Take my word
for it never get interested in a dancer they are tired *all* the
time. I was in the wings and she came off after her number
and I kissed her, it was like kissing a racehorse after six
furlongs. Sweat? My God! So that killed it for me." . . .
"And make it VERY rare please, and the green salad with a little oil and vinegar." . . . "*Prejudiced* against Jews! I said
why what are you talking about why I'm Jewish myself my
ancestors were the only Jews on the *Mayflower* well of
course he didn't know whether I was kidding him or not so
then we went down to the Village of course in ten minutes
he was surrounded by about six hundred of his faggish pals
I just can't stand that kind of an evening so I went up to a
re-run of Caligari. Waiter, I wanted *iced* coffee please not hot
coffee I haven't had any hot coffee in two years my doctor
told me, you know, all my troubles *actually* stemmed from *hot*
coffee." . . . " 'Oh,' she said to me so cleverly, 'where do
you have your *leather things* made?' I felt like saying, 'I come
from Montana, dear, and I have all my leather things made
in the dearest little shop in Butte.' 'Oh,' she said, 'I've found
the most *wonderful* man on Lexington Avenue he's a perfect wizard with leather he's made me the most divine sort of
handbags.' Well, I thought, honey, you will need more than
a divine handbag to get on the main line with me." . . .
" 'The script needs tightening,' he said. 'Hell,' I said, 'we've
been tightening it for thirteen months when are we going to
have some action here and where is the rest of the money
coming from what we need is a choreographer let's quit mum-
bling about the script incessantly and kick out this dummy
Razatkov and get ourselves a choreographer and start moving
and where is the rest of the money coming from?' I said,
'Harry, tell me please where is the rest of the money coming

from are we going up to Central Park and pick it off the bushes?' . . . I'm sorry, I didn't order the beef bones, I had the *Cannelloni*. Yes. The *Cannelloni*. No, I didn't have the beef bones. Never in my life. Thank you. That's fine. Yes." . . . "So Rudy Lorraine was there, with the cigar. 'You know how many records I sold last year?' he says. 'Just guess how many records I sold last year.' 'How the hell do I know?' Snow said. 'Well I sold two million,' he says, and then he says, 'and I couldn't care less.' 'Oh no,' says Sam Snow, 'you couldn't care less. That's why you sent out those hundred bottles of whisky to the deejays at Christmas, just friendship. And you don't care when John Crosby says your lyrics stink.' 'That bum Crosby they ought to send him someplace,' Rudy says. 'But he doesn't bother me. Let him rave on. Say, do you suppose people take him seriously? I wonder what kind of a following . . .' 'What the hell do you care,' says Sam Snow. I'm telling you that Lorraine is a bird from the dizzy far-off places. He's not satisfied living with one girl, he was living with *two* the last time Bud was up to see him about the trouble with the Blue Label people. Anyway I hear Snow and Crosby have got Rex Ives to play the lead, that big ham, well I know he has a voice so what, this is a different age, these guys got to *act* not just shoot their cuffs and let go with the pipes." . . . "So I said, 'Listen, Gadge, what I'm saying . . .'" "Oh no, Jesus, get out of here with that 'Gadge' stuff will you. I can't take it. I get headaches real easy." . . . "So he said, 'Who is Jack Jordan for godsake who ever heard of him? And what makes Hackett think *he* can write a show; Hackett hasn't written a show for twenty years has he?' Well, Irene Lovelle overheard this so she came in aflying. 'Don't you tired old cynics ever run down?' she said. And she says to Don Wallstein, who had been doing most of the talking, she says 'When was your last big hit, Smarty?' She hates him anyway you know because he had Buzzy Randell tossed out of *Flying High* and Irene was completely insane over Randell, she was on the rebound from the Campbell affair. 'And don't run down Jack Jordan while I'm around either,' she said. 'That's what we call New Talent in the theater. Did you ever hear of it?' Oh boy she was mad." . . . "Say listen, Clarkie, I want a biog from you by Monday at the latest. Has your agent got a biog on you or are you gonna hafta write me up one, but listen, *please* do it for me I need it. I can't get anything for you publicity-wise you understand without the biog so try and get me a biog by Monday. And don't clean it up too much. Say, the boy musta put the gin in this Collins with an eyedropper." . . . "If you don't want the part, dear, just say so right now don't wait until New Haven and then do the artistic-temperament bit. Sure we want you, honey. I think, and I mean this sincerely — I think you can do this part to perfection and frankly, dear, you need some good notices after that last disaster. . . . I *know* it was Brewster's fault, I'm just saying . . . But just think it over, we don't want to be hung up in New Haven when you decide you don't like it after all it's not big enough for you or Betsy is stealing all the laughs." . . . "Well wait a minute, wait a minute, I didn't give you the punch yet — listen will you — and so the Madame got sore and kicked the whole bunch out and there's Charlie laying at the bottom of the stairs and he looks up and he says, 'Hey, Flossie, this doesn't kill it for Saturday night, does it?' Oh that Charlie was some kid; we came into Omaha on the day coach one morning in March 1916 — about 6 A.M. it was so we got into the cab and Charlie says to the driver he says, 'Hey, bud, where's the hook joints at?' 'At 6 A.M.?' says the cabbie. 'What's the matter with 6 A.M.?' says Charlie. Well it was like that all the time; in East St. Louis he would go till he dropped." . . . "I wish them all the luck in the world and I really mean that sincerely, Paul, but you can't tell me a love duet between that square Rex Ives and Irene Lovelle is going to do anything to Kerr, Atkinson, Chapman and Co. And you know what Watts thinks of Ives, I guess you read that famous review. If Hackett can get a performance out of this block of basalt then they better put up a statue of him on top of the Bond Store instead of the Pepsi-Cola bottles." . . . "You know what's the trouble with Kazan? He's too successful, that's the trouble with him." "I wish I had some of that trouble." "Guys like you and me, what chance have we got? Take *This and That* for example. Did you read the notices I got in the Westport paper? 'A smooth job of direction by Merlin Crump.' 'A director worth keeping an eye on.' So what's it add up to? I can't even get an assistant stage manager's job down here." "Let's eat." . . . "What's it about? Nobody *knows* what it's about. Hackett's got this Jordan guy in to help write it. Jordan's from out in the sticks someplace, Oklahoma or Ohio or one of those places. The other day Hackett says to him, 'I'll meet you at Sardi's,' and Jordan says, 'Where's that?' So you can imagine what kind of a script that'll be." . . . "Listen, Julie, I wish Sam Snow every success in the world and I mean that sincerely, but if Sam Snow thinks for a minute he's a producer, then . . ." "Rudy Lorraine? Don't make me laugh. On *Broad*way?" . . . "I hear they're in trouble already." . . . "Richard Hackett? So what?" . . . "And I mean that sincerely." . . . AND MAKE MINE VERY DRY PLEASE, WAITER.

Chapter 18

People who agree with me that morning café au lait tastes best out of a big European-style cup are likely to find the homey earthenware cup that Bonniers has imported from Sweden completely irresistible.

— S.H. IN THE NEW YORKER

THE DAY before Christmas began at 6 A.M. when Katie came in and poked me and told me that she was worried that Santa Claus had not received her letter.

"Listen, honey," I said. "You go in your room and write another letter and I'll send him a telegram."

"Oh, goodie," she said. I closed my eyes.

"Mama, wake up. Mama, listen, Daddy's going to send a telegram." Katie was now over poking Frankie.

"No, he isn't, dear. It's all right, go back to bed," Frankie mumbled.

"He IS TOO!" Katie screamed. "He's just said so!"

"Quiet, dear, you'll wake up the others," Frankie said. "What's he going to do?"

"Send a telegram. He promised. So he's got to. When you promise something and then you don't do it, you have to go to *hell.*"

Frankie had fallen asleep again.

"Who told you that?" I said, rolling over.

"My boy friend," Katie said.

"In the First Grade?" I said.

"Sure. I can have a boy friend if I want to. So there!"

"What's his name?"

"Ronald Kaplan."

"Kaplan? Listen, honey, you better not count on much of a wedding present from Grandmother," I said. "I suppose you're going to marry him?"

"I don't know yet," Katie said, doing a little dance, slipping on the rug and falling down with a crash, "maybe I'll marry my other boy friend."

"Uh-uh. What's his name?" I said.

"Melvin Kaplan."

"Haven't they got any kids up there at Willard School except Kaplans?" I said.

"They're twins," Katie said. Having put on Frankie's mules, she was clumping around in them. "I'm in love with both of them."

"That's swell," I said. "Now you get out of here and go play in your room or something. And if you come back in here before eight o'clock I won't send that telegram to Santa Claus."

"How can I can't come in until eight o'clock when I can't tell time yet? Gee, that isn't fair."

"Beat it," I said.

"You're mean," she said. "I can't even tell time and you meanly go and tell me not to do something until eight o'clock. I'm mad at you."

"Just pretend mad," I said.

"Real, real, real," she screamed and went out slamming the fine, warped, unclosable eighteenth-century door.

I fell asleep again and tried to dream something happy. After a while I woke up. Downstairs, the kids had turned on the TV already, and Dave Garroway was booming through the floor. Dave quit, and the Colonel gave us the facts on those chicken pot pies. Then I heard Frankie coming from the bathroom and I said, "Hello, Nebraska, what's going on?"

"Where did you hide the Christmas tree?" Frankie said, sitting down at the dressing table. "Seems to me I used to look better when we lived out in that horrible town."

"Out behind the barn," I said.

"Are you *sure* you don't have to go in town today?"

"The day before Christmas? Christmas Eve? Certainly not. I just said, 'Boys, I'm a family man, and Christmas is one time when Show Business is out the window.' "

"That's good, because you've got a million things to do. Tommy has more presents than Nat, so you'll have to go down to Springdale to Bongo's and find him something. And you can pick up the turkey for me at Ridgeway and we need a couple more strings of lights, and some bulbs, and there's presents to wrap . . ."

"Listen, honey, we've got to have the Kaplans to dinner," I said.

"Who are the Kaplans for example?"

"Katie says she's going to marry one of them as soon as she makes up her mind which one. I think it's only right that we ask them over. Find out what kind of folks they are. Give Kaplan a cigar and talk things over. Play bridge and have some clever little sandwiches. How about a covered dish? That's what I like, a covered dish."

"Get up out of there and start moving around," Frankie said.

"And it seems like only yesterday I was holding our little girl on my knee and listening to her childish prattle," I said, moving toward the bathroom. Then I stopped and went over and looked out the window.

"Quaint old New England," I said. "Why, it's a regular Christmas card outside. Old King Winter has laid his cheery mantle of fog and rain o'er hill and dale. Bells on Bobtail ring, making spirits bright. Say, honey, do you suppose it's required to wear Bermuda shorts around here on a sleigh-ride party?"

"Keep moving, Jack, please," Frankie said.

"Goddamn the whole state of Connecticut and all the lousy no-good bums in it," I said. "I never saw such a crummy assortment of weather in my life. The whole layout looks like E. A. Poe was in charge here."

"That's a nice Christmas thought," Frankie said. "Oh-oh, another gray hair."

"Never mind that," I said. "I expect to wake up some morning and find mine has turned white overnight like in the horror stories."

"Poor you. Now hurry up and shave and start generating a little Yuletide joy."

"Frankie," I said.

"What?"

"I wish we were home for Christmas. I bet there's three feet of snow out in the old side yard."

Frankie got up and came over to me and put her arms around me and gave me a good old kiss.

"You wanted to get out," she said. "And you're out. You're writing a play with Richard Hackett. Darling, I'm so proud of you I could bust."

"Are you, baby?" I said.

"You bet I am. You're terrific. Now get going. We'll have a real old Indiana Christmas right here in this lousy, crummy state of Connecticut."

"I'm glad I located you, Nebraska," I said. "You're pretty hot stuff yourself."

So I went in and wasted another good fifteen minutes out of my life with the razor and the genuine badger hair shaving brush and the lotion with the manly North Woods smell. I thought maybe I ought to send Irene some flowers for Christmas. I didn't think very hard about it.

Breakfast was the usual dignified affair, with Father, the Autocrat of the Breakfast Table, leading the conversation into intellectual channels for the instruction and improvement of his little brood. For what ties bind the family more closely in mutual respect and love than the partaking of our daily bread together?

"What the heck kind of a winter do they call this anyway?" Nat said. "Gee whiz, no snow."

"That's a very interesting point, Nat," said Father. "It's because we are so close to the seacoast, I imagine."

"The heck with the dumb seacoast," Nat said. "I want some snow."

"Don't be such a twerp, Nat," Tom said.

"The science of the weather is 'Meteorology.' Can one of you sturdy lads spell that for me?" Father said.

"Mology," said the Baby.

"Baby, be quiet," said Katie. "You can't spell."

"Me can too," said dimple-darling, bursting into tears and dropping his spoon on the floor for a new course record.

"Hey, Nat, Katie was bad and Santa Claus isn't going to bring her anything," said Tom.

"Thomas, you may leave the table," said Father.

"Don't you dare leave the table," Frankie said. "Eat that egg."

"It's got a lot of stringy white junk in it," ejaculated Thomas plaintively.

"Fine discipline," Father said. "I sure cut a lot of ice around here."

"Can I go to the movies this aft?" said Tom. "There's a neat show down at Springdale."

"What's the name of it?" Father said.

"It's a double: *Island of Desire,* and *Reform School Girl.*"

"Can I go, Papa? Please, come on. Gee, I never get to do anything," Katie said.

"Well, I'll tell you," Father said as Nat dropped his jam toast upside down in his lap. "If Tab Hunter is in it, okay."

"Don't listen to your father," Frankie said. "He's just being funny."

"What's funny about it?" Nat said.

"Well, can we go?" Tom said. "Come on, Pop?"

"What's the matter with you, are you out of your head or something?" Father said. "Do you think you're going to some movie called *Reform School Girl* the day before Christmas? Damn it, what ever happened to Tom Mix anyway?"

"I knew it," Nat said. "Typical."

"Why don't you kids ever go out in the barn and make something out of an orange crate or have a lantern slide show or something?" Father said. "When I was a kid . . ."

"This egg has got some old sticky goo in it," Katie said. "I'm not even going to eat you, you stupid egg."

"Now you're going to make nice Mr. Egg cry," said Father. "Is that polite?"

"What's a lantern slide show, Pop?" said Nat, casually hiding his egg under some reject toast.

"How can an egg cry?" said Katie. "Gee you're silly, Papa."

"My teacher asked me if you knew Clark Gable, Pop. Do you know him, Pop?" said little Thomas.

"Sure, Clark and I went to reform school together," said Father.

"I knew it. I told her you did," said Master Tom. "Last week she asked me if you knew Joan Crawford."

"Hey listen," Katie said. "This old egg *is* crying," and she stuck her ear down to her plate, getting her braids well egged.

The phone rang and it was the handy colored girl advising Frankie that she had contracted logos on the bogos and paralysis in both arms which would render her unfit for work for at least forty-eight hours, or until the Yuletide festivities were over.

Frankie went out into the kitchen and began slamming things around.

"Now listen, gang," said Father. "We'll all have to pitch in and help Mother. It'll be a lot of fun, really, and we'll all give Mother a nice Christmas present by being little old Santa Claus's helpers; how about it?"

And then the phone rang again and it was Hackett.

"Jack," he said. "can you be at Rudy Lorraine's so-called studio at two o'clock? He's got a new number and frankly the lyrics have me badly worried. I've called a meeting — everybody will be there."

"Well," I said, "as a matter of fact things are pretty balled-up here. Christmas, you know, and the kids."

"Jack, if you were to hear these lyrics you'd know what I mean. I'm very much upset."

"My wife will probably . . ."

"I think your opinion will be of great value. If his stuff doesn't fit in with your idiom, we're in trouble."

"I'll be there," I said.

I hung up and went out in the kitchen and broke the news to Martha Hoople. Her idiom was immense.

I took a script along with me and was looking at it without interest on the train to New York and the chap next to me struck up a conversation regarding his activities in the theater which consisted of the fact they don't have any shows nowadays like *Abie's Irish Rose,* which he admitted having witnessed nine times.

"Now you take this *South Pacific,* for example," he said, lighting a Wheeling stogie. "I seen that one. I got an open mind. But if anybody can tell me what that baby was about I'll give 'em the keys to Pawtucket. One time this girl comes out and sings a song about washing her hair. Call that romance? Might as well have some bird come out and sing about how he's on his way to the barber for a shave. Take this here Martin dame they are all the time yippin' about. We had ten better lookers in my home town of Wilmington, Vermawnt, and the dang town is only a wide place in the road. Then she come out in a sailor suit that is five sizes too big for her and the audience howls like they was away from home for the first time. I seen that act so many times on the B. F. Keith circuit the sight of a dame in a sailor suit gives me the headache. I hope this here show you're tied into ain't got no sailor suits in it."

"Well if it makes one tenth as much money as *South Pacific* I will be a happy boy," I said.

"If they say that show made any money they was lying," he said. "It couldn't of. They just faked them figures to get the public interest."

In Grand Central there was a choir up on the balcony singing "Silent Night."

I grabbed a cab. Stanislaus Grzli, driver, had the radio on. Bing Crosby was groaning "Silent Night."

When I got over to 47th Street, Harry Paige was out on the sidewalk with his camel's-hair coat draped over his shoulders.

"What are you doing here on Christmas Eve, you with four kids?" he said.

"Same thing you're doing, Harry," I said. "The Boss told me to be here and here I am. My wife is no doubt consulting the lawyers right now."

"This won't take long," Harry said. "You get out of here and back to those little kiddies after a while. What's it all about?"

"They're worried about the lyrics to some new number Rudy came up with. Hackett was in an awful sweat when I talked with him."

"I'm worried myself about this Lorraine guy," Harry said. "I was talking to Brisson at Vegas the other night and what do you think? He's never even *heard* of Rudy Lorraine. The guy has no Coast background at all. I don't believe he's ever *been* in California. Hell of a thing."

"Come on, Harry, let's go up to the musical annex," I said.

"I could have borrowed a couple of song writers from the studio," he said as we went up the grimy stairs.

"Listen, Harry, don't say that to Hackett."

"No? Why not?"

"Just don't. Wait awhile and see what happens."

"He's prejudiced against picture business, huh?"

"Not prejudiced. But he's Broadway, Harry. These guys have funny ideas."

"You don't have to tell me that," Harry said. "And look at the way they dress. White shirts."

The room was small and there were so many of us there we resembled that Marx Brothers skit in the stateroom.

"All right. Play it," Hackett said.

Rudy played the melody through on the piano and it was marvelous. I nudged Sam and nodded at him. He nodded at me. Ted looked at me and nodded questionably. I nodded back. Harry Paige nodded at himself.

The second time around Rudy sang the words. This num-

ber was supposed to be sung by our hero after he has met the
girl and fallen for her. The girl in this show was an inde-
pendent type, passionate in her opinions, and full of fire. The
guy had been around; he was having no illusions about anything.

Rudy didn't have any title yet, but some of it went like this:

> When a feller and his gal get together
> The weather
> Is fine.
> They wonder whether
> The sun will ever
> Forget
> To shine.
> Billing and cooing is lots of fun. . . .

Well that's enough and it'll give you a rough idea. Later on,
much later, Sam used to sing it for us when he was feeling gay.
Or Ted would say, "You know, Jack, billing and cooing is lots
of fun."

"Well, Jack, what do you think?" Hackett said. "Aside
from the fact that 'whether' and 'ever' is *not* a rhyme."

"You don't understand, Mr. Hackett," Rudy said. "In pop
music . . ."

"Harry, will you let Jack talk?" Hackett said.

" 'A Feller and His Gal' . . . ?" Harry Paige said. "That's
right off the cob. Sounds like George M. Cohan. This isn't
that kind of a . . ."

"Harry, will you let Jack talk?" Hackett said.

"What'd you think, Jack?" Sam said.

"Well it — uh — just hearing it once," I said, "it's kind of
hard to say." Hell, I'm not used to hurting people's feelings.
That's my trouble, always trying to keep everybody happy.

"Well, it's not right," Hackett said.

Rudy looked very unhappy.

"Let me explain my thinking in regard to this number," he said, and he launched into a long complicated statement while we all listened with sad faces. Plenty thinking going on, and plenty frowning, eye-squinting, lip-pursing and other facial antics indicating heap big mentalities strained to the cracking point.

"Rudy, let's not intellectualize too much," Hackett said when he was finished. "This is just musical comedy, not Ibsen. There are words and phrases here that make me uncomfortable."

"I couldn't agree with you more, Dick," Harry said, earning himself a look of scorn turning to hate from Rudy. Harry had decided he was just as good as any Richard Hackett and if Jerome Robbins and Helen Hayes and Alfred Vanderbilt called him Dick, why by god he was going to call him Dick too. "I'll be frank, Dick, these lyrics are out of key story-wise, as far as I'm concerned."

Yes, I thought, and not only that but they are out of story key-wise, also.

"I'll tell you what I think . . ." Sam said.

"Perhaps it would be helpful if we . . ." I said.

"Don't get me wrong, Rudy, but . . ." Ted said.

"This is for Broadway, not for the juke . . ." said Sam.

"One thing we've definitely learned in pictures," Harry said, "is that you can't pawn off inferior material on the public of today, and try to justify it because the project is 'just a musical.' We find that the exhibitors resist any attempt to . . ."

"Listen, Rudy, here's what I mean," Ted was saying. "Now you take this girl. We don't want jam on her puss. She's not that type, she's . . ."

"Yeah, yeah," Rudy said. "Listen, this guy is just expressing every man's universal — just a perfectly obvious — you guys, what are you getting so *exci*-ded about? Just a perfectly natural bunch of emotions this guy is expressing. What's the madder with that?"

". . . and Metro threw out the whole score, the whole lyrics, everything . . ." Harry was telling Ted, who was looking at Harry and listening to Rudy.

"I don't think we can get away with it," I said.

"What?" said Sam.

"What'd you say, Jack?" Hackett said.

"I said I don't think we can get away with it. It's too soupy. It don't go with the characters."

"Spoken like a man, Jack," said Hackett. "You're dismissed. Go back to the country and don the Santa garb."

The phone rang and Rudy picked it up and said "Go to hell" into it and hung up.

Hackett got up and put on his hat.

"No use in wasting a lot of time in frustrating argument," he said. "We don't like your lyrics, that's all. So you've got to write some new ones. That's all. Perfectly simple. Happens all the time."

"Maybe I see this love story from a different angle," Rudy said.

"Well if you do you're in a bad way," Hackett said. "There's only one way to see this love story and that's my way."

"Well, we better have a long talk," Rudy said.

"That's a good idea. I'll work with you tomorrow. How about 10 A.M.?"

"But tomorrow is Christmas," Rudy said.

"Excellent day to work," Hackett said. "Nice and quiet. I'll see you at ten. Now I've got to go."

He went out and I followed him out onto the stair landing.

"Well . . ." I said. "I hope I didn't hurt Rudy's feelings or anything."

"Never mind, he's just a song writer," Hackett said. "Thanks for coming."

"That's okay," I said, and turned to go back in. Already I could hear voices being raised. While Hackett was there everybody would be polite — after he left the hostilities always broke out.

"Well, Merry Christmas," I said.

"Oh, I don't know about that," he said. He started off down the dark dismal stairs to the street and I leaned against the wall. He got about halfway down the stairs and he turned and looked back up at me. He had his hat kind of pushed back, the way he looked best.

"What are you doing?" he said.

"I don't know," I said. "Just standing here looking down the old stairs."

"You're a pretty good writer, Jack," he said, and turned and went on down to the street.

So that was my Christmas present. None of the stores all up and down Fifth Avenue had anything in them for me like that.

Chapter 19

So I went back in to get my coat.

"Well maybe you guys are all scared to death of him but I'm not," Rudy said. "So he's 'uncomfortable' with my lyrics is he, well he can knock out some of his own then by god if this is what I have to put up with you can take the whole lousy show and shove it. You know what the American people are doing right now, you know what? They're sitting around, millions of them, from goddamn coast to coast, shoving dimes into the jukeboxes just to hear my lyrics; just in the last hour while he's telling me my lyrics stink probably ten thousand people paid to hear my lyrics. Down in those dreary coal towns in Pennsylvania, out on the plains, up on Park Avenue . . ."

"Aw can it, there's no jukeboxes on Park Avenue and what's it prove anyway?" Sam Snow said.

"Yesterday," Rudy said. "Take yesterday for example . . ."

"I don't want it," Ted said.

"Yesterday 'Chief of Love' was played over the air thirty-eight times *before noon* in the New York area *alone*."

"Rudy, listen," Harry said. "Listen to me a minute will you, old boy? Listen, fella . . ."

I was putting on my coat. Ted Crosby had on his Lee Tracy hat. He walked me over into a corner.

"Of *course* we have confidence in you, old man," Harry Paige said.

"You just simply can't act like this with Richard Hackett," Sam said. "Damn it, man, we're all in this together."

"——," Rudy said.

"Hackett is the greatest . . ." Sam said.

"Double ——," Rudy said.

"Jack, listen," Ted said. "Listen, I want to talk to you. Say, roll me one of those cigarettes, will you?"

"Okay. Make it quick. I'm going home," I said.

"For Christ's sake shut up will you about the goddamn jukebox business. It has *ab*-solutely nothing to do with a Broadway . . ." Sam was saying.

"Listen, Sam," Rudy said, "you're a very smart young fellow, so they say, but right now before we go any farther I might as well tell you . . ."

"Now cut it out, you guys," Harry said. "Rudy, listen fella . . ."

"What the hell do you want, Ted?" I said.

"Listen, Jack," Ted said. "Remember that funny scene in the original book where they were on the streetcar? Jack, believe me that's rich material. You've got to get that into the script."

"Ted, we've been all through that a million times," I said. "Hackett hates it, he loathes it, he abhors it, he thinks it's cheap, vulgar, and terribly un-funny. So what the hell am I to do?"

"Listen, Jack . . ." Ted said. "Say, which end of this do I light?"

"The end that's twisted," I said.

"Like this dialogue on the streetcar where the guy says to

the girl some crack about her hat, remember? Man, that's pay
dirt, that's gold, man."

"Man, Hackett don't dig it, man," I said.

"I'm *not* being a damn bit stubborn, Rudy, I'm simply
saying . . ." Sam said.

"Rudy, listen fella, take it easy, will you?" Harry said. "We
certainly are aware of your success in the pop field and we
certainly appreciate your talent. But listen, old man . . ."

"I'm listening I'm listening," Rudy said. "Go on, say something."

"I'm going, Ted," I said.

"Think about what I said, will you?" Ted said. "Just think
about it, will you?"

"I'm not thinking about anything, but *anything* to do with
this show for at least forty hours," I said.

"*Now* who's being stubborn?" Sam said. Rudy threw his
sheet music into the air.

Ted followed me out onto the landing.

"Well, Merry Christmas," he said.

"Yeah, very," I said.

"And thanks for everything, boy," he said. "We've got a
nice tight script. Next year is our big year."

"On the streetcar," I said.

"I'm not kidding about that," he said. "You're passing
up one of the funniest sequences in the whole damn
book."

"Listen, producer," I said. "You've got a bigger problem on
your hands right now."

"Yeah, what's that?"

"Go in there and get Harry Paige to quit calling our Mr.
Lorraine 'fella' or you won't have any composer at all in about
twenty minutes."

Sam came out.

"Hey, where you going?" he said. "Come on, stick around, this is important."

"I got to get home, Sam," I said. "I got to get home to those little old kiddies. It's Christmas Eve, man."

"You're right, you're right," he said. "Run along, boy. And thanks for coming in."

"Thanks, fella," I said.

I walked up to 49th and over toward Fifth Avenue. It was cold and damp. Everybody was rushing around with packages. By the rink in Rockefeller Plaza some choir was shivering and singing "Silent Night" for a change. That's a dandy little tune but the lyrics make me uncomfortable.

I ran into my agent, Max Davenport.

"What are you doing in town?" he said.

"Working," I said.

"Well how's it going?"

"I don't know," I said. "Craziest business I ever got mixed up in."

"Hackett ever let up?"

"Never. He's working tomorrow at 10 A.M. with the composer."

"How's Lorraine like that?"

"He doesn't like anything. He's an unhappy boy. We're all picking on him, his lyrics."

"That's no surprise to me. How come you got him in the first place?"

"Damn it, Max, we couldn't get anybody *else*. They didn't like the script. They were afraid of it."

"It's a tough break," he said.

"You think it's that bad?" I said.

"Maybe not. Hackett ought to know. How's Irene Lovelle?"

"Just absolutely perfect, that's all," I said. "She's the woman I love."

"Uh-huh," he said. "How's the family?"

"They'll live through it, I guess."

"Well, boy, have a Merry. Don't worry."

"Why not? Everybody else does. I haven't met anybody that wasn't worried since I left Indiana."

He went off toward Sixth Avenue. He was "the best in the business." Everybody told me so. Down here when you meet somebody they say, "How do you do? Who's your agent?" That's a Milton Berle kind of a joke but it's true. So then they say to me, "Gee, how'd you get in with Max Davenport? I hear he's pretty hot."

"Yeah, don't worry," I thought. "But what am I going to eat on if this show is a big flop?" So I figured it all over in my head again: (a) I haven't earned a dime in five months except royalties. (b) BUT we would play a week in New Haven and three weeks in Boston anyway, and since this was a musical even if the show was a complete bomb we'd probably play say eight weeks in New York before throwing in the towel, so that was twelve weeks of royalties at least. Okay, say we averaged forty thousand a week to be safe, my percentage of the gross would be a thousand a week. Twelve weeks would be twelve thousand bucks. With that I could get the gang back home to the sticks again and hold on until I could find a position at the vinegar works.

I went down to the bar by the skating rink. Man what a crush. There were TV executives three-deep at the bar. I fought my way to a White Label and soda. One thing they do there is put in a generous slug. Over on Eighth Avenue you can get a Scotch highball for fifty cents but the shot glass is one of these glassblower's triumphs and is all glass and no hooch. And no peanuts either. And no thrilling Communications executives telling of victories in the deodorant field. And sometimes here by the rink some boys from the *Time* and

Life building across the court would be around; they had all the inside dope on everything, they were very authoritative — it made a person feel real stupid to listen to them. They knew the true story behind Eden's meeting with the Archbishop, and believe me it had nothing to do with what you read in the papers. And they were all greased up on doings in Costa Rica, Addis Ababa, and Omsk. None of this information was available to the public.

I began to feel homesick again and sorry for myself. I could stand there for a year and nobody I knew would ever come in, whereas out home at the International or the Four Deuces, why, Cousin Archie would be there with some good ones and Uncle Dumpington would be singing "Lovely Hoolihans" and everybody that came in I would know their history for the past thirty-five years. They might not know the difference between Tennessee Williams and Tennessee Ernie but they knew *me.*

I had another White Label and soda, jammed against this bird in a Homburg with a dude accent, who was telling a long complicated joke that I first heard in Superior, Wisconsin, about twenty years ago; I can still smell the sawdust and the soft coal smoke. That was when I was on the bum. And as the second White Label began to make the circuit I began on that old theme: "I Was Better Off in the Old Days When I Was Just a Bum," with words by J. R. Williams. Those were the good old times, etc.: a day's work, a slab o' yearlin, and the old bedroll out in the sagebrush. We were sloggin down to Rio in a rusty-sided tramp, me and my buddy Slim; first the deckhouse carried away and after the old girl went down it was eighteen days in the longboat with the two Lascar firemen stark ravin mad with the thirst.

So the hell with this town anyways. When I was out there where the wind blows through the telegraph wires and the Big

Ten keeps on scoring I thought that if you were a big successful writer like me in New York you were constantly sitting at a round table with Neysa McMein and Murdock Pemberton, or hanging around McSorley's saloon with Abe Burrows and George Ade, or playing poker all night with a bunch of wisecrackers from the daily papers. And what the hell has it added up to? Lunch at Schrafft's, lunch at the Plaza, lunch at Torino's, lunch at the Automat, lunch at Moore's, lunch for godsake all the time lunch! And who with? Am I having lunch with famed raconteurs and international polo champs, or am I having lunch with Sam Snow, Boy Producer and his electric Meccano set, Ted Crosby who is a former bum just like me, and Richard Hackett who paralyzes me so bad that I can't even think of any Ford jokes, much less new stuff?

At this point the Funniest Man in the World, who kept elbowing my drinking arm, began to recite the Funniest Christmas Poem You Ever Heard:

> 'Twas the night before Christmas
> And all through the house,
> Father was cockeyed, drunk as a louse;
> The chauffeur and mother were snuggled in bed
> While sister was nursing her hangover head. . . .

You see, folks, the story of the Nativity is old yet ever new, and watch the papers in January for the sales, it's crazy to buy anything you don't actually need until the sales.

And while all this was going on, and the waiters were busy bringing the wrong orders to the customers, and the shivering, shaking choir outside was bringing joy to the world of those who like to hear a choir singing Christmas carols (pardon me I have to make a phone call but I'll be right back) — while all this good cheer was flooding the joint I was in the usual 4 P.M. dumps, and trying to figure out how to justify calling up Irene; what I had in mind was a little December twenty-fourth romancing on Park Avenue, instead of dashing to the station and going home to start hunting for the Christmas tree stand.

I thought about Frankie and all the hell we'd been through together. "Man, they don't make many dames like that," Ted Crosby always said. "I hope you know how lucky you are, wife like that." So I began to choke up but before the tears started to roll I went over to the booth in the corner and called Irene.

"I think this is a lousy town and I'm going back to Horners Corners," I said.

"What are *you* doing in town?" she said.

"Honey, I had to come in. Something about Rudy's lyrics. Listen, why don't I come up there and tell you all about it? It's a thrilling tale that requires a more personal delivery."

"You better hop right down and get on that train," she said. "You and your three dozen children. I don't know why it is every time I meet some boy I can stand he has a wife and seven kids with braces on their teeth."

"Listen, honey," I said. "I've been over at the Rockefeller Plaza where all the dark and light folks meet and I'm feeling pretty good and I'm coming over to see you, so slip into something comfortable. In fact, if I were a bell I would ring like the beat beat beat of a tom-tom."

"Wow!" she said. "Where'd you tie this one on?"

"And moreover," I said, *"ich bin von Kopf bis Fuss auf Liebe eingestellt."*

"Okay," she said, "I suppose."

"Strike that 'I suppose' from the script," I said.

"Say, you're flying," she said.

I got out of there in a hurry and went up the steps and over to Fifth Avenue. Saks Fifth Avenue was playing "Silent Night" to the rubes. I got a cab in front of St. Patrick's.

"These here architects are the ones draggin' down the big salaries," the driver said. "I'm a draftsman myself, but I give it up. I figured 'Where am I goin?' I can make more money drivin' a cab."

"Yeah, them goddamn architects have it made," I said.

By the time we got through knocking the bastards we were at Irene's.

She was wearing white toreador pants and a white blouse with gold inlay all over both pieces. She had a canary bird named Melvin in a gold cage.

We started out very refined with drinks and cigarettes but the party soon degenerated into a feeble love scene with dialogue by five TV writers. Kissing Irene was like going over Niagara Falls in a barrel. Except that you wanted to do it again.

"I love you, darling," I said. I have a compulsive neurosis which forces me to tell every girl I kiss that I love her. After I've said it a few hundred times it sometimes turns out that I do.

"That's good, let's get married," she said.

"Shut up," I said. "Just because you get your picture in the paper you don't have to be so fresh."

So just then the door buzzer began to buzz.

"Let it buzz," I said.

"Damn," she said. "Wipe off that lipstick. Comb your hair. I bet it's my script. It was supposed to come over this afternoon."

So she pushed the button and I went in the bathroom and combed my hair. I went back to the living room and got my glass and was making myself a new one when somebody knocked on the door and Irene opened it and Sam Snow came in.

"Here's your script," he said. "Snow's Personal Delivery Service. We never sleep. Merry Christmas, darling." And he went into the New York hugging act. So far he had not seen me.

"Hello, Mr. Snow," I said.

"What the hell are *you* . . ." he said, breaking the clinch and turning red.

"You want soda or plain water?" I said.

"Soda," he said. "Say, for an out-of-town boy you sure cover a lot of ground."

"Listen, Sam," I said, "you're just the guy I've been wanting to see."

"Yes," he said. "We haven't seen each other for over an hour."

"Well this is serious, I mean," I said.

"Yeah, what is it?"

"I mean I don't want you to think I'm a heel or anything but there's something I've gotta tell you."

"Yeah, what is it?"

"I've been meaning to tell you for a long time now but I . . ."

"Is it something to do with the show?" he said. "Look, tell me what's bothering you. We'll fix it up somehow."

"It's not as easy as all that," I said. "See, I've been pretty busy."

"I'll say you have and you've done a damn good job, too. Gee, we've all been busy."

"Well, Sam, you know I think a lot of you. We always got along real good, didn't we?"

"Damn right. Right from the start."

"So listen, don't get sore."

"I *won't* get sore. What the hell's the matter, boy?"

"I guess I better get it over with."

"That's the best way," he said. "We're all in this together."

"Sam, I didn't send you a Christmas card," I said.

Bing Crosby sang "White Christmas" to us over the Radiola.

I was doing my best to live it up very carefree and get into the big city act. I figured every decent self-respecting young man with a copy of *Variety* in his side pocket had an obligation to the industry and to society to have at least one love affair a month. What the hell, I didn't want people to think I hadn't never read Norman Mailer and *Playboy* magazine.

Love among the tall buildings is nothing at all like love and the motions, notions, and preliminaries of same out in the fried-potato precincts. But I was in training and my right-cross was working fine and I figured I would get into at least the semifinals before long.

Irene was a handsome opponent and we made a lovely picture as a "cozy twosome at Armando's" or "in the clouds at El Morocco last night" as the columnists say. Love means five bucks to the maître d'hôtel and getting a soaking for the dinner. Love means bouncing down to the Village at 3 A.M. to hear "the most wonderful piano player." Love means a soiled dawn over the East River with two forgotten highballs ("Let's have a nightcap") slowly approaching room temperature on the fake mantelpiece. Love is "Hasn't it been a wonderful evening! Hasn't it been a ball!" Love is two lines by Leonard Lyons.

"No, no, don't be silly. Run along now, like a good boy."

Chapter 20

How well I remember it all — the sense of ease and well-being that was over this place, and over all Broadway; the loud clothes, the bright straw hats, the canes, the diamonds, the hot socks . . .

— THEODORE DREISER

January 3 we went into rehearsal in a warehouse across from a gasworks on 77th Street, near the Hudson River but not near enough. The streets we walked through were, like O'Casey says, "a long drab gauntlet of houses, some of them fat with filth . . . long kennels of struggling poverty and disordered want . . . the lacerated walls, the windows impudent with dirt . . ." By the time I got over to the rehearsal studio I didn't care any more.

This was where we rehearsed "the book," while it rained outside on the cobblestones. Upstairs above us in a dirty room with a grand piano in it the singers rehearsed, and a few blocks away the dancers worked in another "studio," over a vulcanizing shop. So there was a constant rushing to and fro, and endless complications as to when the principals, the singers, and the dancers would be available for their rehearsals. They don't just all get together like I thought and "rehearse." They have singing, dancing, and book rehearsals, all separate. And they also have appointments at the costumer's. It goes like this:

"When can I have Irene?" says the composer. "We're doing 'Nearly Mine' at three o'clock."

"Sorry, she's going to costumes at three. You can have her at six," says Hackett.

"That's no good. Rex has to rehearse his dance at six," says De Marco, the musical director. "And right after his dance rehearsal I want Rex for at least an hour," De Marco adds, and rushes out the fire door.

"Well, then, tonight, eight o'clock," says Hackett. "You can have Rex and Irene both at eight."

"Mr. Hackett, you called book rehearsal for eight tonight," says Ted Crosby.

"Oh god! So I did," says Hackett. "You'll have to wait until tomorrow for Irene, I guess."

"That's terrible! I'm not getting enough rehearsal time," Rudy says. "When can I have the boy dancers, man they need plenty work. Such voices. They're awful."

"Ask De Marco," says Hackett.

"What good is it to ask him? He don't know what's going on."

"Where's Al St. James?" Hackett says. "Where's that funny man? Let's rehearse the front-door bit."

"He's gone to costumes," Sam says.

"Well who *have* I got?" Hackett says.

"Let's see," says the stage manager. "We've got Mrs. Fondemeyer, and the fat girl, and we've got Irene until three o'clock. We could do the second beauty parlor scene."

"All right, let's go," Hackett says and he gets them on their feet and they go through it again, while we hold our scripts and smoke cigarettes that make us sick. Hackett is all over the place, showing *exactly* what he wants. Every once in a while he says, "I don't like that line. Jack, give me a new line." You sensitive boys who have to spray the room with lilies of the valley before you can start to write, how would you like to write some great stuff under those circumstances, with six bored actors standing there watching you think of a screamer? Well, don't think I could do it because I couldn't. Not very much.

Then Rudy Lorraine is usually having a riot with De Marco, the musical director, about the choral effects. This Lorraine knows from nothing and back again about music but he is out there in front all the time saying, "I can't hear the words. That was terrible, girls." Then the girls get mad and De Marco gets mad and goes to Hackett and Hackett takes Lorraine aside and tells him to quit bothering De Marco when he is rehearsing the singers, and Lorraine gets mad at De Marco for going to Hackett and blows his top and stomps out of the rehearsal room and the singing girls nudge each other, and De Marco goes to it again:

"Push it, Johnny," he says to the piano player. "If you feel the six-eight it'll go better. *Whoa,* whoa, get the retard, kids, get the retard."

By this time Lorraine is back to see Hackett again and he says he doesn't think Irene will ever be able to sing "You and Me" with Ives because of the A-flat or something and not only that but the expensive comedian Al St. James has got to go because he may be a good comic but he can't sing. "Can't sing at all," says Rudy to Hackett. "You won't be able to hear him past the third row. Besides that he swallows his lyrics. I hate to say it because personally I like him very much. I personally respect his very great talent. But he can't sing, Mr. Hackett, and he's got three big numbers to carry in this show. He's got to be replaced, that's all."

"Now just cool down," says Hackett. "This boy was singing

in musical comedy before you were born. He's been in twenty Broadway hits. He's been in two R. and H. shows in the last five years. Good solid parts, too."

"Then Rodgers and Hammerstein are tone-deaf," Lorraine says. Oh-oh, this is greeted by a stony silence. You know, that's not so good, a young punk song writer from the Brill Building, with a few pop numbers to his credit, saying things like that about Rodgers and Hammerstein. That's like making jokes about the King and Queen when you are playing Toronto.

Of course there are some of the kids standing around and they hear it and they repeat it around at ballet class, or up at Hanson's Drug Store, and in a day or so it is all over New York and everybody getting a big laugh out of it:

"Didja hear what Lorraine said about Dick Rodgers?"

Pretty soon the story gets even worse than it was to start with.

Great personal publicity.

Then Harry Paige would show up at rehearsal, parking his Rolls-Royce drop-head saloon across the street by the gate to the gasworks, and he would come in and sit quietly for an hour or so watching the book rehearsal and when we would have a break he'd say to me, "Let's get a cup of coffee," and we would walk up to the corner in the rain.

"Listen, Jack, this script is lousy," he would say, stirring his coffee with a bent spoon. "It's simply not *funny*. We'll never get away with it."

"Well, Harry, what the hell are we going to do about it? I'm the guy they hired."

"Listen, I've got the greatest gag writer in Hollywood. This guy is terrific. Brother, we *need* him. Right now."

"Well, talk to Sam and Ted about it, Harry, not me."

"I already did."

"Well?"

"They thought I was *kidding*. Then when they saw I wasn't kidding, they just laughed it off. Boy, is Broadway in a rut! It's like I always say, you can tell people by the shirts they wear. Sam, Ted, Hackett — look at them! All in the white shirts. Sam puts on a blue Oxford, and figures he is raising hell. And you can see it in their thinking. All their ideas are dressed in white shirts."

Fortunately I was wearing a nice lavender stripe.

And we had an old character actor who had fifteen or twenty lines and he was worried about his lines all the time. He was always getting me off in a corner against some steam pipes and telling me he could get a lot more out of "Hello there, Charlie!" if it was changed to "Hello there, Charlie, what do you hear from the mob?" More of a joke to it, see? And he would slip me scraps of paper with jokes for other people's parts, too. And he also clipped the magazines and newspapers and would hand me a clipping saying, "There might be something here you could use for that barbershop scene," and it would be some news item about a barber in Glens Falls, New York, who also owned a pet alligator.

We had a good-looking lead dancer who had a minor part, Sonia Ilanova (née Mildred Kerrigan) who took a fierce shine to me, giving me the gladdest smiles, and caressing my nice flannel arm, and I thought, "Say, this is more like it, you are a terribly attractive fellow, Jack," until one day when she was busy fondling me and she whispered, "Give me some *lines!*"

Sam was all over the place, hollering into telephones, watching the book rehearsal for ten minutes and then rushing off to hear the singers, and from there dashing out struggling with the sleeves of his topcoat as he charged over to the dance studio, then way back across town to the office, more phone calls, publicity meetings, trips to the costumers, arguments with the set designer. Ted was a little calmer, a little less distracted; he stuck pretty close to Hackett and kept things running smoothly — well, not smoothly, but running somehow.

Everybody loved Irene. She didn't put on any crap. She was always appearing for rehearsals in something nutty: maybe toreador pants, bell-bottom sailor pants, or a skirt with a crazy blouse. With that blond hair, she filled the dirty rehearsal hall with something resembling sunshine. And she worked. She wasn't at lunch at the Plaza any more.

"Mr. Hackett . . ." She always called him Mr. Hackett at rehearsals even though she had frozen half to death with him on the road to Westport . . . "Mr. Hackett, would you please help me out here a bit? I just don't get what this girl *wants* in this scene. I'm sorry but I just don't get it. What's she driving at?"

"Tell her what Susie wants in this scene, Jack," Hackett would say.

"Guess I'm pretty dumb but I . . ." Irene would say. "Could you clear it up a little for me?"

"It's like this," I would say. "She's pretty damn mad at Chuck since she got the phone call from Margie, but she's trying to draw him out. For all she knows Margie made the whole thing up. She still doesn't know what Chuck thinks of Margie, but she'd sure like to know. Get it?"

"I guess so. Well, let's go," and she would turn back to Rex Ives who was standing there like the spreading chestnut tree.

Rex was all the leading male singers in the universe rolled into one.

"Rex, you've got to break yourself of this cheap stock-company style of acting," Hackett would say. "Now you've got to listen to me. Do *exactly* what I tell you. Stop *acting*, in the first place. All right, now let's run through it again. Irene, I think you better be upstage just a bit — so — like that. You'll have to have some business here. How about looking in your handbag for your lipstick? Would you be carrying a bag here? I think so. Now time it so that just as you find the lipstick and take it out, Rex says, 'What happened to you last night? Did you get lost?' *Then* you pause, turn, and say your line and then on into the scene as before. Got that? Now, Rex, loosen up, boy, this isn't operetta at Montclair High School. *Think* the lines. *Think* what you're doing. Ready? Go ahead."

Occasionally Irene would flip a wink in my direction but mostly she was just all work. This is a grueling profession, friends, believe me you have got to want to get up there and have people looking at you mighty bad to work this hard and not fall dead.

After days of rehearsing all day, and nights sometimes until twelve or one, and not much sleep, Hackett would ask Irene if she wasn't getting tired.

"I'm all right," she'd say.

Irene was friends with everybody, that's the way she was. The gang used to go up to the corner to eat at this real awful dump called Morty's; it was a counter and three or four booths. I lived in joints like this for years and it was no change for me and no treat either.

"I don't see *how* you can eat there," our old character actress used to say. She always took a cab to Rumpelmayer's or someplace and was always getting back late from the lunch break.

There were never enough booths and I was never with Irene but with Rudy Lorraine, or three chorus boys, or

Hackett and Sam and the rehearsal piano player, or Ted and a couple of girl dancers, or with the assistant stage manager and Al St. James, the great comedian. Al was a real riot.

"Say, where do you live?" he'd say to me.

"Out in Stamford. I'm renting a place," I'd say.

"What kind of heat you got?"

"Hot air."

"Listen, take it from me, throw it out and put in steam or hot water. You'd be way ahead in the end."

"Well, I just rent this house."

"Oh."

So we would eat our fried eggs or beef stew and pretty soon he'd say, "Next time that landlord of yours comes around tell him you want steam heat. That hot air isn't healthy."

Then we'd eat some apple pie and he'd say, "I wouldn't live in a house with hot air heat."

Then the assistant stage manager would tell us about his wife's operation and then we'd walk back to rehearsal in the drizzle.

"This rain isn't doing my bad leg any good," Al would say. "Goddamn climate. I was nuts to leave the Coast for this lousy show."

Irene loved all of it including the bum apple pie and the rain. What she liked was show business, all of it. She was a performer.

It is pretty hard going even under the most ideal conditions to light up all the lights with an actress, but even worse when she's in rehearsal. Like a wife who says, "You know, I think we ought to change the wallpaper in this room" just when things are getting right, Irene would look at me dreamily across the coffee cups, with the violin music and the potted palms, and I would be telling her how great she was, and she would say:

"Darling, I want to tell you something . . ."

"What is it, sweetie?"

"Jack, I hate that blackout line in Scene Three."

And then there was her big overwhelming indiscriminate love for everybody in the show. I guess I admired and loved her for it, because it made everybody love her, too, but I used to get fed up to see her kidding around with a couple of the chorus boys or having some long boring talk with our old character actor about the time he played with Maude Adams. If you think the boys in the club car talking about their sales quotas are boring you ought to talk to a few actors. Wow.

"What are you looking so sad about?" Irene would say.

"What are you gonna do, write a book about Maude Adams?" I'd say. "You're gathering material, huh?"

"Oh quit being such a big baby," she'd say. "The poor old guy. Nobody ever listens to him."

"How about listening to me for a while? How about going to Romeo's for supper?"

"I can't. I've got to work with Rex and De Marco. How about after rehearsal tonight?"

"I can't. I've got to go home. I've been in town for three days."

"Don't look so sad," she'd say.

Then she went out with Sam and he took her to the Stork Club.

"I didn't have much fun," she said.

"Uh-huh," I said.

The only one in the show she didn't like was Rudy Lorraine. Once in a misguided moment at rehearsal he told her her diction was poor, and that was enough for her. The next day he asked her for a date and she told him No and he said Leonard Lyons was a big pal of his. She said No and he told her Columbia wanted him to do the score for a picture. She said No and he said Danny Kaye wanted him to do some special material for him. She said No and he said "Chief of Love" had hit the two million mark. She said No and he said Winchell thought the world of him. She said No and he said NBC wanted him for a special consultant. She said No and he said he had a recording date with Patti Page and went away mad.

Hackett kept things going:

We had our first run-through and the next day Hackett told Sam to fire the old man and the girl comedienne. We picked up replacements.

Harry Paige told Hackett what they needed was a good gag writer and Hackett told Harry Paige what they didn't need was a good gag writer.

One of the chorus girls changed her hair. Hackett made her change it back. She cried.

Two of the chorus boys had a lover's quarrel. Hackett canned them.

Rudy wrote a new song and Hackett said it was no good and he'd have to try it again. Rudy said if they had left it in it would have been a smash hit.

Rudy wrote another song and Hackett said it was good. Rudy said it would be a smash hit.

Sam got a cold and had to stay home. Hackett sent his doctor around.

Hackett told me to rewrite the big love scene. I told him I liked it the way it was.

I rewrote it.

Hackett told Al St. James to quit worrying about what was going on on the Coast and learn his lines.

Hackett took one of the dancers home with him.

The choreographer didn't like the costumes. Hackett refereed the battle.

And then January was gone and we moved into a theater to rehearse. We had our last run-through.

The show looked terrible.

The next day we left for New Haven.

Chapter 21

W<small>AIT</small> till we get to New Haven! We'll have a ball!" Rudy Lorraine told me repeatedly.

"We'll have a ball when we get to New Haven," Irene told me.

And others in the cast also predicted that balls would predominate during our stay in the historic city.

The next event will be an essay contest on the subject: "New Haven, Connecticut, As I See It." Please write on one side of the paper only, and Neatness Counts.

New Haven is a very modern city with gas mains, city water, and electric lights and is chiefly noted for being the home of the famous college called Harvard. There are Harvard boys all over town wearing gray flannels and carrying footballs under their arms. Some carry oars over their shoulders which at times presents a nasty traffic hazard. The curriculum consists of trying to sneak into the Shubert Theater when a musical comedy is rehearsing. Any lad who succeeds in this with every show that comes to town for one whole season is permitted to sit on the "Harvard fence," even when it is raining.

New Haven is near enough to New York City for all

those "in the know" to be constantly coming up to see the shows trying out. This gives them a big social advantage at Lindy's as they can say, "I seen it in New Haven. It hasn't got a chance unless they get a whole new second act and shoot the director."

The Hotel Taft, named for the family of the same name, is considered by the international set to represent the finest American example of the art of l'hôtelier. Its lavish appointments and de luxe cuisine beggar description.

New Haven is also the birthplace of Elvira, the Alligator Girl, who travels with the Ton o' Fun Carnival.

Everybody in New Haven brushes their teeth twice a day. This is typical of the progressive spirit of the "Citrus Capital" of New England.

We all went up from Grand Central in a "show train." One of the bit players insinuated himself into the car with the management and the principals, much to Sam's disgust.

"Forget it," Ted said. "Once a ham always a ham. You always expect actors to be like *people* for godsake."

Rudy Lorraine lit up a large cigar in the Panatela shape and blew smoke in Hackett's face and did some ponderous kidding with the girls. While Sam was waiting to see if Hackett was going to ask Irene into the dining car for lunch I asked her. So we had some damn poor pot roast together.

"How do you feel, honey?" I asked her.

"I feel like I was on my way to New Haven again," she said.

"Yeah. We'll have a ball," I said.

"Yeah, who says so?"

"Why, that's what you told me."

"I did? Well, maybe we will. Sometimes it's fun, sometimes it's a pain in the attic."

Rudy Lorraine came in with Harry Paige and sat down at the next table to ours.

"Dig the Great Lorraine working on Hollywood," Irene said.

"We budgeted it at two million," Harry said. "So we went nearly a million over. But what did we care, we had Frankie."

"You gotta have names up there," Rudy said.

"That's what I mean," Harry said. "We'll be all right. Same thing in the trucking business, shirts, or anything else. You gotta build that name. That's what worries me about this show. I mean let's face it. We've got no *names*." Harry's *sotto voce* was carrying out pretty well. He was projecting just fine.

"Sure we've got Hackett," Harry said. "But what else have we got? Who in hell ever heard of Jack Jordan?"

I turned around and tapped him on the shoulder.

"Listen, Harry," I said, "I am the toast of the town in Chippewa Falls, Wisconsin."

"Listen, I'm serious," he said. "I'm just thinking of the show."

"Well, we're all thinking of the show," I said. "I wish I could think of something else for a while but I can't," and I turned back to the pot roast and Irene, a girl with no name whatsoever.

"Take yourself," Harry said to Lorraine.

"Oh-oh. Look out," Irene said.

"I mean sure you've had some pop hits but who pays any attention to . . ."

"Now wait a minute," Rudy said. "You know how many bottles of whisky I sent out to the deejays last Christmas? Two hundred. So don't tell me that nobody . . ."

"Listen, the disk jockeys don't buy theater tickets," Harry said.

"I got second place in the *Down Beat* poll last year, that's all," Rudy said. "You mean to tell me . . ."

"So who reads *Down Beat?* The guy from Battle Creek in New York on a convention who wants to take some dame to a show? Listen, don't get mad. I'm just thinking of the show."

"Let's think about the show," Irene said.

"Okay. What do you think of it?" I said.

"It needs names," she said.

Sam came in with Hackett and Sonia Ilanova, but he didn't say hello.

"Well, it's beginning," I said.

"What is?" Irene said.

"Trouble in paradise," I said.

When we got off the train in New Haven a fellow with glasses and a fly-front topcoat herded us all together and shoved a mike into Hackett's face and said:

"And here's Robert Hackett, producer of this grand new show opening right here in New Haven on Monday night. How do you feel about the show, Mr. Hackett? Is it going to be another Hackett hit?"

"I think I'll be better equipped to answer that question on Tuesday morning," Hackett said. "We've got a lot of work to do, and that's why we're in New Haven. We've got a good cast, a good book, and a good score. So we should have a good show. And incidentally, *I'm* not the producer. The producers are Paige, Crosby, and Snow. Here, boys, thrill the radio audience," and he gave the mike to Harry, who happened to be nearest.

"It's a very great pleasure to be here in New Haven . . ." Harry said.

Two tired cameramen popped their flash bulbs.

I hung up my topcoat in the closet and went over to the window and looked out over the gray towers of Yale. The phone rang.

"Have you got a bottle?" It was Sam.

"Strangely enough I have," I said.

"Bring it to 535," he said.

Sam and I had a drink out of water tumblers.

"Can you believe we're *here?*" he said. "Did you see that marquee? Did you see your name up there on that marquee? God! Isn't it the greatest!"

"So far," I said. "It sure is the greatest."

But after that first jolly burst of boyish high spirits Sam changed. For Sam Snow in New Haven with Sam Snow's first show was not entirely the same person familiar to all in the coffeehouses of Broadway. He was playing his role to the last lonesome fare-thee-well, in fact he was hamming it; Hackett should have knocked off and given him some direction. He was capricious, moody, violent, proud, sad, severe, and repulsively gay by turns. He ran around brandishing telegrams. Sometimes he sat with chin in hand, as sad-eyed as Henry B. Walthall, thinking. He allowed his hair to become impressively mussed. Sometimes he loosened his tie, to show that he was in New Haven. He waved letters and pieces of script and held endless phone conversations with New York in the small office at the Shubert as people climbed over him going to and fro.

Ted had come up three days before the rest of us, and was out in the theater getting that scenery hung and working with the electrician among a tangle of wires and three giant switchboards.

If "having a ball" means having a real miserable time then we were "having a ball." After twenty-four hours practically everybody was sore at everybody else.

Rudy Lorraine screamed like a stuck pig when he saw the scenery. We were all sitting around down in the orchestra watching the struggle on stage.

"I thought this was supposed to be a real low-down American story. Look at the goddamn park scene. What the hell are those pink and lavender pigeons doing there? Who ever saw a pink pigeon? What do they think this is, *Peter Pan,* or some big fag fantasy? All you boys been telling me is Realism! Now here we are in New Haven and all of a sudden we got ART! How can Rex Ives get out there and sing a real love song to his lousy girl friend with some pink pigeons over his head?"

"Shut up, you bastards. Wait'll we see the whole picture before you start all this screaming," Ted said from up on stage. "Hey, Props, strike this telephone and give us a French phone."

"That's supposed to be an old-fashioned phone on purpose, Ted," I contributed from the third row where I sat with my coat over my shoulders.

"Well if you use my music in front of sets like that you might as well throw your money in the sewer," Rudy said.

"Oh be quiet, Rudy," Sam said, coming down the aisle. "Let's get the show at least set up. Then you can have all the fits you want."

"Pink pigeons," Rudy muttered.

"What'd you say, Jack?" Ted called down from the stage.

"Hold it, hold it, the drop is fouled," one of the stage hands hollered.

"I said it's supposed to be an old-fashioned . . ."

"Get Eddie! Where the hell is Eddie?" somebody shouted.

"You better go over and stick with that orchestra rehearsal," Hackett said to Rudy. "We'll talk about scenery after it's hung."

"I can't hear you, Jack," Ted said, coming down stage. "What'd you say about the telephone?"

"I said it's *supposed* to be an old . . ."

"Look out! It's clear!" hollered a stage hand.

"The action is supposed to be in a hick town in Indiana, isn't it?" Rudy said. "Since when is Indiana all pastel shades? When did Indiana get to be a tone poem?"

"Aw go tell it to Eddie Fisher," Ted said.

"Eddie happens to be a very dear friend of mine and I don't think it's so funny," Rudy said.

"I must say I rather agree with Rudy on this," Harry Paige said from under his Borsalino. "It certainly isn't what I . . ."

"Oh, Harry, goddamnit . . ." Sam said.

"Shut up, here comes Telesco," I said.

Telesco was the scenery and costume designer. He was pale and wore a full haircut and his hands were long and slender. He wore a dove-colored coat with a velvet collar. We shook hands all around.

"Buddy drove me up," he said. "I can't endure the New Haven Railroad."

Buddy was his boy friend, a "brilliant" dancer; so brilliant in fact that he could never find a vehicle suitable for his talent. ("I'll bet he's a bellhop from the Astor," Ted used to say.)

"Everybody busy as little beavers, I see," Telesco said. "How's everything going?"

"Your pigeons are giving Mr. Lorraine several new ulcers," Hackett said.

"Oh, really?" Telesco said. "My lovely little birdies?"

"I got nothing against the birds except their color. Who the hell ever saw any cerise and aqua pigeons, especially in Indiana?" Rudy said.

"Ah, but my dear Rudy, you miss the point. I'm seeking an effect. The visual impact is . . ."

"Well it's a lousy effect, my dear Telesco," Rudy said. "I'm going over to Kaysey's and have an impact in a glass."

Rudy went up the aisle.

"Rudy, listen, I want to talk to you," Sam said, and followed him.

"Ted!" Hackett called. "I want a scrim in front of that."

"Mr. Hackett," Ted said, "we're mighty tight back here. There's not enough room left to hang a string."

"It can go on the same pipe, can't it?" Hackett said. "Hang it on the same pipe."

Irene appeared on stage with the wardrobe mistress. She had on a pink dress. She just came out and stood there.

"Good God!" Telesco said. "Irene dear, *where* did that dress come from?"

"That's what I'd like to know," Irene said. "Larry brought it up from New York yesterday."

"Larry's an idiot," Telesco said, and walked down to the pit. "Go take it off. I can't stand it."

He disappeared backstage.

"There goes another two hundred dollars in the ashcan," Hackett said.

"Is this Telesco always as disorganized as this?" Harry Paige said.

"He's the best in the business," Hackett said.

Ted came down to the footlights.

"Can you imagine putting a dame with Irene's coloring into a pink dress that color?" he said.

"Watch your head, watch your head," somebody in the wings shouted. Ted turned and began to talk to Props, who was chewing a cigar.

"How do you feel about the scenery, Dick?" Harry said to Hackett.

"I haven't seen it yet," Hackett said.

Pink dress, purple dress — what did it matter? Darling, you look so wonderful up there. You are my Chief of Love. And outside her windows, and down below, the cars were so quiet in the snow all up and down Park Avenue that very first afternoon just as though nothing very wonderful was happening.

"How do you feel, Jack?" Hackett said.

"Scared," I said.

Chapter 22

I found out the reason that Gloria Swanson has been in complete seclusion since she's been in Hollywood.
She's been on a water diet for eight days.
— LOUELLA PARSONS

WE HAD supper at Kaysey's, across the street. I couldn't eat much. Just watching Hackett pack away the broiled swordfish and three cups of coffee made me sick.

"You're not eating much, Jack," he said. "What's the matter?"

"I don't feel so good," I said.

"You'll get used to it," he said.

"I doubt that," I said. "I don't think I was cut out for this exciting life."

"How's everything at home?" Ted said, busy with liver and bacon, which the sight of it alone makes me want to go away. "How's all the kids?" He never came any closer than this to saying anything about me and Irene.

"They're okay," I said. "The boys are sore because there's no snow in the lousy state of Connecticut, and the colored girl says if the Baby sucks his thumb it will bring on the false teeth."

"That's ridiculous," Hackett said.

"That's a great little wife, that Frankie of yours," Ted said. "One in a million."

"Okay, Marconi, I'm getting the message," I said.

"What?" Hackett said.

"How's the swordfish?" Ted said.

Sonia Ilanova stopped and showed her dazzling smile and other charms to Hackett and Ted. She had about given up on me because I not only hadn't built up her part with more lines, but in fact Hackett had cut some out and she blamed me for it.

Irene was over in a booth with Sam Snow. I guess that was another reason I couldn't eat.

"I just wonder if that ballet in the sordid dive is going to come off," Hackett said, as Ilanova went away.

"I just wonder if any of those dandy jokes are going to come off," I said.

"Irene is in an uproar over her costumes," Ted said.

"Naturally," Hackett said.

"And Schatzie wants you to go on the radio with Rex Ives. An interview."

"With *Rex*? What's the matter with Schatzie, is he out of his mind?"

Well I don't care, I thought, let her eat supper with that old dumb Sam Snow if she wants to. She'll find out who her true friend is someday. By that time it might be *too late*, don't forget that, Irene. When you're huddled by the stage door in the rain and I come out in my silk hat with Olga Baclanova on my arm. There's a broken heart for every light bulb on the Great White Way and a tear for every bubble in the champagne. I can see you now in a furnished room on Tenth Avenue. The shade is all cracked, there's a hole in the rug. The child cries — Sam's child. You put your last quarter in the gas meter . . .

". . . in Scene Four," Hackett said. "What do you think, Jack?"

"I'm sorry. I wasn't following," I said.

"We're in New Haven," Ted said. "There's this show we're putting on, remember?"

We went over to the theater and had a complete run-through to set the lighting. Ted kept hollering up into the dark to the control booth, way up in heaven someplace at the top of the theater.

"Can you hear me up there, Dave?"

Then we'd hear a little voice out of a cloud.

"What'd you say, Ted?"

"Hit Irene with a small spot."

"O-o-okay!"

"And, Dave! Hey, Dave!"

"What'd you say, Ted?"

"Take this spot *out*, when that goes on. Got it?"

"O-o-o-okay, Ted."

"The sets are a disappointment," Harry Paige said.

"All right, that's fine!" Hackett shouted up to the stage. "Ted! Ted Crosby!"

Ted appeared from the wings, pale in a white spotlight.

"Ted, that's okay. Strike and go into the next scene," Hackett said.

"Roll me one of those cigarettes, will you?" the Choreographer said. "Have you ever read any Kafka?"

"Not today," I said.

Sam came in and sat down in the fourth row with us.

"De Marco says the orchestration needs more work. He wants Schlussel up here tomorrow."

"How much did we pay for orchestrations already?" Harry said.

"Nine thousand," Sam said.

"I told you it would be closer to thirteen before you were through," Hackett said.

"I'll call him," Sam said.

"How's that working, Mr. Hackett?" Ted said from the stage.

"We're getting too much spill. Too much hilation. It'll never work."

"Can't we do a stylized thing here?" Telesco said. "We'll see them move anyway."

"Jack, I have a feeling this scene will have to be all rewritten. It looks lou-say," Hackett said.

"Well it won't work this way," Harry said.

"If you handled it in a stylized way you wouldn't have to depend on lights," Telesco said.

"All right, go on!" Hackett said. "Jack, think about that."

"Ted!" Telesco said. "Now on this, give me a back light at a low reading."

"Okay," Ted said.

"Girls, get back out of the wings, we can see you out front," Hackett said.

"Girls, move back, move back until you get your cue," Ted said.

"No hat in this scene please, Irene!" Telesco said.

"But I need the hat," Irene said, coming down to the foots.

"Why no hat?" Hackett said, turning back to Telesco.

"You want the hat? All right, leave the hat," Telesco said. "Personally I've always seen this without the hat."

"Lovely hat," said the Choreographer.

"All right, dear," Hackett said. "Keep the hat."

"Hold it, hold it, the drop is fouled," Ted hollered.

Props came out of the wings smoking his cigar.

"Not now, not now," Ted said. "Come on, boys, clear it up, let's go." Props trudged back into the wings.

"Ted, aren't you going to use the ground rows? We need 'em. Telesco, that's an awful dress you've got Irene in," Hackett said.

"All right, all right. We'll change it, we'll put her in dungarees."

"It's too frilly and fussy," Hackett said. "This is a working girl out in Indiana, not a plantation belle at her first grand ball."

"You can buy a dress like that in any shop in Indiana," Telesco said.

"I'm sorry, there's too much dress," Hackett said.

"Much too fancy," Harry Paige said.

"I'll take her out shopping tomorrow," Sam said. "Maybe we can find something right here in town."

"Go ahead," Telesco said. "Don't mind me." And he walked out.

"I didn't mean it like that," Sam said.

"He'll be back," Hackett said. "Rex! Rex Ives! Take your coat off for this scene. Try it with your coat off."

Back home we used to close the factory at 5 P.M. and go home and forget about it. It seems like here we worked all the time. We didn't get through until 1 A.M. and while we were having some scrambled eggs at the Waldorf cafeteria Hackett said, "Jack, see if you can come up with something by tomorrow for Rex and Irene's number in Scene Five. Try and get Mrs. Fondemeyer out of it. She doesn't have to introduce the number and her dialogue is poor, anyway."

"Scene what?" I said.

"Scene Five," he said.

I wrote this damn play but I don't know the scenes by number even now, and I can't remember the sequence, I'm always forgetting whether the front porch scene comes before or after the bit in the drugstore; it's like the road from

New York to Boston, I can never remember whether Bridge-port or New Haven comes first.

So I was in for a restful night. I was supposed to get some sleep and simultaneously eliminate Mrs. Fondemeyer and think up a whole new way to get Rex and Irene into a number.

I brushed my teeth and looked at myself in the mirror. Boy, you're in the wrong business, I thought. You better get the hell back to Indiana before they catch onto you.

And I looked out the window at Yale. Those boys are in fine shape. They are busy writing term papers on entasis in the columns of the Parthenon, on the Baron de Charlus, on Fra Filippo Lippi, on schist, gneiss, and varved clay, and letters to girls beginning "When I said that about Betty I didn't mean at all what you thought I meant. What I really meant . . ." Then they sit in the window seat under a sign that says No Parking and play a few novelty numbers on the mandolin and go to bed and sleep like a piledriver hit them.

Richard Hackett, having caressed the lush contours of a girl with a fine chest-voice and lain with her, has dismissed her and is in bed in neatly pressed pajamas rewriting Scene Five in his head and has already had six splendid ideas. No naughty little gnomes labeled "Incorrect Speech Habits," "It Might Have Been," and "Upset Stomach" are dancing gleefully on the headboard or grouped around his pillow chipping at his head with geologists' hammers. Let others seek physic. Hackett stands alone, filling out no coupons, rejecting filters of all kinds.

The phone rang.

"Say, have you got a bottle?" Sam said.

"Oh my," I said. "Saints preserve us!"

"Listen, we're down here talking things over. I think we're

having some pretty damn constructive thoughts, too. We just ran out of whisky. Irene is here and she . . ."

"I'll bring it down," I said.

Sam and Ted and funny Al St. James were there, and a girl from the chorus who never said a word, and Ilanova, who never stopped talking. And Irene Lovelle.

"The whole last half of the second act has to be *completely* rewritten," Sam said, taking my bottle. "Ted and Al and I all agree."

"Hi, sweetie," I said to Irene. "What are you doing here with these drunks?"

"Oh, we're just rewriting the show, that's all," Irene said. "You know, tightening up the good old script."

"You better quit smoking so much," I said. "That's not good for your voice."

"I mean the show . . ." I said.

"I mean . . ." I said.

"Aw forget it," I said. "I don't know what I'm saying up here. I'm gone."

"I didn't like the second act in the run-through and I read it over last night and I liked it even less," Sam said.

"The motivation gets lost," Ilanova said, draining an enormous slug of my whisky. "In fact there is no motivation. The whole thing's a muddle. I'm sure *I* don't understand what happens or why."

"Or why! That's the point!" Sam said.

"Motivation is important," Ted said. "Motivation is the most important . . ."

"You've got to talk to Hackett about it, Jack," Sam said.

"Sure," Irene said. "Jack's just the boy to tell Richard Hackett where to head in."

"Well why not?" Sam said very sharp and ornery. "They're collaborators aren't they?"

"You're damn right," Ted said. "Damn tootin'."

"You say to him, 'We had something wonderful and somewhere it got lost. We've simply . . .'"

"Motivation," Ted said. "How the hell can we bring a show in without motivation?"

"Take Ibsen," Ilanova said, pouring herself three ounces.

"It's up to you to put this over with Hackett," Sam said. "Listen, you and he *wrote* this script. You just say, 'We had something wonderful here but somehow somewhere we lost that wonderful quality. We've simply got to . . .'"

"Wonderful quality," Ted said. "Gotta get it back into the script. *I'm* gonna tell him. You know what I'm gonna say, I'm gonna say, 'Mr. Hackett, we had a wonderful quality here, but somewhere it got lost. On the playing fields of Yale.'"

"And I'll play the violin accompaniment while you tell him," Irene said.

"Aw come on, Irene, get serious, will you?" Sam said. "I think we're in trouble. I *really, sincerely,* think we're . . ."

"I got work to do," I said. "I gotta go. Irene, you better get some sleep."

"Never mind about Irene. Quit worrying about Irene. She's okay," Ted said.

"You know what Balanchine used to say?" Ilanova said. "He always used to say . . ."

"All the time worrying about Irene," Ted said. "Irene's okay. Are you okay, Irene?"

"Yes, I'm fine," Irene said. "Talented, too."

"I'm going to BED," I said. "Hackett gave me WORK to do."

"Goddamn it, aren't you even *interested* in what we're telling you?" Sam said. "He isn't even interested. He doesn't care. You wanna come in with a lousy flop show? You wanna find yourself back in Indiana?"

"Al agrees with us, don't you, Al?" Ted said.

"Sure," Al said. "You got any more Coke?"

"I'll talk to him," I said. "Okay?"

"Attaboy," Ted said. "Listen, tell him the whole goddamn second act stinks."

"No, no, shut up, Ted," Sam said. "Just the last half. Just tell him we feel . . ."

"No motivation," I said. "Unresolved, inconclusive, lacking drive and conviction."

"Script, penned by Hackett and Jordan (latter wrote original book), sags badly in second act. Dearth of comedy material had New Haven preem audience dozing until so-so finale," Irene said.

"Plenty rewrite indicated," I said, "to bring this one in for a chance at coin."

"Right!" Ted said.

"Well, not that exactly," Sam said.

"You got any other little chores you want me to do?" I said. "Orchestrations? Ham sandwich? Press your pants while you wait?"

"Well, if you feel that way about it . . ." Sam said.

"Lousiest second act any show I was ever with," Ted said.

"Come on, Irene," I said. "Let's go. I'll walk you home."

"What I like about pictures," Al St. James said, "you work for six or eight weeks and it's all over."

"Aw forget it, Al," Ted said. "You don't like pictures. All that lousy smog."

Irene got up and draped her coat over her shoulders.

"Bye-bye, Producers," she said. "Don't get so down. Wait till we see some reviews. This is a wonderful show and you know it!"

"You doll!" Sam said, embracing her. "Do you really think so?"

"You're damn tootin' it is," Ted said. "We're gonna be so rich. We're gonna knock Broadway right on its can," and he moved in on the hugging act.

"See you tomorrow," I said, and Irene and I finally got out.

"You guys got any more Coke?" Al's voice came over the transom.

"*I* don't think he's going to say a *word* to Hackett," Ilanova said. "I think he's *scared* of Hackett. That's what I like about you, Sam, *you're* not scared of him, are you?"

"Certainly not," Sam said. "Don't be silly."

"Get that Ilanova," Irene said.

"Yeah," I said. "Do *you* think the second half of the second act is lousy?"

"Darling, don't worry about those things now. Sam and Ted are just excited. All there is to do now is wait until we open. Leave it to Hackett."

Pretty soon we got to her room.

"How about it?" I said, while she was hunting for her key.

"I'm dead, Jack," she said.

"Just for a minute or two? Christ I'm dead too. I'm no menace to anybody's virtue tonight."

"No you better not," she said.

"But I *want* to," I said. "I want to *talk* to you."

"You run along," she said. "You have to work, remember?"

"Irene, I'm sorry I told you you smoked too much. I didn't mean it. I mean it was pretty rude."

"Jack, baby, sometimes you get the most woebegone look on your face."

"I guess this is kinda silly," I said. "I mean standing in the hall like this."

So I kissed her good night. But nothing came of it.

Chapter 23

> *In selecting a store building for a motion picture theater it should be remembered that the ceiling should be high enough to accommodate the operator's booth over the entrance and still leave head room enough so that the audience can enter without stooping.*
>
> — MOTION PICTURE MAKING AND EXHIBITING

ALTHOUGH I mooned about Irene I was in no condition for the romantic bit. I wasn't getting any sleep, wasn't eating enough; I was smoking too much, and worried that I wasn't doing my part.

I had an awful night, arose at 8:30 and concocted a completely phony new Scene Five. It stunk. I read it aloud and groaned, it was so terrible. So I sat down again and racked my aching head for an idea. Writing had become utter torture to me. Even the simplest ideas eluded me. My mind was sliding off into crazy sloughs of idiocy: a long forgotten conversation with Cousin Archie, Ty Cobb's all-time batting average.

Until finally Zeus sent a thunderbolt down and conked me on the head with it and I had a good workable idea. It was 10:15 and the call was for 11 A.M. I pulled myself together and wrote it all down, oh it was going lovely, such nice dialogue, such a clever idea. I was saved. Hackett couldn't help but like it.

I rushed to the theater. Hackett had all the principals in the lobby.

"Here," I said, handing my pages to him. "Maybe we can use this."

"Ah words, words, that's what we like to see," and he put on his glasses and read it while everybody stood around.

He read it through and handed it back to me.

"I don't think that's just what we want, Jack," he said. "Anyway, I already rewrote that."

I remember reading someplace about some kid who drew a picture of a horse. He worked hard on it and he was mighty proud of it. It was the most beautiful horse in the world. He took it to his old man and said, "Look at the horse I drew." He looked at it and said, "Uh-huh. Well, you're on the wrong track, that doesn't look like a horse. Here — I'll show you how to draw a horse." So the kid went away and cried because his horse was no good.

I'm a big boy now and it doesn't get you noplace to cry and anyway what would all the actors standing around think if I busted out crying?

"Jimmy," Hackett said, "have you got a copy of that new stuff for Jack? Give him his copy."

Jimmy handed me two typewritten sheets and I sat down and read them while Hackett got started with the cast, "giving notes."

I didn't like his stuff any better than mine, really. His idea was better but his dialogue was worse.

"What do you think?" he said.

"I think it's okay," I said.

"If you can brighten up the dialogue go to it," he said.

"I'll see what I can do," I said.

That's one thing about Hackett, he's not proud. If you can improve his stuff it's okay with him. But you have to show him it's really better, not just different. Once in a while, though, like all writers, he'd fall in love with some terrible line and I couldn't blast it out of the script no matter what. But the theater is a funny area. He had one line that used to make me cringe every time we came to it. Man, it was embarrassing I mean. It stayed in and when we played for an audience it rocked the house. Just crazy, no sense to it. Meantime a real hot line *I* was in love with played to an utter, dead silence. It was such a funny line in rehearsals it broke everybody up. When we played it — Nothing.

"Now you tell him about the second act at lunch," Sam said.

"Oh hell," I said. "Now? Why not wait till after the dress rehearsal?"

"Listen, tell him *now*, so he'll start thinking about it."

Sam and Ted and Hackett and I had lunch together around the corner at Ceriani's. I had two Martinis to loosen my tongue and build up my manhood. We ate a lot of antipasto and spaghetti but I couldn't get into the subject. Sam kicked me a couple times and kept making eyes at me. Finally he couldn't stand it.

"Jack, tell Mr. Hackett what you were telling us last night. I mean about the second act."

"*I* was telling *you*?" I said.

"What was it, Jack?" Hackett said.

"I thought it was very sound," Ted said.

"It wasn't really anything, nothing to worry about *now,* I mean," I said.

"Now is exactly the time to worry about everything," Hackett said. "What's bothering you?"

"It's the second act," I said. "The last half and the finale. The motivation seems a little weak."

"Motivation?" Hackett said. "Where do you get words like that? You sound like that crazy Ilanova. Anyway, the motivation is just the same as it's always been. It's all perfectly clear."

"In the first draft we had a sort of a wonderful quality that seems to have got lost someplace along the line," I said.

"I don't know what you mean by that," Hackett said. "What quality?"

"I think I know what Jack means," Sam said. "Did you feel it, Ted?"

"Yes, I did," Ted said.

"That's all too vague, much too vague," Hackett said.

"In the night club scene," I said, "Irene gets lost. In fact she's lost for two scenes. Just when the audience gets all interested in her she disappears for two scenes."

"That's what I mean," Sam said, beaming at me.

"But how are we going to change that?" Hackett said. "Both those scenes are vital to the plot development. And she can't possibly be in them. No, boys, we'll have to sink or swim with what we've got."

"Well, there's something wrong with the second act," Ted said. "It bothers me."

"I don't agree," Hackett said. "I wonder what kind of pie they have here."

So that was the end of that. Two weeks later, in Boston, we rewrote three scenes in the second act and moved one scene into the first act.

That afternoon Sam took me over to the orchestra rehearsal at the Eagles Hall. De Marco was up front with his sleeves rolled up and his tie loose talking a strange language:

"I *must* have that rim-shot on bar seventy."

"Stanley, in thirty-five, thirty-seven, and thirty-nine, don't play those afterbeats."

"Take the cowbell and the woodblock out. And I also want you to play your part."

"The *fermata* is out."

"*Tempo primo* for the vamp again is what it amounts to."

"*Tacet* please for me from sixty-four through seventy-nine."

"And kill the castanets."

"Take the *fermata* off the third beat."

"Cello stay out of bar twenty, please."

"All right, everybody play this very legitimately and watch me for the dynamics."

After hearing the numbers with a rehearsal piano for weeks it was beautiful to hear the orchestra. It was like hearing the music for the first time. I think it was the most exciting thing I ever heard.

On the way back to the hotel I met Rudy Lorraine.

"I was just over at the orchestra," I said. "Boy it sounds terrific."

"We need at least eight more pieces in that band. We've got no sound at all. Goddamn cheapskates."

"It sounded okay to me," I said.

"It's lousy," he said. "Goddamn cheap outfit."

"Aw come on, cheer up, will you?" I said. "Every time I get steamed up around here somebody dumps the grates. Now cut it out, will you? The music sounds great. You're a great composer!"

So we walked along together and after a while we got to the theater and we stood under the marquee looking at the cards.

"You said something back there," Rudy said.

"What did I say?"

"About me being a 'great composer,'" he said. "Do you really think so?"

He says these things with complete lack of self-consciousness.

"Why sure, Rudy," I said. "I think your stuff is wonderful."

"I guess I am pretty great," he said, staring dreamily upwards.

That night we had dress rehearsal. We were all excited and Sam and Ted each had three Martinis before dinner and Hackett had a double brandy and soda.

I knew because I was in the next booth to them, with Irene, and I was trying to be lovesick and attentive but it was very difficult because I was trying to hear what Hackett was saying all the time.

"Look," Irene said. "Why bother with the sweet talk? I'll tell you what. I'll eat, you listen to Hackett and the boys."

"How's your voice feel?" I said. "Are you nervous? Don't you want a drink?"

"I'm all right. It's only the dress rehearsal. How do *you* feel, honey?"

"I wish we were back in New York," I said. "Under the canary cage. I don't like the road much, I guess."

"If you were happy you wouldn't be a writer," she said. "When you're down, then I know you're a writer. The further down you get, then I know you're really a great writer."

"Yeah. I guess I am pretty great," I said. "But do you know why I like you so much?"

"You tell me."

"Because you're the only person in the entire world that when I start to roll a cigarette *doesn't* say: 'Can you do that with one hand?' You don't know what it means to me, honey. Not once. You never said it even once."

"You don't want to be back in New York," she said. "You hate New York."

"That's true," I said.

"And you didn't like it out in Indiana."

"No."

"And you don't like Connecticut."

"That's right."

"You're in a hell of a way, Author," she said, "aren't you?"

"Yes," I said. "I'm in a bad way."

At the theater I went over to Left Center and sat by myself in Row E for the dress rehearsal. The Overture sounded great and I had lump-in-throat, watering eyes, and chills up and down the spine. For the remainder of the evening, though, I just had the chills. Things seemed to go slowly downhill all the way. I slumped out to the lobby at the intermission for a drink of water.

The Choreographer was there in a suéde leather suit and Greek peasant shoes.

"Looks good, doesn't it?" he said. "Say, what do you think of Ronald Firbank?"

"I don't think of him at all," I said. "You really thought the show looks good?"

"I thought the dances were fine," he said.

"But what about the book?"

"Oh, I wouldn't know anything about that," he said. "You mean you've never read any Ronald Firbank?"

Sam and Ted were over in a corner having a private talk and a lot of head shaking with Hackett and Harry Paige.

I went in again and sat down away off by myself and the second act began to creak away. After a while Rudy Lorraine came over and sat with me.

"What a turkey this is going to be," he whispered. "Hackett's lost the old touch. Look at the staging of my numbers.

Strictly from Ziegfeld. Listen to the orchestra, it needs ten more pieces at the very minimum. Damn cheapskate outfit. Look at the scenery. They tried to save money on the scenery and look at it."

"Oh, be quiet," I said.

"I tried to get 'em to use Mooch Minchin for the orchestrations but oh no, 'He's too expensive,' so they take this bum Schlussel — and listen to the sounds coming out of the pit."

"What are you always kicking about?" I said. "My god, we're getting a break working on this show."

"A *break! Who's* getting a break? Man, you've got that backwards. *I'm* giving *them* a break. Where the hell would this show be without my music?"

"I don't even know where it is *with* your music," I said.

"And the way Sam is always sucking around Hackett. It's just disgusting."

"Aw shut up, Rudy," I said. "Give us a rest, will you?"

Irene and Rex went into their reprise of the love song. When I looked at her up there, I couldn't believe that this divinity from some other world was anyone I knew on earth.

"Say," Rudy said. "What goes on with you and Lovelle? You getting any? Mmm, look at that! Isn't she something? Ooooooh, would I ever like to —— —— —— and —— —— —— —— and —— —— —— and —— —— —— —— and —— —— her!"

"Say, you're a regular cannibal," I said.

"I think Rex's voice is going," he said. "It'll never last till New York."

One of the major problems of being in New Haven with Hackett is waffles. He is always wanting to go to this waffle joint across the street and have some waffles swimming in butter and imitation maple syrup and talk things over in a sticky booth where you have to keep your elbows at your sides and do all the cutting with your wrists. So that's what we did after the dress rehearsal. To make it worse, Ted had a jelly doughnut. The jelly kept oozing all over. Who says show business isn't a tough life?

When I got up to the room I looked at Yale for a while but there was nothing doing. That's a dead bunch of boys, they are never dropping bags of water out the windows or burning Julius Caesar in effigy or anything.

So I called up Frankie.

"Jack," she said, "how are you making it? How's it going?"

"Well, we had a dress rehearsal tonight," I said.

"How does it look?" she said.

"It looks like that operetta you were in in high school," I said. "Only not as funny."

Chapter 24

> *It is also said of me that I now and then contradict myself. Yes, I improve wonderfully as time goes on.*
>
> — GEORGE JEAN NATHAN

Frankie came up to New Haven for opening night. She had spent a week's royalties on clothes and a hair-do and looked great. You'd never think to look at her that she came off a farm in Nebraska. She's a jet-black brunette with beautiful white skin and blue eyes. I like to walk down the street with Frankie and see them stare, because she's a real looker.

"There's my girl," Ted said, when we got to the theater after an enormous dinner and too many cocktails. And he went into the hugging bit. "Oh, if I were only a few years younger," he said.

"You look pretty good right now," Frankie said. "Let's shake Jack and go down to Atlantic City for the week end."

"Say, that place would never be the same," he said.

"Hello, Sam," Frankie said.

"Hello, you doll," Sam said. "Are you excited?" and he kissed her.

"What have you boys been doing to Jack?" she said.

"The poor boy is a big bundle of nerves. Or has he got some cute chorus girl wearing him down?"

Ted had a coughing spell and then Harry Paige came in escorting Jayne Marchal, the star of his latest movie, so we all exchanged some idiotic conversation and the crowd tried not to stare and stared all the harder.

"Who's that she's with?" says one matron in furs.

"Rex Harrison," said her chum.

"Well, Harry," I said, "I see you've got on a white shirt."

I went downstairs to the men's room and was sick.

We went in and sat down and looked at all the people and I read my name over a hundred times on my program. Then De Marco got up in front of the band and raised his arms.

"Well here we go," I said.

"Oh, Jack," Frankie said and reached for my hand.

I have been a writer for quite a while and have had some big moments; like when I sold my first piece, and when I got the telegram about the Book Club selection. And a lot of others. But there is no thrill for a writer like hearing those lines spoken in front of an audience. Three minutes after the show started Al St. James opened his mouth and spoke some lines that I had written and the audience roared. All the sweat is worth it, believe me. I felt like Hillary and Tenzing at the top of that big hill.

I leaned over to Frankie.

"I wrote that," I said, when I could talk.

When you write books you write them all alone in a hole someplace, and the people who read them might as well be on Mars. In the theater you can hear them laugh and see them being moved by your words. There's no feeling in the world so strange as watching an audience ride along with a play that you have written.

"I'm going crazy, honey," I said to Frankie.

"So am I," she said. "Isn't it insane?"

Everything went off pretty well in the first act, except Ilanova stopped the show with a little dance bit in one that we hadn't paid too much attention to. They really howled.

"I don't get it," I said to Frankie.

"What's the matter?" she said.

"We just put that in last week instead of a talking cross-over," I said. "She wasn't supposed to get anything on it."

We ran into Sam in the crush going up the aisle at the intermission.

"Circulate around," he said. "See what they're saying."

"I need a drink," I said. "I'm going over to Kaysey's."

"No, no," he said. "Circulate around. Get the audience reaction. Plenty of time for a drink after the show. Big party in Harry Paige's suite."

So Frankie and I circulated around. There was a lot of mink from New York up for the evening, and a lot of the boys in the know, as well as Governor Lodge and a couple of movie moguls.

"Keep your ears peeled now, honey," I said, lighting Frankie a cigarette.

"I think it's just terrible," said a cultured female voice behind me.

"But isn't there a chance . . . ?" said another.

"Darling, not a chance in the world. The whole thing's a complete mess."

"Well, it's simply a tragedy, that's all. And after everybody tried so hard. Are you absolutely certain?"

"My dear, Madge called me this morning. She's off to Reno. The children have gone to stay with her mother in White Plains and Kenneth is at the Harvard Club. It's all over."

"Poor old Madge," I said to Frankie, and we wedged over another ten feet.

"They never should have cast her in the part in the first place," a man said. "I told Sam that right at the beginning."

"She certainly didn't project," said a fellow with a pipe.

"But what could she *do?*" said a woman with a stole. "What could she do with material like that?"

"Yes," said the pipe. "The script was certainly weak."

"Weak?" said the first guy. "It stank to heaven."

"They opened at the State-Lake in Chicago, played it three days and yanked it and put in a cowboy picture to fill out the week."

"Well you know how Sam Rogers is, stubborn as hell."

"I'm getting a lot of swell nuggets here," I said. "Come on, little mother," and we squeezed along the side of the lobby to the foot of the stairs and I planted myself back to back with a couple of smart-looking big-town girls.

"I think it's *simply* divine."

"I *simply* adore it."

"Hey, get that," I said.

"Where on *earth* did you find it?"

"At that *marv*elous little place I was telling you about on 64th Street."

The lights blinked and the crowd began to get back inside, but we waited.

Rudy Lorraine spotted me and came over.

"I told you," he said. "I told you." He glared fiercely, popping his eyes, and rushed for the door, bumping into an usher and nearly knocking him down.

Hackett was leaning against the pillar talking to Harry Paige. Harry was doing a lot of talking. I went over.

". . . and I think we should start looking around for a

replacement right now before we get into any worse trouble," Harry was saying.

"We'll see, we'll see," Hackett said. "Hello, Jack. How do you like hearing your immortal words before an audience?"

"Damn weird sensation," I said.

"We'll be all right," he said.

The second act started out fast and fine.

"Hackett says we'll be all right," I said to Frankie. "Man he's a cool one."

"How can he *tell?*" she whispered.

"I hope Kenneth is getting along okay at the Harvard Club," I said.

But in Scene Two the scenery got stuck and from then on things got worse. Al St. James forgot a quarter of his lines, the aged character actor failed to appear at all in his big one-line crossover, and Mrs. Fondemeyer had to cover it, the orchestra played the underscoring so loud in the tender love scene that the dialogue was lost, Irene failed to make the quick-change in Scene Five and there was a thirty-second stage wait; the jokes went sour, Rex Ives was way down, and the big dynamic night club ballet never got off the ground at all. Worst of all, the book dragged. The whole thing was permeated with a certain terrible quality.

The audience gave us a big hand, though, and a lot of curtain calls and all that, but it all added up to nothing. There were so many friends, relatives, and backers in the audience that applause didn't mean a thing. Rex and Irene took their curtain calls in their costumes from the preceding scene, he in his swim trunks and she in her bathing suit, and when she stepped forward they screamed and whistled.

"Jack, listen to them. It must be a hit," Frankie said.

"Pay no attention to all that," I said. "An audience like this always overdoes it. Doesn't mean a thing."

After the audience got out of the house they raised the curtain and there was a crowd milling around up on stage so we went over to the side and through the door and up to the stage too. The place was swarming with backers of the show; that's what they put money in shows for, so they can go up on the stage after the show in New Haven or Boston and tell the management what's wrong. And everybody's agent is there, and two tall men from *Life,* and eighteen Yale boys talking to each other and pretending they are important characters from the big city.

"Well it certainly wasn't Cole Porter," says one.

"No, it certainly wasn't Cole," says another, sucking on a briar pipe in a very manly way.

"Or Harold Arlen, for that matter."

"No, it certainly wasn't Harold Arlen."

And everybody involved in the show, from the wardrobe mistress up, has a mother and father up there wanting to say it's the greatest show they've ever seen (the last show they saw was Lew Leslie's *Blackbirds*). And some cousins from Kansas City who happened to be in New York on business "saw it in the paper" and have come up to say hello and that they think it's a real nice show if you're broadminded.

Sam introduced me to a Mr. Pfalz, or Falls, or False, or maybe Walsh.

"Congratulations," he said. "It's a sure hit. Don't worry about the lyrics, they're not as bad as they seem at first — maybe. As for the scenery, well, it's a shame but you can do a lot with repainting. Too bad about Al St. James, guess he's had his day. Grand comedian — once. You won't have any trouble replacing him though. Frankly, I see Jerry Lewis in that part."

"And Dean Martin in the Rex Ives part," I said. "Say, that's not bad."

"Breathe it to Hackett," he said. "I'll bet he'll buy it," and he winked solemnly and turned away.

"I'll do that," I said.

"Frankly," Frankie said, "I see Bebe Daniels in the Irene Lovelle part."

"I'll buy that," I said. "Breathe it to Hackett, honey."

"No, you breathe it," she said.

Mrs. Fondemeyer appeared, with a skinny youth in tow. He had on one of Robert Hall's finest two-tone leisure coats.

"Mr. Jordan, my nephew is just dying to meet you, you don't mind, do you? It'll give him such a thrill. Ronald, this is Mr. Jordan. He wrote the show."

"Gee whiz, I know that much," he said, shaking hands.

"This is Mrs. Jordan," I said and they shook hands with Frankie.

"I guess you must be an actress," Ronald said.

"Well, I'm at liberty right now," Frankie said.

"Mr. Jordan," Ronald said, "do you get your ideas from real life or . . ."

"Now, Ronald, don't pester Mr. Jordan. Come along, now," Mrs. Fondemeyer said, and dragged him away.

"Doggone it, Aunt Louise, all I was doing was just asting him a simple question," Ronald said. "How can I learn to be a writer unless I just ast a few simple questions once in a while?"

The crowd thinned out after a while and Hackett got the cast on stage and gave them a little fatherly talk and told them he was satisfied and that anybody that had goofed knew it anyway and he wasn't going to dwell on it tonight. And he called rehearsal for 11 A.M. and told them not to

stay up all night carousing because there was plenty of work
to do. And he told them to go to bed.

Everybody went away and the rest of us talked about all
the things that needed to be done and we all disagreed and
got into an argument and Hackett said to knock it off, we
would sleep on it and meet at 10 A.M. in his room. So we all
got our coats, wives and girl friends and left. As I was going out the door I turned and looked back into the empty
theater, and the Choreographer was up on stage under the
work lights with two of the girls planning out a new routine.
It was quarter to one.

"I hope he puts a safety repeat on that intro," I said.

"What's that mean?" Frankie said.

"How would I know?" I said. "It's just something he said
to De Marco once."

"Ah, what an ear!" Frankie said.

That ball we were all supposed to have in New Haven
was taking place up in Harry Paige's suite. All of the
principals from the show were there, and all the rest of us,
and some of the backers, who were shivering with the
thrill of it all, although it was hard to shiver because the
temperature was around 110° and the room was filled with
smoke.

Harry had a photographer there and he was taking one
million pictures of Jayne Marchal. She had to keep putting
her highball down on a window sill every time they took
another shot, so it wouldn't show in the picture.

Harry introduced Frankie and me to a Mr. Krauss with
steel-rimmed spectacles and Mr. Krauss told me that Harry
certainly was an operator and you never knew which way he
was going to move. You had to keep a close eye on Harry
because he moved mighty fast. When Harry had formed

Paige Intercoastal Transport the bankers had shaken their heads but that didn't faze Harry a bit. And he had proved they were wrong because Paige Intercoastal Transport was on solid ground. Harry always put things on solid ground, that was what he liked about Harry's projects. And another thing about Harry was his loyalty. Harry was mighty loyal. If you kept your nose clean Harry would take care of you. And he never forgot a friend. Picture business was getting to be a rat-race these days and you never knew where you stood with most of them, but with Harry you were on solid ground. With Harry you were all right.

Behind me, leaning against the wall, a young man in a Shetland jacket was talking to Sam Snow.

"I guess I'm talking too much but you want my honest criticism don't you? I mean this is strictly a business proposition. Listen, Sam, I'm in the eighth row and I can't even *hear* half the lines," he said.

"I know, I know. The orchestra was terrible," Sam said. "The underscoring was much too loud. We know it. We'll fix it. I already spoke to Mr. Hackett about it."

"I thought the book was okay. Let's say serviceable. I did feel though, *very strongly,* and so did Jean . . ."

"Now keep Jean out of it, Bruce, I don't give a damn what Jean thought," Sam said. "And I'm just drunk enough to tell you I don't think Jean knows a good show from soap opera."

"Okay, okay, so maybe she doesn't. We'll start over. *I* felt very strongly that you should build the love story sooner, and cut down on the funny stuff between Chuck and the other girl, the one that does that eccentric number. As for the Mrs. Fondemeyer stuff, I'm sorry but it left me cold. If I were you I'd cut the part completely. Throw it clear out and forget it."

"In other words you liked the book fine except it's lousy," Sam said.

Frankie got caught in an eddy in the current and was swept over to where Hackett and Ted were talking to a woman in a gold dress with earrings as big as silver dollars.

Irene's agent grabbed me by the arm, spilling my highball, and said he wanted to talk to me privately and propelled me to the bathroom. Somebody else was in there talking privately so we went to the bedroom. There were three different private talks going on in there. So we had our private talk in the hall where there were two more private talks being held.

"Listen, Jack," he said, "you got to get Irene on sooner. Hell, half of the first act is over before we even *see* her. Couldn't that duet . . ."

"We *can't* get her on any sooner," I said.

"Couldn't that duet between Irene and Rex be shoved up to the first scene? It should *open* the show, actually."

"Now, Morty, listen for God's sake," I said. "Talk sense. The whole story is built around her meeting with Rex in the third scene. So how in the hell can she come on after the curtain goes up and start singing a duet with him?"

"Well I don't mean the same song. Lorraine can write a new song for the opener, can't he?"

"Sure he can. Go tell Hackett. Go tell somebody else."

I went back inside and ran into Irene.

"Baby, you were terrific," I said. "How did it feel?"

"It felt pretty terrible," she said.

"But you were great. Really great. Hasn't everybody told you so?"

"Your wife told me so," she said.

"You met Frankie, hey? How'd you girls get along?"

"She's a doll, Jack."

"Everybody's a doll," I said.

"You never told me anything about her," she said.

"Such as what?"

"She's a real person, Jack. A real, live, honest-to-God person. They're hard to find, as the song says."

"Yep," I said. "Frankie's okay."

"You never told me she used to be in show business, either."

"Say, you kids had quite a talk. Well, she wasn't really in show business. She used to sing around those night clubs in the Middle West. You know, one week a year at the Blackhawk or the Sherman and the other fifty-one in Peoria."

"That's the hard way and the long way. Say, what was Morty yakking at you about?"

"He wants you and Rex to open the show with the duet," I said.

"I told him to keep out of it. I think I'll get rid of that silly jerk. First thing you know he'll go to Hackett with that crap and queer me good."

"Everybody's re-writing the show tonight," I said. "Everybody except the writers."

"Jack, honey, go and find him before he gets to Hackett. Tell him to lay off."

"Here she is," Harry Paige said. "Come on, darling. We want a shot of you and Jayne chumming it up."

"What a thrill," Irene said. "My big moment."

They went in and started taking pictures and I looked for Morty.

I found him in the bedroom sitting on the bed talking to Mr. Krauss.

"Naturally we were afraid of TV at first," Krauss said.

"There's room for everybody," Morty said.

"But we met the challenge," Krauss said.

"All we need now is some pictures the public wants to see," Morty said. "Pictures Are Worse Than Ever."

"Hey, Morty," I said. "Listen, you know what we were talking about out in the hall? Talk it over with Sam or Ted. Don't say anything to Hackett."

"You been talking to Irene?"

"Take it from me the worst thing you could do is go to Hackett now. Wait and see how things work out. Wait till Boston."

Sam and Ted and Harry Paige came in and they were all red in the face and mad.

"I just don't approve, that's all, Harry," Sam said. "I just think it's a hell of a lousy trick."

"Why, I'm amazed. Simply amazed. It's just publicity. Damn good publicity," Harry said.

"Harry, what the hell are we promoting, anyway, your movie or our show?" Ted said.

"Both, for godsake," Harry shouted.

"Keep it down, keep it down," Sam said.

"Say, would you fellows mind clearing out for a few minutes?" Ted said.

We went out and they shut the door.

"Mr. Snow and Mr. Crosby don't understand Harry's *modus operandi*," Mr. Krauss said.

"I can see that," Morty said.

Shows Out of Town

The Girl from Indiana

New Haven, Feb. 8.

Paige Crosby and Snow Musical Production in two acts (22 scenes). Book, Richard Hackett and Jack Jordan, adaptation of Mr. Jordan's novel, *Down Home*. Music by Rudy Lorraine. Staged by Richard Hackett. Co-stars Irene Lovelle, Rex Ives, and Al St. James. Setting, lighting and costumes, Telesco; orchestrations, Bernie Schlussel; musical director, Vincent De Marco; dances and musical numbers staged by Frederic Shaw. At Shubert, New Haven, Feb. 8, '54; $5.50 top.

Susie .... Irene Lovelle

. . .

New producing firm of Paige, Crosby and Snow has enlisted Richard Hackett to direct their first offering, another bucolic saga of love in the stix. Script, involving small-town girl, played by Irene Lovelle, and city slicker Rex Ives, isn't a compeller in its present form. Musical score by pop-composer Rudy Lorraine is far from inspired and cries for a socko earbender or two. Lyrics stick to familiar patterns. Preem audience at Monday night's opener fidgeted through overlong second act which is filled with extraneous material and numbers which fail to click. Terp segment could stand drastic telescoping, and an overelaborate "Dance to the Moon" number should be returned to the trunk. Scripters have doled out meager fare to veteran comic Al St. James. A torrid routine by newcomer Sonia Ilanova provides only real lift and pew holders begged for more. Master builder Hackett has rough four weeks ahead of him in all departments to bring this one in for Broadway acceptance.

First act gets off to slow start with . . .

Chapter 25

BOSTON: FIRST STANZA

IN BOSTON it was raining. Raining on Stuart Street where the sailors from Charlestown stood looking in the display windows at the TV sets with the giant screens, raining on the cobblestones along Atlantic Avenue as the ships slid silently out to sea, bound for far-off Cathay and Newport News. And raining on the uneven sidewalks in front of the frame apartment houses in Dorchester, Everett, and Chelsea, where all the sad secrets of life are spelled out with a smudged forefinger on the flowered wallpaper, behind the lace curtains.

I SHOT HIM — MALDEN HOUSEWIFE

It even rained on a Coolidge and a Saltonstall, and on two members of the Somerset Club as they umbrellaed their way down Beacon Street toward Charles. It rained also on the doorman at the Ritz, and on the dwarf selling papers by the Park Street subway station.

"MALDENMURDER! READ IT!"

Puddles were forming in Harvard Square. Wiggly wetness trickled down the glass at Leavitt and Pierce. Radcliffe girls splashed their way to Liggett's.

HARVARD GETS $10,000,000,000,000.00

The field at Fenway Park was sodden.

RED SOX SIGN PLOTSKI

President Pusey spoke a few warm words of welcome. Hasty Pudding voted him in.

"Plotski is another Honus Wagner" — *Record*.
"Plotski is another Ty Cobb" — *American*.
"Plotski is another Rabbit Maranville" — *Post*.
"Plotski is another Red Grange" — *Globe*.
"Plotski is another Ralph Waldo Emerson" — *Herald*.

Plotski sent to minors in July.

The Hub populace, flat-faced, dressed in holiday attire from Raymond's, shuffled down Tremont Street lost in dreams of Irish glory.

MANHOLE COVER BLOWS OFF — SOUTH BOSTON TOT INJURED

"I'll have the souvlakia," Hackett said.

"Just a plate of soup. Gimme that vegetable soup," Ted said.

"I want that stuff with the vine leaves," Sam said.

"No vine leafs today, sir," said the waiter. "Maybe tomorrow we have vine leafs. Nice lamb chop, sir?"

"Okay. Nice lamb chop," Sam said.

"Souvlakia," I said. "And two sidecars."

That night we opened. In the rain.

THE THEATER
By Chauncey Crabbe

Boston's newest musical comedy, *The Girl from Indiana*, arrived in town last night at the Shubert Theater. The per-

formance resembled wet firecrackers. There were fitful and
infrequent explosions of wit and gaiety in the course of the
long, long evening, but in between, the show fizzled along,
threatening at times to go out entirely.

The libretto, fashioned by the indefatigable Richard
Hackett in cahoots with one Jack Jordan, is a compendium
of theatrical clichés. The dusty script tells of life and love in
a small town in Indiana, a state henceforth to be avoided like
the Black Death. Struggling in the lead role is Irene Lovelle,
whose agent should be shot at sunrise for involving her
in this tawdry enterprise. Boston audiences who have ap-
plauded her brilliant style in the past will squirm with em-
barrassment as she fights her way through a jungle of impossible situations and trite lyrics.

The tedious score, by Rudy Lorraine, king of the jukebox
trade, a man who is personally responsible for the recent
public-torture scheme called "Chief of Love," maintains an
even level of banality. One can scarcely imagine what the
new producing team of Paige, Crosby and Snow could have
had in mind when they hired Mr. Lorraine to write a full
musical score.

Rex Ives, the man with the big chest, big muscles, and
big voice, goes through his chores with a creditable willing-
ness, but the charm of his past performances is not quite
here. Only in "Say, Darling," a love ballad, does he have a
chance to show a *soupçon* of either his acting ability or his
voice.

Al St. James, a casual comedian who deserves better things,
wanders on and off stage, seemingly puzzled by the pro-
ceedings. He has a few good moments in a comic ballet. He
has many more bad moments.

The story revolves around the love affair of a small-town
girl and a city slicker, hardly a novel theme. The lovers are
surrounded by an enormous and professional cast of support-
ing actors, most of whose identity and purpose are not quite
clear.

Relieving the general monotony much too seldom is a
zany youngster, Sonia Ilanova, whose lines are unintelligi-
ble but who dances with a wild and beautiful frenzy. We

must watch this pixie, she seems destined for wonderful things. She is pure delight.

Miss Ilanova, however, is hardly capable alone of lifting matters out of the doldrums. Mr. Hackett, we expect better things of you, sir.

"We're dead," Sam said.

"Gawd Almighty," Ted said.

"Crabbe panned *South Pacific*," Hackett said. "Just relax, boys."

"Wait until Irene sees this," Sam said.

"She's gone," Harry said. "She'll be in New York by noon. She's packing right now."

"Aw hell no, Harry," I said. "Irene's not like that."

"Like what?" Ted said. "Any actress is 'like that.' She gets slaughtered and some kid just out of the chorus gets a rave? Chauncey, you bastard. I wouldn't blame Irene if she did walk."

"Well, the other reviews weren't so bad," Sam said.

"They weren't good," Harry said.

"No, they weren't good," Hackett said.

"How about that 'dusty script'?" I said. "Get that."

"I wonder if the show *is* possibly lousy," Sam said.

"No," Hackett said. "We'll be all right."

"I don't see how we're 'all right,'" Harry said. "Looks like we're all wrong. Ask me we need somebody to punch some laughs into the script. The audience is sitting there like they were at a goddamn wake. You guys think I'm nuts, but what we need is a gag man. Loosen things up. Get a few boffs in there."

"Harry," Sam said. "Not now, Harry. I've had it. Don't tell me about the gag man. I just can't take it."

"You think we need some boffs in there, Harry?" Hackett said.

"Dick, I've got a lot of money riding on this show," Harry said. "When I read a notice like this crazy Crabbe guy, I'm worried. Notices like that just about wrecked my last picture. ' "A cinemistake" — *Time* magazine.' That funny crack cost us about two million at the gates."

"Maybe the picture was no good, Harry," Hackett said.

"A real stinker," Harry said. "That's just what I mean."

"Okay," Hackett said. "Jack, you've got a new job."

"Nothing simple, I hope," I said.

"You're our new gag writer," he said. "Get the script out and loosen it up."

"Loosen it up?"

"Yes. Punch some boffs in there."

I had an enormous suite at the Touraine with three big windows looking out over historic Boston Common. The furniture was Vilma Banky modern. I like the Touraine because of those big marble washbasins. Everybody else stayed there because it was near the theater.

I called Irene and asked her to come on up. Then I called Room Service.

While I waited I stood looking out the window at the cars going up and down Tremont and tried various new blackout lines for the second scene. We had already tried four and none of them worked. Everybody except the wardrobe mistress had passed me suggestions written on little scraps of paper.

The bellhop brought in the tray.

"Well, now you got Plotski," I said while I signed.

"That won't make no difference," he said. "He's all burnt-out. By the time Boston gets 'em they already had their usefulness."

"He had a hell of a season with Cleveland," I said.

"He won't have no hell of a season with Boston. None of 'em do. Don't matter whether it's baseball or what it is, this lousy town makes a wreck out of any man."

"Say, you're a real booster," I said.

"Well sir, take a look at it," he said. "Just look out the window at it."

He went away and I made a drink and walked around trying lines out loud. I felt a little dizzy and worn down. Maybe it was true, Plotski and I would go down together, swinging. Me in February, Plotski in July.

Irene came in. She had on her leopard coat.

"This lousy goddamn town," she said, throwing the cat over a chair. "Why the hell didn't we go to Philadelphia in the first place?"

"Hackett likes Boston," I said.

"Yeah, he likes the show, too. But nobody else does."

"Now listen, honey, here, have a drink and cool down. Those reviews weren't bad. Except dear old Chauncey."

"A name like that. Big Back Bay fruit. I bet he went to Groton or one of those fakeout places where they play cricket."

Her drink was gone already. I fixed it up.

"Well, Golden Boy," she said. "It's all your fault. Indiana wasn't good enough for you, you had to write a book and come to New York."

"Yeah, I wrote it," I said.

"Some book. Some show," she said. " 'A compendium of theatrical clichés.' "

" 'By indefatigable Richard Hackett in cahoots with one Jack Jordan.' " I said. "Listen, what are you gonna do?"

"Have another drink," she said. "What are you going to do, one Jack Jordan?"

"Well, that's two in four minutes. You'll be flying in a minute."

"I'm flying already. I had a couple down in my room. I feel lousy, Author, and I'm washing those blues away with that good old White Label."

"You better take it easy, sport," I said. "We have a lot of work, new lines and everything. I hear two new songs are going in."

"Well good luck to you, Mr. Lorraine," she said. "You self-inflated idiot. Write a couple of good ones. Get out your rhyming dictionary. Quit admiring yourself in the mirror and sit down at the eighty-eight and get started. Forget about the payola and brother Mitch and Make Believe Ballroom and grind, boy, grind. Jack, turn off that damn radio, it reminds me of Lorraine."

I got up and went over and turned it off. In the last second before it snapped off the disk jockey said: ". . . by Rudy Lorraine."

"What the hell!" I said, and quick turned it on again.

". . . my sleeper of the week," he said, "from the new musical now on the road, *The Girl from Indiana*. It's called 'Say, Darling' and I'm going right out on that well-known limb and predict that it'll be right up there near the top. And here it is: 'Say, Darling.' "

"Hey, get that," I said. "From the new musical now on . . ."

"Who is that, Clooney?" Irene said.

"Hey, Rudy," I said. "You self-inflated idiot."

Irene got up and came over to the radio and we stood there listening.

"That girl is good," Irene said.

"That song is good," I said. "How do you like them onions, Chauncey old fruit?" And Irene and I danced around the room, with the business like when she did it on the stage with Rex. At the end of the song they go into a kiss and then he picks her up and carries her off to the hay for the blackout. So I did the same, and carried her in and laid her down on the bed. Then I leaned over and kissed her again but she pushed me away.

"I'm still mad," she said.

"You don't look mad," I said. "You look beautiful, Irene. Like Hackett says, you're not only beautiful from out front, you're beautiful all the time."

"When did he say that? You're just making that up."

"In the lobby of the Shubert in New Haven last Friday night at 10:15 P.M."

"What else did he say?"

"He said he liked to work with you because you had an instinctive grasp of the material."

"Richard Hackett said *that*?"

"He sure did."

"Tell me some more."

"Okay. I think I better lie down beside you so I won't have to shout."

"Turn off the light," she said. "It hurts my eyes."

Three minutes later Sam Snow was pounding on the door and we all had to sit around cussing Crabbe for an hour and then we went over to Steuben's and had coffee so as to make sure we would have a good night's sleep.

Chapter 26

WHAT ARE THE DANGERS OF DESIRE?
THE TRUTH ABOUT LOVE FEARLESSLY TOLD!
JAZZ-CRAZED CHORINES AND THE BEASTS
THAT PREY UPON THEM!
(ADULTS ONLY)

IT WAS 10 A.M. and Sam Snow stood clasping Jeri Brooks halfheartedly in his arms. Miss Brooks, a prominent jazz-crazed chorine, was wearing Sam's pajama tops. Over her shoulder, across the street in the Little Bldg., Sam saw the dentist on the fourth floor remove the drill and the patient lean over to spit. Sam was thinking about the costumes in the Finale. Miss Brooks was wishing he'd brush his teeth before kissing in the A.M.

Chapter 27

> *I am glad to say that in the march of civilization the best dramatic critics now receive salaries almost as great as those paid the worst actors.*
>
> — ASHTON STEVENS

THAT FIRST WEEK in Boston we had plenty empty seats but that didn't bother Hackett any. He knew what was wrong or he thought he did and he began to chop up that book with a meat ax and he and I put it together again. He had Rudy Lorraine chained to an upright piano up in his room at the Touraine with a boy to bring him coffee and cigars; every ten hours Hackett would go up and unlock the leg irons and give him a raw steak, three Martinis, and pour two girls into the room for thirty minutes. Anyway he *was* up there working and he came up with "It Had To Be Me" and "I Couldn't Care Less," both in five days, and then Hackett and I had to write them into the show and the Choreographer staged them and Irene got sore because one of them was a featured number for Ilanova as a result of the reviews.

So her agent came up and we all had a big smoky meeting in Hackett's room where I sat embarrassed and miserable not looking at Irene, who was crying off and on. Sam was being pretty rude to Irene, and Hackett was being pretty rude to the agent, and the agent was being pretty rude to everybody and panning the show and blowing cigar smoke all over the place.

"If I didn't have a contract I'd advise Irene to get out right now," he said. "I gotta notion to break the contract."

"Do you honestly think we'd be smart not to build up the Ilanova part after those notices?" Sam said. "What do you think we are, complete morons? This is a two-hundred-and-fifty-thousand-dollar show, Morty."

"If you woulda built up Irene's part in the first place it woulda been more on the point," he said.

So that went on for a while.

"Mr. Hackett," Irene said, "do you honestly think I'm being unreasonable?"

Hackett gave it a couple of beats and then he said, "Yes. I think you're being very silly. I'm surprised at you."

"Ooooh," Irene wailed, and began to blubber some more.

In another half-hour Hackett was getting pretty sick of Morty and told him to tear the contract up in little pieces if he wanted to, but to make up his mind so they could get a replacement for Irene.

"Replacement?" Irene said. "You mean you want somebody else to play the part?"

"That's not what I said," Hackett said. "I want *you* to play the part. But if you feel persecuted and unhappy — well, your performance will suffer. And I need everything you've got. So I think you better make up your mind."

Irene made up her mind. She stayed, and Morty went back to New York. But by the operation of some mysterious law of female psychology I never could get back on the main line with her, hell I could never even get on the siding; she was friendly enough but somehow or other she had it figured out that I was responsible for The Rise of Sonia Ilanova, that zany youngster, that pixie. Not only that but I hadn't leaped to Irene's defense at the waterworks session in Hackett's room. I suppose I should have got up and punched Richard Hackett in the eye for picking on my girl who wasn't my girl at all.

But she put it another way, as dames are sometimes wont to do. It seems that Frankie was the swellest person and the greatest girl ever and Irene was looking out for Frankie's interests and going to get us two grand people back together again. It was useless to point out that Frankie and I had been together for fourteen years and it would take the combined Russian armies to get us apart; she had Frankie sitting by the fireside in the gloaming alone and rejected instead of up at the P.T.A. giving a speech about why Johnny can't read, the little twerp.

So I dried my tears, wrote a moving sonnet called "Why Can't It Be in Boston, the Same As Like What It Used to Be in New Haven?" and gave my fraternity pin to Jeri Brooks. I had lost the first fourteen rounds but I was still on my feet.

Meanwhile Irene had been so impressed by Sam's rudeness, and he by her tears and pathos, that they had fallen into each other's arms and taken to sitting around together at Locke-Ober's consuming lobster Savannah and the better California vintages while I had Jeri Brooks down at Jake Wirth's filling her up with sauerkraut.

This girl was a tiny little thing, a raving brunette with big eyes and a pony tail, and an ardent conversationalist.

"This reminds me of the funniest thing that happened when I was in *Beautiful Sea*," she would say.

"What does?" I would say.

"These frankfurters and kraut. We had a wonderful com-

pany, just the swellest bunch of kids you ever saw, and Miss
Booth was such a doll. She's a doll. Anyway the frankfurters
reminded me of this funny time — there was *always* something funny happening we just had a ball — but anyway we
had this boy Jimmy Stagg a wonderful boy, and talented!
He's been on Ed Sullivan and everything. He . . ."

"He has?" I said.

"Has what?"

"Nothing. Go on. Jimmy Stagg."

"That's his name. I honestly think he's one of the most
talented boys I know. There's nothing I respect so much as
talent. Especially in show business. You know what I respect
about Al St. James? Talent. Boy, has he got it. Just natural.
Effortless. A real natural. I just love to stand in the wings and
watch him work. A lot of the girls kid me about it. They say
'What interest do you see in him? He's just an old vaudeville
hoofer and comedian.' But I don't let them bother me. He's a
pleasure to watch. Don't you agree, Mr. Jordan?"

"Listen, sweetie, quit calling me Mr. Jordan, will you? I'm
not a day over sixty-two."

"I'm sorry, I didn't mean it. I forget. All these weeks you've
been Mr. Jordan to all of us girls."

"What about the humorous sauerkraut incident?" I said.

"Frankfurters. Not kraut. Well not really frankfurters
either. It was knackwurst. See Jimmy — Jimmy Stagg — was
just crazy about German food so one night after the show
some of us kids went to the Blue Ribbon there on 44th
Street, you know where it is, across from the China Bowl
someplace in there. I remember Kitty Stone was with us, she
had the understudy to Edith Adams in *Wonderful Town*. I
just love Edith don't you. What a doll that girl is. And
talent! Gosh! Helen didn't want to go to the Blue Ribbon
because she doesn't care much for German food. She doesn't

like it for some reason. Jimmy comes from Milwaukee and
was practically raised on German food or something I guess.
Anyway he's mad on the subject. Personally I can eat anything. So Jimmy ordered *knack*wurst. I'm not crazy about it
so I think I had some of those huge potato pancakes. Well
you can't guess what happened. We all simply howled!"

"What happened?" I said.

"The waiter brought him *brat*wurst. Well you can imagine
how he felt. He had this terrifically simple look on his face
like he was some terrible square. You never saw anything so
funny in your life!"

"Gee," I said. "What did he do?"

"Oh, he told the waiter about the mistake and the
waiter brought him knackwurst."

"That's a hot one all right," I said.

"Another funny thing happened, when we were in Philadelphia. We had this girl from Kansas City, one of the
singers . . ."

"Listen, honey, we gotta get out of here, we'll be late for
the call."

The only way to get this doll to shut up was to . . . Oh
well, she was okay to bum around with and she used to come
up and lie on the couch and read *Variety* and *Confidential*
and my mail while I was working, which was almost all the
time I wasn't at the theater or eating, and it's nice to have a
girl around. She even gave me a line one time and I used it
and Hackett liked it so we put it in. It got a ripple, which
is not a very big laugh but they all help.

I figured I would score with her and pay my debt to the
industry but when I brung the subject up after feeding her six
dollars' worth of assorted cocktails she said, "Oh, Jack," she
said, "but you're married. I saw your wife in New Haven.
She's a doll."

So I gave up and contented myself with reading *Captain Billy's Whiz-bang* every other day.

By the end of the week we had one of the new numbers in but the house was still feeble on Saturday night. Everybody was low, except iron-man Hackett.

When I got back to the hotel that night there was a special from Cousin Archie out home and he said Uncle Bill wanted me to come home and take over the foundry at fourteen thousand to start. He said I was the only one in the family that understood the business and I could write my own ticket. Archie said he had bought a Stanley Steamer and needed me to help him overhaul it. They had eight inches of snow and were going out for a sleigh ride. He said everybody wanted to know what Irene Lovelle was like, and when was I coming home and stay put.

I wrote Uncle Bill and told him to give me two weeks to think it over.

I turned on the radio and read the paper. Clooney sang "Say, Darling" to me.

Boston, Feb. 18.

With show and performance winning mild nod from crix, except mauling by Chauncey Crabbe, "Girl from Indiana" grossed a weak $31,200 in its first stanza at Shubert.

Chapter 28

Now really," Irene said. "I mean why this Brooks girl?"

"You mean you have Learned to Care?" I said.

"You're gone," she said. "What's the matter with you anyway?"

"Oh just anyway," I said.

I met Rudy Lorraine coming out of the Union Oyster House with his two girl friends.

"Hey," he said. "You been in this crazy joint?"

"It's the end," said the brunette.

"It's the most," said the blonde.

"Yeah," I said. "Dig those crazy clams."

"Hey, how you like the two new numbers?" Rudy said. "They're going to knock the good old customers right on their cans. I'd say they're as good a pair of show tunes I ever heard. How you like those crisp lyrics, man? Who is this Cole Porter? Tell me any song writer who can knock off two hits in five days, tell me that."

"Well let's see," I said. "Berlin, Frank Loesser, Rodgers and Hammerstein, Van Heusen and Cahn, Adler and Ross, Harold Arlen, Harold Rome, George Cohan . . ."

"Aw come on now, cut the funny stuff. Say, Columbia is

waxing 'I Couldn't Care Less' with the Rock 'n Rollers this afternoon."

"What's on the flip side, Rudy?" I said.

"Who cares," he said. "It'll be groove-dusty. Oh boy, wait'll Jack Lacy and Jerry Marshall spin this one."

"The indie diskeries are bankrolling plenty deejays for top plugs, Rudy," I said.

"Yeah, that payola is gettin' to be homicidal," he said.

"Jerry Marshall is a doll," the blonde said.

"All deejays are jerks," said the brunette.

The call was for eleven o'clock at the theater every day and we rehearsed until one, took an hour break and rehearsed from two to five, then came back at eight and put on the evening performance. After the show we worked some more.

I never understood about rehearsing until I got into this business. I thought once the actors knew their lines you ran through it a couple of times until they had it and that was that.

Hackett used to "work the book" in the lobby while the dancers and singers rehearsed on the stage. Hackett would go over and over that book until it nearly drove a person crazy. Every day we added new stuff and yanked old stuff; we not only changed lines, we changed whole scenes. The stage managers and I, with scripts on our laps, sat on gold chairs brought out from the boxes, following the action and ready to prompt and to mark down the new action, movements, and business. The actors not working sat around in the theater in the back rows; sometimes they waited all day to come in and say one line.

Hackett was working with Irene and Rex on a new bit.

HACKETT: All right, again, and give it a beat after "You've been neglecting me."

IRENE: You've been neglecting me — don't think I haven't noticed.

HACKETT: Listen: You've been neglecting me — don't think I haven't noticed.

IRENE: All right. You've been neglecting me — don't think I haven't noticed.

HACKETT: You're saying You've been neglecting me — don't think I haven't noticed. Think it, see if you can feel it. You've been neglecting me — don't think I haven't noticed.

IRENE: All right. You've been neglecting me — don't think I haven't noticed.

HACKETT: Don't *rush* it. We have to hear the words.

IRENE: I'm sorry. You've been neglecting me — don't think I haven't noticed.

HACKETT: Not as glib as that. Your feelings are hurt. You've been neglecting me — don't think I haven't noticed. Make yourself clear mentally here, dear.

IRENE: All right. You've been neglecting . . .

HACKETT: Hold it, hold it. This isn't *tragic*. Now think what you're saying.

IRENE: You've been neglecting me — don't think I haven't noticed.

HACKETT: There, you've almost got it. Can you hold that?

IRENE: You've been neglecting me — don't think I haven't noticed.

HACKETT: That's good. That's fine. All right, go ahead. Come on, Rex.

IRENE: You've been neglecting me . . .

"How do you think it's going?" Sam said, as we stood outside on the sidewalk having a smoke.

"I don't know, Sam," I said. "The new stuff seems pretty

good. Rudy's new numbers are great. But I don't see any stampede there at the box office."

"Did you talk to Hackett about the finale? Jack, that finale is a bomb."

Schatzie came up in his oversize overcoat.

"Hey, Jack, just the man I'm looking for. You're writing a piece for the *Herald,* I've got it all set up, they're waiting for it. For the Sunday edition, it's all set. They want it by six o'clock. Great publicity. Boy, we need it."

"By six o'clock?" I said. "What kind of a piece? What about?"

"About the *show*. You know, about how you happened to write it, working with Hackett, chorus girls, Rudy Lorraine, dear old Boston, any damn thing. Just so it's in that good old Jordan style."

"I don't feel like good old Jordan today," I said. "I can't write a piece in two hours and have it make any sense."

"Who said anything about it making sense?" he said.

"Go on, Jack. Write the piece for the *Herald,*" Sam said.

"Get Hackett to write a piece," I said.

"He doesn't write that stuff," Sam said.

"But I do," I said. "Why me?"

"Look, why argue about it?" Sam said. "Schatzie knocks himself out selling the idea. So write it. You're a writer. So write."

"Yeah and you're a producer, so go on in and produce," I said.

"What's the matter with you?" Sam said. "You sore about something?"

"No, I'm not sore about something!!" I shouted, getting sore.

"Louder," Sam said. "They can't hear you in Cambridge," and he glared at me and went into the theater.

Schatzie took me over to the hotel and fed me White Label and squeezed a piece out of me for the *Herald.* He said it had a wonderful quality and the *Herald* printed it and several ladies in South Boston read it while wrapping the garbage in it.

"Where were you all afternoon?" Hackett said when I saw him in the lobby before the evening performance. "I needed some lines."

"I was writing a piece for the *Herald,*" I said.

"We're trying to pull this show together," he said. "No time for that kind of nonsense."

"But Sam told me . . ."

"Never mind about Sam," he said. "You just stick close to me. That's what you're here for. Never mind the personal publicity."

After a while Sam came in but he made a big show of buddying up to Rudy Lorraine. Finally I cornered him by the orange juice counter while they were playing the overture.

"Well I saved the show," I said. "I wrote that piece for the paper."

"Very nice of you," he said.

"We're out of the woods now," I said. "Monday morning they'll be knocking the box office down, screaming for tickets after they read that piece."

Sam walked away.

"Who is your favorite author?" said the Choreographer.

"Mary Mapes Dodge," I said.

"Roll me one of those cigarettes, will you?" he said.

"I hear MGM is here tonight," I said.

"Can you do that with one hand?" he said.

MGM was there and I met him in the intermission; a pleasant fellow in a dark business suit. Sonia Ilanova had got so excited about her notices that she had lost most of her voice.

"I came up to see Ilanova, confidentially," he said.

"You picked a great night," I said. "The kid is exhausted."

"She's pretty good, I hear," he said.

"How do you like the show?" I said.

"Too offbeat," he said.

He said it was a nice show but the public didn't want it. He said the public wanted glamour and when the public didn't get glamour they stayed away from the wickets.

The Bostonians filed in from the lobby to their seats and the Second Act groaned to a start. The Bostonians were puzzled by the word "Indiana." Did it have something to do with Indians? And if the girl really loved this young man, why was she being so beastly to him? The songs were pleasant enough, but what did the words mean? Well, one had to keep up with things, but thank heavens D'Oyly Carte would soon be back.

After each song number, Rudy would come striding out to the lobby muttering and making notes on the backs of envelopes. We would pass each other, as I, having sat out the song in the lobby, rushed in to hear how the dialogue was going. When the words were over I'd leave, bumping into the Choreographer as he came in to see his dance number. None of us could any longer endure any part of the show with which we were not directly connected.

During Ilanova's big dance number Rudy and I leaned against the orange juice counter while the doorman swept the cigarette butts off the floor of the lobby.

"I gotta send a telegram to Johnny Ray," he announced.

A dowager stormed out followed by a middle-aged woman in tweeds.

"Ordinary vulgarity I can endure," said the dowager. "But this passes all the bounds of decency."

"But, Mother . . ." said the other.

"I shall call the Watch and Ward Society in the morning" — and they went through the doors.

"Wonder where I can send a telegram?" Rudy said.

"What are you gramming Johnny Ray about?" I said.

"My god, don't you read the papers? He's in the hospital."

"Yeah? What's the trouble?"

"Why, he's got this abscess on his foot. I guess it's pretty bad."

"Gee, that's tough, how'd he get that?"

"Well, he stepped on a Martini toothpick beside somebody's pool at Palm Springs."

"Man, you can't tell where it'll hit you these days," I said.

"He had to cancel out of his date at the Mocambo," Rudy said.

"What kind of a guy is he?"

"I don't know him," Rudy said.

"How come you send him a gram then?"

"Why, it's good for business. This guy sells millions of records."

"You're crazy," I said.

"Whadda you mean I'm crazy?" Rudy said. "I'm the only sane person in this whole foolish organization. You're just like the rest of this bunch, too goddamn bright."

"Yeah," I said, "I take them smart pills right along."

"You think you're big stuff because you wrote this novel. I make more royalties in a week than you make in a year. And don't forget I'm a writer too. The best goddamn song writer this country ever saw since Stephen Foster."

"You mean the guy that wrote 'Yes We Have No Bananas'?" I said.

"Aw why don't you go back to Indiana?" he said. "I bet you kill 'em out there."

"Listen," I said. "I gotta send a gram to Hemingway. I hear he cut his finger opening a can of soup. Excuse me."

I went back in and had a look at the show.

The audience was sitting on their hands. I went backstage.

"For godsake who's out there tonight?" Al St. James said. "I can't get to 'em."

Irene was in the wing waiting for her cue.

"Hi," I said. "Pretty bad house."

"Say, Sam's mad at you," she said. "What's it all about?"

"It's that old Boston magic working," I said. "I give Plotski about two months."

She got her cue and went out under the white spot and into her number.

The kids began straggling in from the dressing rooms for the next number. I spotted Jeri Brooks and went over to her.

"How about after the show?" I said.

"Gee, I'm sorry," she said. "I've got a date."

So I went to Hayes-Bickford's after the show with Ted Crosby. Ted had a jelly doughnut.

"How's the family?" he said. "How the kids like their school?"

"They like their school fine," I said. "The schools down here have even more assemblies, movies, rallies, and square dances than back home; they don't have hardly any classes at all."

"That Frankie is a wonderful girl, Jack. You're lucky."

"*She* likes it fine too," I said. "I don't know why. Me, I've had enough of it."

"You mean you don't *like* it down here?" he said.

"I should have come down here fifteen years ago," I said. "I'm tired, man. I've worked like hell all my life and played

like hell and I'm tired. I can't keep up with you boys.
Hackett is driving me crazy. I haven't had a night's sleep in
two months. I think I'm going nuts."

"Listen, you're doing a swell job. Ten more days of this —
we open. Then we charter a yacht and go to Trinidad."

"I've been in Trinidad," I said.

"Well where the hell do you want to go then?"

"Indiana," I said.

"Man, you're sick," Ted said. "You mean you want to go
back with all these goofs you write about in your books?"

"Yeah. I know all the goofs and all the goofs know me.
That's the difference."

"You can't go back there now. What would you *do* for
godsake?"

So I told him about Uncle Bill and the Foundry and I
gave him the net sales, and the dividend picture, and the
distribution setup, and Grandpa's patents, and the expansion
program, and the price of scrap, and the deal with A.C.F.
— talking about something I knew about for a change made
me feel better. Ted was so amazed he went up and got
another jelly doughnut and a dish of fruit salad.

"But listen," he said. "Don't you want to be a writer? Don't
you want to do another show sometime? Man, you have
talent, you can't throw that up and go run a peanut stand
someplace because it's *easier*. Nothing that comes easy is
any fun."

"Running a business isn't easy," I said. "But I understand
it. I was in that lousy foundry for sixteen years."

"Quit it, quit it," he said. "You're a writer, get it? A
writer."

"How's this show going to do on Broadway, Ted?" I said.

"I think it's going to be a flop," he said. "But I'm not
running back home to Bellows Falls and go into the shoe

factory. I'm gonna do another show. And if that's a flop I'm gonna do another one. And if that's a flop I'm . . ."

"Yeah, well you don't own that shoe factory, baby," I said.

"Thank God for that," he said.

Boston, Feb. 25.

"Girl from Indiana" in its second stanza at Shubert picked up a so-so $38,000.

Chapter 29

BOSTON: THIRD STANZA

An actor is much better off than a human being.
— JOHN BARRYMORE

Being in Boston in winter is like having the
hives; you know it will soon be over but it's miserable while
it lasts. By the time we got to our third big smashing week at
the Shubert all I wanted to do was get out and get far away
from any further possible views of the State House dome
and the triple-decker sandwiches at Steuben's.

Hackett asked me if I was getting any sleep and I said I
wasn't and he said why didn't I take a pill? I said I didn't
have a pill. He said, You mean you never take a pill? And I
said, No, I never take a pill, I don't approve of it. He said
that's a noble attitude but you don't look so good. I feel a
little worse than that, I said. I will give you a pill, he said.
You mean you take pills, I said. Why of course, he said; how
in hell would I get any sleep some nights?

Those pills are great stuff all right. I took one on Wednes-
day night after dancing Jeri Brooks around and around at the
Statler during which the orchestra played "Say, Darling"
twice, once for Jeri and me and a few minutes later when
Rudy and his two girl friends came in. I took the pill and

hopped into the sack and concentrated on feeling drowsy; this was going to be great, that good old Land of Nod, come on, you Sandman, here I am right over here at the Touraine. By the way, I wonder if I am paying too much for this room I sure couldn't get a room like this for sixteen dollars in New York but then remember that room I had in Toledo that time what in the hell was I doing in Toledo anyway that must have been in 1934 I guess that was the Toledo Tube deal or something no it couldn't have been because Ed Temple was with me I wonder what happened to Ed — *Wait* a minute, how about that sleep? Sleep, that knits up the raveled sleave of care. Now what in hell is a raveled sleave of care anyway? If I wrote that kind of stuff they would tell me to go home. . . .

An hour later I was with Grant at Vicksburg so I took another pill. This was the Big One. Fifteen minutes later the first earthquake in the history of the Bay State occurred, the center of the disturbance being concentrated in the southeast corner of Tremont and Boylston Streets. At 5 A.M. the room quit shaking and I went over to Hayes-Bickford's for a cup of coffee.

"Did you take that pill?" Hackett said at 11 A.M. "How do you feel?"

"I feel fine," I said. "What have we got to do?"

"I've decided to throw out the finale. We'll attack the problem from an entirely new point of view."

"I have a little idea," the Choreographer said.

His little idea turned into a big idea and we put it into the show, throwing away five thousand dollars' worth of costumes all covered with sequins and rhinestones while Telesco howled.

Warner Bros. came up to look at the show. He had a mustache and a cigarette holder.

"It's too offbeat," he said. "The public wants glamour and when they don't get it . . ."

"How about *Waterfront?*" Sam said.

"Oh well . . ." he said.

"I guess you heard what Warner Bros. said," Rudy said to me during the evening vigil beside the orange drink, Jordan almonds, and chocolate creams. "I've risked my reputation and lost."

"But we're having a ball," I said.

"It's different with you," he said. "I mean what did you have to lose?"

"No reputation, that's for sure."

"That's what I mean," he said. "I just happen to be the hottest thing in the business right now, and being associated with a flop show . . . well."

"It's going to hurt, career-wise," I said.

"But I'm gonna fool 'em," he said. "This pop stuff is all okay but after a while you get sick of one hit after another, I mean the thrill is gone. I've always felt my talent was really wasted in the pop field. For instance, would Mozart be writing hit songs today?"

"Gee whiz no," I said.

"Keep this under your hat but I'm gonna write an opera. Did you see this Menotti show? Man, it was strictly from Alabama. I could write a better show than that in a week. A folk opera, get it? I've even got an idea. Listen, what's this Sacco and Vanzetti bit? What the hell did they do? Give me the bones, just the bones."

"You're going to write an opera about Sacco and Vanzetti?" I said. "Isn't that pretty esoteric?"

"Esoteric?" he said. "Hell no. It'll be the cleanest show in town. The sets and costumes will be sensational. Old-time

Boston — hoop skirts and all that, and the men in those
pearl gray toppers. I see Beaton for the costumes."

"Listen, Rudy, this was in the twenties. Upton Sinclair
wrote a book . . ."

"Okay, so much the better. Those crazy cloche hats . . ."

"And Sacco and Vanzetti can sing a duet for the finale, in
twin electric chairs."

"Now you're with it. . . . Hell, did they get burnt?"

"A little," I said, as Rudy rushed in to check the bones of
that great folk song entitled "I Couldn't Care Less."

I went backstage and up to Irene's dressing room.

"Hello, Author," she said. "Say, we have an audience out
there tonight."

"Rudy says he has risked his reputation and lost," I said.

"Have you seen Hackett? How does he like the show
tonight?"

"I just saw him out front."

"What did he say?"

"He said one time when he was deer hunting in Maine the
fellow he was hunting with got shot and killed by another
hunter."

"Didn't he say anything about my new exit from the
porch?"

"The tough part of it was, this guy had a wife and three
kids and a big career ahead of him."

"Well anyway, *I* thought it worked."

"Brooks Atkinson is the baby I worry about," I said. "God,
he's so important."

"And so unpredictable," she said. "You'll have to get out of
here now. I have to change."

"Look at *A Time for Heroes*. You'd have said it was practically written for him. And he panned the bejesus out of it."

"Only five more days of suspense. Run along now."

"Bye-bye," I said.

Backstage Rex Ives was kidding a couple of the chorus kids.

"Say," he said. "How'd that exit go? I hope it's set now."

"I guess it's set," I said. "I think the whole show is set, as of tonight."

"I won't count on it," he said.

"I've got a chance to go into Freddie Friedberg's new show," one of the kids said.

"You better take it fast," Rex said. "In two weeks those big trucks will be hauling the scenery away from this one."

I went out into the alley and had a smoke. Sam came out and grabbed my arm.

"Come and have a drink," he said.

"I have to see the waltz," I said.

"The hell with the waltz," he said.

We went over to a crummy bar and threw down a couple.

"It's set," he kept saying. "It's set. God I keep thinking about Walter Kerr."

"How about Atkinson?" I said.

"Watts can be tough as hell," he said.

"Chapman could really take this thing apart if he was in the mood," I said.

"It's set," he said. "What do you *honestly think?*"

"Sam, I have only seen three or four musical comedies in my life and one of them was *The Student Prince*. I don't know anything about this business."

"You're always playing dumb, Hackett says," he said. "I wonder about McLain . . ."

We stared at the bottles at the back of the bar, and at ourselves in the mirror above them. We looked awfully intelligent.

When I went back to the theater the stage door man,

kindly old Pop Beloved, said, "There's a couple letters in the box there for you, Mr. Jordan."

I took the letters and went around to the front and into the lobby.

DEAR PAPA
MY DOLLY HAS A CO
LD. MAMA SAYS WE
MINTE GO BACK TO
INDANANA.
LOVE X X X O O O X X
O O X X O O O X X X X
KATIE

DEAREST JACK:
Archie called me about the Big Opportunity. What he didn't tell you was that Uncle Bill has had a stroke, not a bad one but a stroke is a stroke. Of course Archie is putting on a big act about your "obligation to the family," etc. — actually, of course, he wants you back there to fix the spark plugs on that Stanley Steamer or something and keep him entertained. And here we go again. After all the years you put in there it's just mad that this should happen now. The way Archie was talking it looks as though you would actually be the mighty Supreme Potentate of the entire Jordan Iron Products Inc. in a few years, meaning those conventions again, and Saturday night at the Country Club, and listening to Rip Ryan's jokes. There is one thing I like about the State of Connecticut and that is that Rip Ryan is 800 miles away. Well, honey, it took you 35 years to get out and now right away they want you back. How is the show going? I went down to Bloomingdale's new store here in Stamford and bought a new dress for the opening. Lots of love and see you Sunday A.M.

FRANKIE

P.S. And not only Rip Ryan but Fatty Hoopes, Lula Belle Ober, and Mrs. C. Roger Leroy.

"Well, it's set," Sam said, leaning on the checkroom counter. "What are you looking so down about?"

"They want me back in Indiana," I said. "The whole state is going to pieces since I left."

"You just left Indiana," he said.

"I know," I said.

After the show three Harvard boys came to interview me. Another one of Schatzie's ideas.

"Mr. Jordan, would you say Mr. Hackett is influenced by the Stanislavsky method?"

"No, I would say he is mostly influenced by the Hackett method."

"Do you have any advice to young writers? How did you get to be a writer?"

"My advice to young writers is to go and live in Indiana for thirty years, preferably working in an iron foundry. This method is almost infallible."

"Mr. Jordan, would you mind telling us something of your work habits?"

"I write all my stuff standing up. I use an old-fashioned quill pen formerly belonging to John Quincy Adams."

And I am not the only famous librettist who works on his feet, boys, because Oscar Hammerstein the Second is also a stand-up writer, and pens his stuff in an upright position on a "schoolmaster's desk" in his lovely home in Bucks County. This article in *Modern Home Magazine* says, for example: "If a phrase eludes him, a word is hard to find, or a meter needs correcting, he may rest one foot on that charming little needlepoint stool — one of the many thoughtful appointments for his comfort that his wife's flair for well-planned detail has provided."

That is one of the troubles with Frankie; she is great to look at and a wonderful cook; but when it comes to well-planned detail *in re* some place for me to rest one foot when I am trying to think of a word to rhyme with "Hammerstein," why she's a complete washout. So to you young men who say to me, "How can I write a hit musical comedy like Mr. Hammerstein is constantly doing?" I say to you, "Look to your footstools!" And stop whining. Out where I come from if a meter needs correcting we call the Gas Company.

So Good-By Boys and good luck in that boat race against the Elis. Is this the way I am to fill out my last lingering hours in the bower of pure thought and high endeavor called Boston, whispering the name Strindberg and the name William Inge and the names Clifford, Arlington, Buckingham, Ashley and Lauderdale in a bit-player's dressing room with soiled towels on the floor? Shall we not sit instead among the teacups behind the lavender panes of Beacon Street and murmur "Bronson Alcott," or talk of transcendentalism over a hot dog at Joe and Nemo's?

Across the street at the Metropolitan Theatre Harry Paige was supervising Jayne Marchal's personal appearance on the mammoth stage, today only, at the Boston première of her new picture *East of Tulsa*. Miss Marchal said it was a real thrill to be here in Boston again. Sam and Ted refused to cross the street for the event, sitting instead on stools in the Paddock Bar and Grill with me, watching the weather report on TV.

"It's set," Sam said. "Anyway it's set. No more changes."

"We oughtta go over and see Harry's picture show," Ted said.

"Sure, we have nothing to do," Sam said. "We're opening in New York next week. Let's go to a lousy movie. What's it about anyway?"

"Well as I get it," Ted said, "Marchal is planted as this

poor girl from Oklahoma and some old Indian she befriended when only a tot . . ."

"How do you befriend an Indian?" Sam said.

"Anyway he leaves her a bunch of oil wells so she goes to New York and then the fun starts."

"And the waiter asks her if she wants a demitasse and she says yes, and a cup of coffee too," Sam said.

"Look, he says more rain," Ted said.

That night Hackett and Ilanova and Sam and Irene and Jeri Brooks and I went dancing at the Statler. Hackett ordered champagne.

It turned out that Ilanova couldn't dance ballroom style so Sam insisted on giving her a lesson. Sam danced hunched up like he was a smoothie down from Andover. He closed his eyes.

Jeri Brooks said to Hackett that one of the funniest things that ever happened was when she was on the road with *Carousel*. There was this boy from Scranton . . . I rushed her onto the floor.

Hackett clinked glasses with Irene.

The orchestra played "I Couldn't Care Less." Rudy's publisher was a live wire all right.

"I just love that number," Jeri said, and sang it as we danced.

> I couldn't care less
> Unless you cared more . . .

But what did it mean?

> With your heart you are so careless,
> Darling, I couldn't care less.

Sam continued to shuffle dreamily. Hackett and Irene glided past the band and the leader grinned even more foolishly than usual.

The band took a break and we all sat down.

"No work tonight, hey, Jack?" Hackett said.

"Yes," I said. "I've been sleeping with Mrs. Fondemeyer and that finale so long I think I'll be lonesome tonight."

"What are you going to do when this is all over?" Hackett said.

"I don't know," I said. "I might go home and join the Kiwanis Club."

"Hmmm," he said, staring into the bubbles.

Sam said Eugene O'Neill was the most tragic figure of the Twentieth Century. Jeri Brooks asked Hackett what he thought of Sean O'Casey. Ilanova mentioned Balanchine. Irene said O'Neill never went to college. Sam said he did too. Irene said he did not did he Mr. Hackett and Hackett said he didn't know. Jeri Brooks said a lot of famous people didn't go to college and it just proved that college wasn't everything.

We took the girls home and then Sam and Hackett and I walked up Tremont Street for a cup of coffee.

"What kind of shape are we in?" I said.

"O Jack," cried stately Lord Hackett, offering me his gold snuffbox, "I Couldn't Care Less."

Boston, March 4.
"Girl from Indiana" in third frame at Shubert picked up a bit but finished only fair at $41,500. House goes dark this week as "Indiana" exits for Broadway.

Chapter 30

"B UT listen, honey," I said, "I don't feel like eating. Least of all at Torino's. Can't I just have a chicken sandwich sent up here or something? I feel lousy enough already without eating at Torino's."

"Here, let me straighten your tie," Frankie said. "Listen, Archie has a table reserved and everything. He's knocking himself out."

"Yeah, I suppose he's hired some Gypsy fiddles to play at us. What the hell did he come down for anyway?"

"Come on now," she said. "It won't be so bad. Archie's all excited. You know how he is when he gets to organizing things."

"Sure, he's probably going to pass out paper hats to Tallulah and all the gang and recite 'Casey at the Bat.' I'm not going."

"But Jack . . ."

"This is the New York opening of the only show I'll ever be connected with and in a week I'll probably be back in Indiana. And I'm *not* going to eat dinner on opening night with Archie. *After* the show okay. Before the show, no."

"Jack," Frankie said, "this has been tough, hasn't it?"

"What has?" I said.

"The show. Working with Hackett. No sleep. Irene Lovelle. Nutty Sam Snow."

"Irene? What about her?"

"Nothing about her. I mean all of it has been wild and you've worked like mad."

"Yeah. I'm beat to the dirt."

"Well so am I," Frankie said. "I've been stuck in that crazy house with the copper bed-warmers for five months. Now your cousin Archie is good enough to come all the way to New York and arrange a nice dinner before the opening and I'm going to it. You can sit here and let your nervous system run wild but I'm going to Torino's."

"Well, have a real jolly time," I said with an uncontrollable sneer.

"I honestly sometimes wonder if you realize there's anybody in this family besides Jack Jordan, the great creative artist."

"Aw now, cut it out," I said. "I don't act like that."

"The heck you don't. Sometimes you act like Philbrick, the Class Poet."

"I am not like that," I said. "I am a virile, two-fisted extrovert. Thoughtful, kind, unselfish — a devoted family man and a doting father."

"And I get lonesome sometimes, but I don't squawk about it."

I was sitting on the edge of the bed. Frankie was in front of the mirror trying on one set of earrings after the other. I had a highball in my hand and I set it on the glass-topped bedside table.

"Come over here a minute," I said, and she came over and I took her hand.

"I like your dress," I said.

"I think it'll do," she said.

"Listen, Frankie," I said. "I try to be as good as I can. I work at it. I have strong inclinations towards being a bum. If it wasn't for you and the kids I wouldn't last a week. I'd be the worst no-good bum in the country. If it wasn't for you I'd never have been a writer in the first place and if it wasn't for you I could never keep it up. So give the poor bum a kiss."

She gave me a kiss and went back to the earring performance.

"How do these look?" she said.

"Okay," I said. "What time are we supposed to be at Torino's?"

"Archie said seven o'clock. You mean you're going?"

"Philbrick the Class Poet has changed his mind," I said.

We walked out of the hotel and down the street.

"Good luck, Mr. Jordan." That was one of the chorus boys in front of the drugstore.

"Good luck tonight." That was one of the stagehands going towards Times Square.

At the end of the street, beyond Eighth Avenue where counter tops are sticky, down past Ninth and Tenth and in the distance beyond the empty lots full of broken bricks and bones, and across the greasy Hudson, smiling Old Man Sun had gone, leaving only a dismal streaked smudge of crimson in the dark Weehawken sky.

LOOK INTO YOUR HEART OF HEARTS FRIENDS AND TELL ME WHAT DO YOU SEE THERE?

Pale, wizened, with lumpy nose and Bodenheim hair, a soul-saver stood brandishing a small Bible. Beside him on the sidewalk was Old Glory in a wobbly stand.

"I hope Archie behaves himself," I said.

"He'll be all right," Frankie said.

"When was Archie all right?" I said.

Four nickels and one is five. Say listen folks i don't care whether you come from up the Mohawk Valley or beside the Great Salt Lake i'm right here to say if you want a real value in a fountain pen that will slip and glide and write both Yiddish Japanese and plain English don't go no further but stop right here. When you give me a quarter you find five dollars laying right in the street.

"Well that's one thing I don't need," I said. "I am all wrote out, for once."

"I wonder how the baby sitter is getting along?" Frankie said.

It's funny, they make the sidewalks out of the same kind of cement but they don't feel the same underfoot anyplace but New York. So there I was, and Frankie, the girl from Nebraska, alongside of me, moving through the trees towards Gettysburg.

Torino's was jammed, as it always is on opening night — jammed with the short fat guys with their tall beautiful girl friends, and with the teeny dolls and their towering protectors with the full haircuts. In the little bar those poor unfortunates sitting on the bar stools kept ducking their shoulders as drinks were passed over to the standees, who stood enthusiastically introducing each other.

"Hello, cousin," Archie said. "What time does the balloon go up?"

My handsome blond cousin was all dressed up in his best Princeton finery. "Whatever you say about Archie," Frankie always said, "he knows the score."

The present score was 14-0 and Archie was winning.

"Come on," he said, and we followed him through the

mob waiting, earning some glares from the dames who had costly furs but no table.

There was Sam Snow, sitting alone at a corner table.

"Hey, Sam," I said.

"Jack," he said, nodding somberly.

"Well this is it," I said.

"I'm sorry, Jack," he said. "Please, I've got to be alone."

"You picked a swell place for it," I said.

Sam mournfully slipped an oyster into his mouth. Frankie and I passed on.

"Big ham," I said.

And then over Archie's shoulder I saw Aunt Roma, and beside her, Cousin Orville, and across from them, sweet, simple-minded Cousin Sue Gay, Orville's little partner on life's highway, who could always be counted on to provide a fruit salad for the church supper, with pieces of marshmallow in it.

"I don't have to put up with this," I said. "There's the Marshmallow Queen."

"Keep going," Frankie said, but she was taken a bit aback, even for Frankie.

"Holy smokes, where did you all come from?" I said with the enthusiasm of a kid receiving an arithmetic book for Christmas.

"Surprise!" Aunt Roma said, with a mouthful of hard roll, her enormous bosom heaving with big-city joy.

"My lands, Sue Gay!" Frankie said.

"Listen, folks," I said. "I can't stay very long. I got a lot of stuff to do and I gotta get to the theater and . . ."

"Siddown," Archie said. "And be quiet."

"You need something on your stomach," Aunt Roma said.

"I always said you never eat enough," Orville said as I sat down between him and Aunt Roma. "I was saying to Sue Gay on the train the same thing. She was kiddin' me I was eatin' too much and I says to her, Well, I says, there is nothin' wrong with a good healthy appetite. Now you take Cousin Jack I says I don't see how he stays alive. That's right, Sue Gay says, he don't hardly eat enough to keep a bird alive. I thought that was a pretty good one."

"Sue Gay always did have a grand sense of humor," I said.

"Jack, you look peaked," Aunt Roma said.

"I feel mighty peaked," I said.

"I wanted a steak," Orville said. "That is, until I looked at the bill of fare. You know what they get for a steak on the train nowadays? Five dollars, that's all. So I got a double order of ham and eggs. It come to three dollars and twenty cents."

"I never order eggs in public," Aunt Roma said. "Cold storage."

"Mine wasn't so bad," Orville said.

Orville had on his gray suit with the peak lapels and a three-alarm cravat. Uncle Harvey, my father's brother, who had the Ford Agency in Goshen, wanted Orville to be a doctor but Orville went to the Mount Union Agricultural College of Applied Arts and Taxidermy. He's got a farm out there, and a lot of alfalfa.

"Well, Jack," Sue Gay said, "I s'pose with the life you lead and all it's pretty tame here sitting around with us here like this and all."

"Aw now cut that out, Sue Gay," I said. "How are the kids?"

She has six of them and by the time she got through telling me about their various batting averages in the 4-H Club the waiters had brought us the food.

"Jack, do you know the headwaiter here?" Aunt Roma said.

"Sure, I know Maurice," I said. "Sometimes he even knows me."

"I've simply got to have this recipe," she said. "I'll spring it on the girls at the next Thursday meeting. It's my turn next. Do you think he'd . . . ?"

The captain was showing Archie the label on the champagne bottle. Archie passed the reading test and everybody was so impressed by the champagne bottle they shut up and sat there looking like they hoped teacher wasn't going to call on them next.

"Jack, are you all right?" Frankie said.

"I'm not sure," I said.

"I bet you know all sorts of famous people, don't you, Jack?" Sue Gay said.

"Well, I've met a lot of them," I said. "It doesn't add up to much."

"Who do you know, for instance?" Sue Gay said.

"Well, who do you want me to know?" I said.

"Do you suppose this salad dressing is made up right here?" Aunt Roma said.

"Too much garlic in it for me," Orville said. "I'll be tasting it tomorrow still."

"Do you know Marlon Brando?" Sue Gay said.

"Who the hell is Marlon Brando?" Archie said.

"Hang on, boy," I said to myself. "Hang on."

I couldn't get through any more of it. I had already had way too much. Yes, I loved them all, Orville and his new tractor and Aunt Roma, now scanning the dessert menu, and even Sue Gay; surely the Almighty had something Good in mind when he dumped Sue Gay in our midst. But I couldn't finish it, I couldn't see it through; the roast beef was churning around in me like molten magma way down in Mother Earth's interior, and the palms of my hands were moist. At the idea of thinking up something humorous to say about Marlon Brando, my mouth began to water.

"The way I see it I figure early-weaned pigs are actually smaller at ten weeks than pigs left with the sow and fed a good creep ration," Orville said. "I'm writing it up for the *Indiana Swine Journal*. Of course they might not print it but . . ."

I had had it too many ways.

"Frankie," I said.

She looked at me and she got it — you can't beat the kid from Nebraska — you don't have to send her no collect telegram.

By now I had met everybody there was to know: Gloria Vanderbilt and Edgar Bergen and Harvey Breit and Rita Gam and Comden and Green, and fifty-six agents, and John K. Hutchens, and Mr. Knopf, and Miss Sohovik, and Sharman Douglas and Miss Monroe, and W. H. Auden and Monte Proser and Bernie Hart and Carmen Alvarez and Turner Catledge and Earl Wilson and Gwen Verdon and Fritz Loewe and Rosalind Russell and Harry Rubenstein and Hoagy Carmichael. Sam and Ted and Hackett were always introducing me to somebody and I had also palmed it with Julie Wilson and Joe Fields and Loring Smith and Conrad Nagel and Edith Adams and Dort Clark and Alfred Vanderbilt and Mickey Mantle and Bill Inge and Nancy Ryan and Zorina and Mr. Capote and Madge Evans and George Abbott and Frank Loesser and MacDonald Carey and Oliver Smith and Saroyan and John Chapman and Lotte Lenya and Hank Fonda and Walter Kerr and Judy Holliday and William L. Shirer and Thomas B. Roshek and Jack Waldron and Emmett Kelly and Frank X. Silk and Nancy White and Ward Morehouse and Jean Lynch and Charlie Baker and Charles Poore and Celia Linder and Percy Kilbride and Happy Felton and Ernie Kovacs and Tina Louise and Leonard Lyons and Merle Miller and Elizabeth Janeway and Orville Prescott and Fran Warren and Brooks Atkinson and Jean Kerr and Patty Wilkes and John Beal and Osbert Sitwell and Shirley Booth and Shirley Maclaine and Shirley Yamaguchi and Shirley Cohen and Harold Arlen and Jake Wilk and Sandy Wilson and Hal Prince and Josephine Premice and Cleveland Amory and Mary Lou Noble and Leonard Bernstein and Steve Sondheim and Victor Moore and Baron Polan and Louis Sobol and Danny Kaye and Freddie Hebert and Freddie Brisson and Goddard Lieberson and Harry Hershfield and Phil Silvers and Shelley Winters and Clifford Odets and Joe Ferrer and Henry Ford Jr. and Cozy Cole. I had ticked them all off and none of them remembered me and I didn't remember them; it was all crackerjack with no prize.

And there comes a time when even Happyface Jack Jordan gets to the end of the line. I couldn't laff it up any more. I didn't even care about the show; I just wanted to get out of there.

Good old Frankie got me out, God love her. She just got up and said we had to go and we went.

So who's standing in front of the theater in his dress suit and a fancy ruffled shirtfront, smoking a fine Optimo? Rudy Lorraine, and he's got this number with him with the blue eye make-up on.

"Well, what do you think?" he said.

"Who's thinking?" I said.

Chapter 31

New York City, March 5

"A luscious lollypop of a show . . . a stem-winder . . ."
— *Herald Tribune*

"Fanciful, gay — the treat we have been waiting for . . ."
— *Times*

"Gets off the ground and stays there . . ."
— *News*

"Pure unadulterated fun . . ."
— *Journal American*

"Irene Lovelle's greatest role . . ."
— *World Telegram*

"A girl from Indiana came to Gotham last night and the town rocked . . ."
— *Mirror*

"Drives home its message under a barrage of laughs and glorious tunes . . ."
— *Post*

"Contemporary, compelling, as new as tomorrow . . . an adorable gamine named Sonia Ilanova . . ."
— *Women's Wear Daily*

Chapter 32

"Fo' de land sakes!" cried Eradicate. "What am de mattah now, Massa Tom?"
"Earthquake coming," answered Tom briefly.
— TOM SWIFT AMONG THE DIAMOND MAKERS

H ow can you stand it?" Cousin Archie said. "Not that I minded, but do you know what that dinner cost me last night?"

"Frankie, where is that Bicar-Seltzer?" I said.

"Listen, what you need is a Dynamite Cocktail." Archie said. "Call Room Service and tell them to send up three raw eggs and a few chili peppers, and an order of papaya juice."

"You call them," I said. "Frankie, where is the Bicar-Seltzer?"

"Who is Jeri?" Frankie said.

"Jerry? Jerry who?" I said.

"Just Jeri. J-E-R-I," Frankie said. She was sitting on the sofa in her dressing gown reading the telegrams in our luxurious suite at the Astor. "She says DARLING BEST LUCK TONIGHT KISSES AND LOVE . . . JERI. . . . J-E-R-I."

"Oh," I said. "Well, she's one of my many admirers. She's that one in the green bathing suit in the beach number."

"Well, well," Frankie said.

"You haven't *got* any chili peppers?" Archie said into the phone. "Why not?"

"I'll be all right if I can find that Bicar-Seltzer," I said. "Frankie, what time is it?"

"Eleven fifteen and it's Today in New York," Frankie said.

There were newspapers all over the end tables, the chairs, the couch, and bottles, glasses, and the forlorn remains of two chicken sandwiches on a tray on the floor.

"Listen to this one," Frankie said. "TO THE BOY FROM INDI-ANA THANKS FOR A GREAT JOB AND WELCOME TO BROADWAY BEST LUCK FOR TONIGHT WHATEVER HAPPENS WANT YOU TO KNOW WE APPRECIATE YOUR CONSTANT DEVOTION TO THE PROJECT HARRY PAIGE. Gosh!"

"Crazy, absolutely crazy," Archie said. "You spent the whole night with him, what did he have to send you a telegram for? No wonder everybody down here dies broke."

"Now, Archie," Frankie said. "It's an old tradition."

"I'll bet Western Union started it," Archie said. "Well they haven't got any chili peppers so I told them to send Tabasco."

"I don't want any Tabasco," I said. "I want a Bicar-Seltzer."

"That stuff is no good," Archie said. "It irritates the duodenum. It actually *produces* ulcers."

"But Tabasco is soothing," I said.

"You don't understand," Archie said. "The Tabasco combines with the egg and forms an emulsion . . ."

"Archie, for heaven's sake," Frankie said. "Do you have to talk about emulsions when my head feels like this? Jack, give me a sip of Scotch and a glass of cold water."

" 'A luscious lollypop of a show,' " I said. " 'A stemwinder.' " And I went in and ran the water.

"All right," Archie hollered. "So the newspapers said the show didn't stink. What's that prove?"

I turned the water off.

"Talk to him, Frankie," Archie said. "For godsake quit sitting there like a moron reading a lot of ridiculous telegrams about nothing — 'YOUR CONSTANT DEVOTION TO THE PROJECT'! How about a little constant devotion to Jordan Iron Products, Inc.?"

"Here you are, honey," I said.

"First since 5 A.M.," Frankie said.

"Well, what about it?" Archie said. "So maybe the show will play a couple of months. Then what? Security is what you want. Iron. Something tangible. Something . . ."

"Something boring," Frankie said.

"I'm thinking about it, Archie," I said. "I'm thinking about it, kid."

"How's Rip Ryan?" Frankie said. "Say, I sure miss that boy."

"How bad is Uncle Bill?" I said.

"He's finished," Archie said.

"You think I could handle the job?" I said.

"Try some of this," Frankie said. "Pull yourself together, Daddy."

The doorbell buzzed and kept on buzzing. Then somebody started pounding on the door.

Archie went to the door and Sam Snow tottered in; he was still in his evening clothes.

"Gimme a drink," he said. "Hello, you luscious lollypop, you pure unadulterated fun," and he grabbed Frankie and hauled her to her feet and gave her a kiss.

"I better order more eggs," Archie said, "and papaya juice."

"Not Atkinson or Kerr or McLain or Watts or Chapman but all of them, *all of them*, ALL OF THEM!" Sam screamed.

"Coffee," Archie said. "Black coffee and ginger ale. Half and half. The ginger ale absorbs the . . ."

"Look out the window!" Sam said. "Look what's happening down there. Give me a drink! Look out the window, you daffy Hoosiers!" He shoved us over to the window and pointed down the street. It was a cold, gray, dirty day. There was the theater, and up on the marquee it said *The Girl from Indiana*, and from under the marquee and extending up the sidewalk was a long, quiet, patient line of people.

"Something tangible," Frankie said. "Iron, for example."

The phone rang and I went over and answered it. Sam had launched into "Say, Darling."

"Hey shut up, Sam," I said.

"Jack, this is Dick."

Dick who? I thought, and then I realized it was Hackett.

"Jack, it looks as though good old Harry Paige has pulled a fast one," he said.

"What's the matter?" I said. "Harry Paige?"

"What's that?" Sam said.

"It seems he sold the show to Paragon Pictures a half an hour ago. Anyway he's got a firm offer."

"Here, you better talk to Sam," I said.

Sam took the phone and leaned against the wall.

"What is it, Jack?" Frankie said.

"Harry made a deal for the picture rights," I said.

"Say that again," Sam said, putting his hand up to his head. "Did you say seven hundred and fifty thousand?"

"If there was a delicatessen store nearby," Archie said, "I could run out and *get* some chili peppers."

Chapter 33

> *"I have been rich, and I have been poor. And believe me, rich is better."*
>
> — JOE E. LEWIS

W ELL, now what'll I do?" I said. "I opened all my toys and Christmas is over."

The colored girl came in and said the dishwasher was busted.

"Why don't you go for a nice long walk?" Frankie said, when Sweet Pea had shuffled out to the kitchen again.

"One reason is, is because I don't want to go for a nice long walk."

"Well then, why don't you go in town to the office?"

"I am just underfoot in the office now," I said. "I can't just go in there and sit around reading *Variety* all day long and kidding the office girls. I've got no job there. If I had to fill the inkwells or lick stamps or something it would be different."

"Well, I'll call the service man on the dishwasher," Frankie said.

"I don't blame you," I said.

So I went into the living room and Mr. Baby and I looked at Ding Dong School for a while.

This here Miss Frances she's cool, man. I mean she can shake my tree any time. The way she rides that horn on Ding Dong Blues — man, she can have me.

You made the side-pocket shot, kid, I thought. Now when are you going to get to work?

The phone rang and I answered it.

"You wouldn't remember me, but I went to grade school with a friend of Archie Jordan's, your cousin Archie; say, how is Archie?"

"Oh I guess he's all right," I said.

"Archie was always quite a character, quite a boy. I never knew him myself, but my friend Earl Krundler, why he went to school with Archie and used to mention him quite frequently. Earl thought a lot of Archie."

"How many tickets do you want?" I said.

"Well, now I don't want to impose on you any. I just called up to say everybody back in Indiana we're sure proud of your success. But now you mention it, if it's really no trouble to you, I'll tell you what it is. See, I'm with the Hotpoint people and I'm here on a sales conference and if I could get a couple of tickets for the President or maybe four, and a couple for the Sales Manager, why it surely would be wonderful and I'd surely appreciate it one heck of a lot."

I fixed him up with a pair and went for a nice long walk among the stone walls and picturesque Connecticut countryside. It all looked fake as hell and then it began to rain so I went home, catching a cold en route.

"It's for you," Frankie said, as I came into the house. "Cincinnati calling."

"You wouldn't remember me, Mr. Jordan, but I used to call on Jordan Iron Products for years with Imperial Coal. How's your father?"

"Father's been dead for eight years now," I said.

So I fixed him up with a pair of tickets for his sales manager.

"Jack, when are we going to California?" Frankie said after I hung up.

"Thank God for the sales managers," I said, "or Broadway would be on the rocks. What are we going to California for?"

"To make the *picture,* of course," Frankie said.

"Oh Lord, honey, how do I know?" I said.

"Well, I'll tell you one thing, we're *not* going to live in some furnished hotel suite. We're going to get a *house.*"

"And a swimming pool," I said. "And a Hispano-Suiza, and I'm going to wear black goggles, a beret, and Murray space shoes."

"Why don't you go in to New York, dear?"

"I haven't got anything to *do* in New York," I said.

"Nothing to do in New York? Why of course you have *everything* to do in New York," Frankie said. What was she thinking of — getting me gone from the house?

"No, my darling, I have no business in New York," I said.

"Well why don't you go for a nice long . . ."

"Walk," I said. "I have just been on a nice long walk. Has it all come down to this, that I must take walks? What is it, are we all going crazy? A walk. I never took a walk in my life before, unless I was going someplace. I've been working all my life, killing myself with either work or worry or both together."

"Maybe you should have taken over the plant," she said.

Well she doesn't know how I feel so excuse it please, a dopey remark like that. She looks mighty good standing there in her nice morning frock all starched and neat, with her beautiful black hair on her shoulders in the Middle Western manner. I wanted to tell her all about it but I couldn't.

"Get the mail," she said. "There's the mailman."

The phone rang as I was going to the door.

"No tickets," I said. "No more tickets. I mean actually, cut them off with nothing. Tell them . . ."

I went across the patch of lawn to the mailbox, beside the stone wall. The drizzle dampened my fine Fenn-Feinstein tweeds, purchased in New Haven on another rainy day, with Irene Lovelle and Sam Snow supervising, and fingering the neckwear and giving out a lot of funny jokes.

"I don't believe it," I said, standing once again in the front hall beside the banjo clock that didn't work, as I looked at the weekly royalty check.

"Oh, of course you can believe it," Frankie said. "Three per cent of fifty thousand a week. And just wait until you get out the road company. Not to mention the London company. And the movie rights."

"You are a cool customer, my love," I said.

"Some of you boys have to make it once in a while," she said.

"We made it, honey," I said.

"Jack, you're so marvelous," she said. "You knock me out."

"Can the colloquialisms," I said. "You live in Connecticut now."

"What are the poor folks doing this morning I wonder?" she said.

That was a crummy old joke of mine.

I kissed her and she said good-by and I put on Baby's Size 3 raincoat and took him out for a walk. He trudged alongside of me with the little fat hand in mine, looking the world over. When we came along to the bridge above the Merritt Parkway I held him up in my arms so he could see the cars whizzing underneath us.

"See car," he said.

"Yes," I said. "Lovely cars, Mr. Baby. All the nice ladies and the nice gentlemen on their way to New York."

"Me see car," he replied evasively.

Underneath us the slick shiny bugs kept streaming on down the slab toward the big city, their occupants plotting, laying their plans for victory. Sure and they all have fine things in store for them.

In fact they are on the very outskirts of salvation.

"Let's get out of here, kiddo," I said.